'*Scream* meets *The B...* ... ...
book made my retro-ho... ...oving heart sing'

Kirsty Logan, *The Gracekeepers*

'*Harrow Lake* is a captivating and creeping mystery full of brilliantly twisting turns and dark secrets. You'll hear Mister Jitters in the deadly whisper of the pages as you race through this chilling, thrilling book'

Holly Jackson, *A Good Girl's Guide to Murder*

'This dark and twisty book will keep you gripped to the very last page and give you sleepless nights. Atmospheric and beautifully written, *Harrow Lake* is a five-star must-read'

Sarah J. Harris, *The Colour of Bee Larkham's Murder*

'What a thrill-ride *Harrow Lake* is. If you like Stephen King, you'd be mad not to snap this up'

Cass Green, *In a Cottage In a Wood*

'A taut, twisting and terrifying read that takes no prisoners as it carves and claws its way into your nightmares. Expect more than just jitters...'

Melinda Salisbury, *Hold Back the Tide*

'*Harrow Lake* is scary, but also hugely fun . . . the claustrophobic Harrow Lake itself seems a fully realized world, a character in itself'

The Bookseller

PENGUIN BOOKS

HARROW LAKE

KAT ELLIS
HARROW LAKE

PENGUIN BOOKS

PENGUIN BOOKS

UK | USA | Canada | Ireland | Australia
India | New Zealand | South Africa

Penguin Books is part of the Penguin Random House group of companies
whose addresses can be found at global.penguinrandomhouse.com.

www.penguin.co.uk
www.puffin.co.uk
www.ladybird.co.uk

Penguin
Random House
UK

First published 2020
001

Text copyright © Kat Ellis, 2020

The moral right of the author has been asserted

Set in 10.5/15.5 pt Sabon LT Std
Typeset by Jouve (UK), Milton Keynes
Printed and bound in Great Britain by Clays Ltd, Elcograf S.p.A.

A CIP catalogue record for this book is available from the British Library

ISBN: 978-0-241-39704-6

All correspondence to:
Penguin Books
Penguin Random House Children's
One Embassy Gardens, 8 Viaduct Gardens, London SW11 7BW

For Ian

Transcript of interview with Nolan Nox, Director of
Nightjar, for *Scream Screen* magazine (*Nightjar*
twentieth-anniversary special feature)

CJL: C. J. Lahey, columnist with *Scream Screen*

NN: Nolan Nox, director of *Nightjar*

CJL: Thanks for agreeing to talk with me for *Scream
Screen*'s *Nightjar* twentieth-anniversary special
feature, Nolan – do you mind if I call you Nolan?

NN: How about this: I'll let you call me Nolan like we're
old pals, and you won't say a damn word about
me smoking while we do this. I'm sick of you people
telling me I'm not allowed to smoke in my own
office.

CJL: [Laughs] Deal. So, it's twenty years since *Nightjar*
first whipped horror fans into a frenzy worldwide.
What do you think it is, exactly, about this movie

that really fired up such an intense and long-lasting reaction from fans?

NN: [Pause] That's really what you want to ask me? *Nightjar* won dozens of awards, including two Emmys, and you want me to tell you why my film is good?

CJL: OK, let's take a different approach. [Pause] In *Nightjar*, we see a small Prohibition-era town cut off from civilization by a freak storm – we're talking fallen trees, floods, a contaminated water supply, and all roads out of town blocked. Nightjar's inhabitants are starving, and they're caught up in this spiralling sense of panic and superstition and fear. That claustrophobic tension you created within the film demanded the perfect setting, and to this day fans still flock to the town of Harrow Lake, Indiana, where you filmed *Nightjar* – maybe looking to capture their own little slice of *Nightjar* terror. What was it about Harrow Lake that made you choose it for your backdrop?

NN: Harrow Lake had hardly changed since the late twenties. As a mining town, it was almost destroyed by some kind of ground disturbance back then, leaving half of it buried under a landslide and the other turned to Swiss cheese with these gaping craters in the hillside. They had to totally rebuild and I guess they couldn't afford to modernize it after that, which was lucky for us. Everything there – the houses, the stores, even the damn

2

people – was in mint 1920s condition. Then there were the caves, of course. When I went with the scout to see Harrow Lake, I just knew. It was perfect.

CJL: You mentioned the caves just now – those are some of my favourite scenes – but filming there didn't quite go according to plan, did it?

NN: [Pause] I assume you're referring to Moss.

CJL: Well, yeah. It's kind of unusual for one of the crew to disappear during filming, isn't it? [Laughs]

NN: Ron Moss was a competent cameraman, and a valued member of my crew. His disappearance wasn't *unusual*, it was tragic – and damned inconvenient.

CJL: Oh, I didn't mean to make light of it. But could you describe what happened leading up to his disappearance?

NN: Are you sure your readers will want to know all this? We're re-treading a lot of old ground here. [Pause] All right. We were nearing the end of our filming schedule for the caves and had just wrapped the scene where Little Bird is cannibalized by the starving villagers. The crew were getting packed up to move on to the next location when we heard noises coming from inside the caves – strange clicking sounds. I'd never heard anything like it. Anyway, one of the other crew members noticed Moss was no longer with us, and all his equipment was just lying there on the grass where he'd been filming. I'm talking expensive kit, and Moss wasn't the type to dump it and wander off. We searched as far as we could, but saw no sign of him. By that point, the noises had stopped, and we called in the local authorities to carry out a proper search. They didn't find him.

CJL: But they did find human remains.

NN: [Sighs] Those were nothing to do with Moss. The ruin of the church where we were filming was inside a sinkhole. It had collapsed when the ground shifted a century before. It doesn't take a genius to figure out the bones they found in the caves were from back then – either from the graveyard next to the church, or from someone who got caught in the landslide.

CJL: So you don't believe in Harrow Lake's local legend, then?

NN: You mean Mister Jitters? Don't be ridiculous. There's no hundred-year-old monster eating the locals, and there never was. Harrow Lake is just a small town that got hit by a terrible disaster and never fully recovered. I'm not surprised they explained it away with some paranormal nonsense – curses and whatnot. It's easier than admitting they mined too deep into their own hillside and damn near buried themselves. [Pause] Actually, cut that last part. People who live in these hick towns are so quick to take offence, and I can't be bothered dealing with the hate mail.

CJL: Sure. Go again, whenever you're ready.

NN: OK. [Pause] I'm not sure what exactly we heard in the caves that night. That clicking . . . maybe it was some natural phenomenon, maybe not. All I know is that I never saw anything unusual in or near the caves, and I have no reason to believe Moss's disappearance was anything other than an accident. We'll probably never know exactly what happened there. Look, these stories – small-town legends about monsters or demons or evil spirits – they're all just an excuse for people to avoid seeing the real monsters all around them. It's a way to shatter the proverbial mirror. That's why I make the movies I do: I'm reconstructing the mirror. [Pause] Make sure you use that, all right? That's a damn good quote.

CJL: [Laughs] Oh, I will. But just to pick up on a point there: don't you think it's a little coincidental – beyond coincidental, in fact – that your daughter also disappeared when she visited Harrow Lake last year?

NN: I don't want to talk about Lola.

CJL: But isn't it strange that –

NN: I thought we were here to discuss *Nightjar*. Let's leave my daughter out of this and move on.

CJL: But –

NN: That wasn't a suggestion. [Pause] Let's take five. Maybe you can use that time to pull your head out of your ass and start asking me relevant questions.

ONE YEAR EARLIER

LOLA

CHAPTER ONE

I bury my secrets in a potted plant on West 17th Street. There's nobody inside the brightly lit lobby of the apartment building next to me, and only a couple of people farther along the street. A man and a woman. From their loud, slurred voices, I guess they've just rolled out of Bar Qua. They're not interested in a seventeen-year-old girl loitering next to an overly primped topiary.

I shove three things into the dirt. Nothing too shocking really: a keychain, a lighter and a lurid pink lipstick.

The keychain I stole from some guy. I saw a girl give it to him outside the public library, and there was something about the heat in her cheeks that made me tell my tutor I was going to use the restroom, and I followed the boy inside. The moment he took his jacket off, I grabbed the keychain from his pocket.

It's not fancy or expensive, only a silver letter *D*. I just wanted to see if I could get away with it.

The cigar lighter is Nolan's – my dad's. I took it because I knew it would piss him off. That's a good, solid reason, right? It's gold, and has the looping double *N* of his initials engraved on the casing. I'm sorry I didn't guess he would accuse and then fire the housekeeper when the lighter failed to show up, but I didn't, and he did, and so it became a secret.

The pink lipstick is my newest acquisition. I stole it tonight from the restroom of Bar Qua – the same bar the couple up the street just stumbled out of. I just couldn't resist hiding one last secret before leaving New York behind.

I don't always take things that aren't mine. I usually just scribble my secrets on scraps of paper and bury those. But I've been stealing more and more over the last few weeks. Small things, like a pen or a pair of sunglasses left on a restaurant table. Easily missed. Easily slipped into a pocket or purse. I know this isn't a healthy development or anything, but at least it *is* a development. My life doesn't have many of those. And it's good to have a hobby, I guess.

There was a farewell party going on in the bar. This guy with hard, over-gelled hair and a loose tie was at the centre of it all. I hung around, having a few drinks, eating hors d'oeuvres, daring someone to notice me.

Look at me. Go on, look.

But they didn't know that I'm the daughter of a legend. All they saw was a strange girl not talking to anyone. Then came the inevitable frown from Mr Hard Hair, the exchange of raised eyebrows with Ms Chardonnay and Ms Lipstick Teeth: *Do you know her? No, you? No.* And then the subtle shift in temperature as that group of connected people closed ranks and froze me out.

Of course they didn't recognize me. Nobody ever does unless I'm next to Nolan. He trots me out all the time at parties. Industry parties. Parties where people know him well enough that they wouldn't dream of taking my picture or paying me more than the most fleeting of glances, because everybody knows that *you don't cross Nolan Nox.*

Twenty minutes after Mr Hard Hair and Ms Chardonnay and Ms Lipstick Teeth looked me straight in the eye, I'd be surprised if even one of them remembered seeing me.

After being dismissed, I wandered to the restroom and saw the garish pink lipstick sitting next to the basin. Two young women – one of them the owner of the lipstick, I guess – were involved in a very animated discussion about some older woman named Celine Reynard who was, by all accounts, *a two-faced bitch.* I washed my hands and pretended to smooth my hair in the mirror.

'And the whole time, she was screwing Joanna's teenage son behind her back! Can you imagine?'

I could imagine – quite vividly, which I probably shouldn't have. Celine, who I'd decided was probably elegantly grey-haired and svelte, with some spotty kid energetically grinding away while Joanna went about her day, making business calls or cooking a lasagne or driving to the liquor store or whatever mothers do, totally oblivious to the skin show going on behind her back.

Maybe Joanna should pay a little more attention to her son.

'What did you do?' the other woman asked.

The first woman shrugged. 'What *could* I do? I wasn't going to be the one to tell Joanna and have Celine call me a liar to my face.'

She used washing her hands as an excuse to break eye contact, her nostrils flaring. Was she lying? Her neck had started to turn blotchy.

Before I could make up my mind, the other woman changed the subject to a boring update on her home renovations, so I tuned out. I was about to leave when my gaze snagged on the lipstick sitting next to the sink. Casually, I reached out and slipped it into my pocket. Walked to the door. Let the throbbing music of the bar swallow me.

And they didn't even glance my way. They were as oblivious as poor Joanna. But did that make me Celine Reynard – stealthy rogue, breaking all the rules? Or was I Joanna's sweaty son, craving attention? I search the cracks in the sidewalk for an answer. If it's there, it's buried too deep for me to see.

It isn't the car itself, but the harsh screech of its tyres that catches my attention. My heart sinks. It's Nolan's car, though I doubt he's inside. This is confirmed when the driver's side window rolls down and my father's assistant glares out at me. 'Get in the car, Lola!'

'Hey, Larry,' I monotone, making no move to get in. I tilt my head and tap my chin. 'Did you do something new with your beard?'

He hasn't, of course. His beard is probably exactly the same as when he first grew it in kindergarten. Larry Brown is a short, stocky man with black hair covering pretty much every part of him you can see. I saw a documentary once about some guy who absorbed his twin *in utero*, but it kept growing inside him like a tumour until it was the size of a raccoon. When they cut it out, the tumour-twin was this mass of flesh with hair and teeth growing out of it.

That's what I think of when I see Larry.

'Nolan texted me, said to come find you,' he says, ignoring the beard thing.

'He texted you? Nolan doesn't text.'

'Well, he did tonight,' Larry snaps. I stifle a wince. For Nolan to text Larry rather than call, he must be too incandescent with rage to actually speak. And I caused that. 'Damn it, Lola! You know you shouldn't be here. He'll be out of his mind worrying about you.' He sighs. He's an aggressive sigher. I guess I've messed up his plans for the night, whatever they were. 'What were you thinking?'

'Oh, *Larry*,' I drawl, channelling Lestat from *Interview with the Vampire*. 'I thought only of oblivion, of course.'

It's easy for me to slide into another persona like this. I watch way too many movies.

If Larry gets the reference, he gives no sign of it. He's probably too distracted by the vein pulsing all the way up the middle of his forehead.

I bite my lip, but stop as soon as I notice I'm doing it. Nolan would tell me I look like an airhead. Not Optimal.

'How did you find me?' I ask.

'You took Nolan's key card. I tracked the chip in it.'

Damn. I didn't know he could do that.

'I don't want to go back yet,' I say. 'Can't I just have a little while longer?'

Just a little more time, a little more air, and I'll be fine. I only need a little bit more . . .

'Lola, for the love of . . . *no.* Just get in the car.'

Down the street, the drunk couple have become long-reaching shadows. If I ran after them, told them a strange guy was following me, would they let me go with them? Maybe for an hour, or a night? Or would they pretend not to hear, and keep walking?

Larry leans against the steering wheel. The horn blares. Larry acts like he meant to do it. '*Now*, Lola.'

I could do it. Just run . . .

I get in the car. The door locks snap into place as Larry starts the engine. I stare at him in the rear-view mirror, holding his gaze as I push the button to raise the privacy partition. He mutters something that sounds like 'damn stupid teenagers' and shakes his head, breaking eye contact before the screen does it for him.

Lights flash past the window as we hurtle between the high-rises of Hudson Yards. My eyes blur, and I start listing all the best things to say when I see Nolan. If I can just figure out a few Optimal things to distract him, I might survive the night. I mean, sure, he'll be angry that I left the apartment on my own and without his permission. But he won't really want a fight, not while all his energy is focused on his new project – and not when we're about to be stuck with each other on an eight-hour flight. Besides, it was kind of *his* fault for not telling me we were moving again.

I arrived home from my tutoring session at the library to find the apartment packed up, my life reduced to a neat stack of boxes with my name on. When I tracked Nolan down inside the cardboard maze and asked him what the hell was going on, he just glanced at me and said, 'Oh, didn't I tell you? We're going to Paris in the morning. I start work on the new movie there next week.'

Then he went back to his study, humming along to that damned jazz record I can't stand.

Oh, didn't I tell you? Just like that. No big deal.

I felt my flesh hardening like volcanic rock, ready to explode at any moment. I couldn't breathe. And he wouldn't even look at me long enough to notice. Wouldn't even look at me.

Look at me!

So I left. He noticed *that* apparently.

I've made a list of Optimal things I can say to Nolan by the time the car sidles to the kerb outside our building. Things like *I overreacted* and *I shouldn't have left* and *You were right*. A list keeps me from saying the wrong thing to Nolan and making everything worse.

Deep breath. Get out of the car.

The Ivory is a beautiful, disapproving beast. It rises ten stories above me with curved art deco stonework. It's easy to imagine flappers skipping out of the lobby on nights like this, all lipstick and gin and looking for a *swell time*.

Nolan is obsessed with the 1920s. He loves the music, the art, the decadence. The architecture, too – it's in the bones of every building we've ever lived in. He once told me ruefully that he wished he'd been around back then to witness the dawning age of cinema – to be able to shape it from that Big Bang moment. I was surprised to hear him say that. Nolan doesn't usually admit to wanting anything he can't have.

'You forgot your purse.'

Larry stands next to me, holding it out like you would to a stranger on a train, his thoughts elsewhere now that he's done Nolan's bidding. You wouldn't think the guy has known me my whole life.

He and Nolan used to be college buddies – before Larry screwed up some big investments and went broke. Maybe he was different back then, before he had to ask Nolan for a job, but it's hard to imagine them as friends. Larry is such a Renfield.

I take my bag and am about to head inside the Ivory when Larry moves to follow me.

'Where are you going?' I ask.

'To check on Nolan. He didn't pick up when I tried calling –'

'Larry. He's fine.'

We both know that's not true; for Nolan to text Larry instead of calling him is a really bad sign. '*Why would I spend ten minutes having a goddamn conversation by text when it can be wrapped up with a twenty-second phone call?*'

This is so, so bad.

The windows of our apartment at the very top of the Ivory are glowing. Nolan's waiting for me, and I don't want to do this in front of Larry. He's still hovering, though. Undecided.

'Look,' I say. 'It's late, and we have things to sort out before our trip.'

There's a tense silence before Larry finally nods. 'If there's anything . . .'

'OK!' I call over my shoulder, already walking away.

The street noise dulls as soon as I'm inside, leaving only the sound of my shoes clicking over the polished floor of the lobby. I pass the reception desk, ready to flash Matty a smile, even though he never smiles back anymore. Once, while he held the door for me, he let his hand curl around my arm and linger there a little too long, his fingers nestled against the side of my breast. I could've just stepped away from him or told him not to touch me, but the contact caught me by surprise. It actually reminded me of a time when I was leaving one of Nolan's film premieres and some guy grabbed me and tried to bundle me into the trunk of his car. The incident was kind of exciting, honestly – like finding myself in a movie with no script. Smiling, I described to Matty how I kicked my would-be kidnapper and screamed the way I thought I should, until the man let me go. Nolan had come running over just as the guy was wheel-spinning away. Then he picked me up and let me sob against his Armani suit. That was kind of nice.

'Nolan didn't report it to the police,' I told Matty. 'That's weird, now that I think about it. But there was a news story a couple of days later about a man who was found burned alive inside a car just like the one I saw that night . . . Maybe it was a different car – I'm not sure. But I think about that guy whenever I smell roasting meat.'

Matty snatched back his hand then, and scuttled off to his spot behind the reception desk. In that moment, I could have said or done anything to him without a single consequence. Stories can be powerful things.

Matty isn't sitting at the reception desk now. He always works the late shift – he has the haggard appearance of a man who's anxious to avoid his wife and kids – but tonight the foyer is empty. He's probably just on a bathroom break, but it feels like the whole building is hollow. I don't like it.

I take the elevator up to the penthouse and step out into a marble hallway that has only one door on it – ours. I'm so preoccupied fishing around in my purse for the key card I 'borrowed' from Nolan that I almost tread in the sticky dark red mess pooling under the apartment door. Looks like one of his fans has sent him another memento.

In the six months since Nolan and I moved into this apartment, he has been the unamused recipient of a box of dead toads, a pie made from what the Police Forensics Team informed us were dog intestines and, most recently, a jar with a human toe in it. If Nolan wasn't so anal that he insists on opening all his own mail, Larry could intercept these *gifts*. But I guess I'd have no reason to send them if he did. (I'm kidding – I didn't send *all* of them. Only the toe. And only because Nolan had been particularly shitty about letting me have my own laptop. He went off – *again* – about

18

'the dangers of the internet' and how I'm 'better off without all those lies infesting my brain'. All the same words he uses when he arbitrarily fires my tutors for not keeping a close enough eye on what I'm up to online.) Anyway, the shine of *gifting* wore off for me when Nolan hurled the jar across the kitchen and it smashed, sending the fake toe sailing into a pot of coffee I'd just made.

I still don't have my own laptop. I don't even have a phone.

Now the 'blood' runs out in lines under the door, between the marble floor tiles, like it's moving, reaching for me. I stop before the toes of my shoes touch the puddle. It's an even deeper red at the edges, drying to a crust.

Before I can swipe the key card down the lock, the door swings slowly inward. I brace myself for Nolan's ice-cold fury, but he isn't standing in the doorway. There's nobody there.

More blood-goop stains the parquet floor. The trail is patchy, like a heavy weight has been dragged and set down a few times. A prickling feeling sweeps over my skin. My grip tightens on the key card and I hold it out like a weapon in front of me as I linger just outside the door.

'Nolan?'

He doesn't answer, but I hear *something*. Like faint music, maybe. Not a conspicuous sound, but enough for me to know that Nolan is home. *Huh*. He never leaves the door to the apartment unlocked.

Sidestepping the mess, I go in. I smell last night's takeout, the coconut oil the housekeeper uses on the leather furniture, and Nolan's Montes – his Montecristo Relentless No. 2 cigars, which he smokes exactly twice a day. But there's another smell, too: tangy and unpleasant.

The long foyer is dim, but there's enough light to see that the trail leads between the stacked boxes lining the hallway, past the kitchen, and disappears into Nolan's study. The door to the study is oak with a coloured glass inlay made to look like interlocking pieces of a geometric puzzle. I'm never entirely sure what Nolan is up to when he's locked away in there. The puzzle door is *always* closed – whether he's inside or not.

It's open now.

'Nolan, are you home?'

Still no reply, but I've identified the murmur coming from inside. That damned jazz record is still playing in his study – 'T'ain't No Sin', one of his favourites. It keeps repeating the same few bars over and over, jumping like it has a scratch. Nolan won't like that.

The red path is wider here; it has spread into the cracks around the parquet blocks, threading outward like bloated veins.

'You left the door open . . .'

The trail thickens as I edge around it and cross to the study doorway, following the path. I know there's too much 'blood' to have come from a package. I *know* that.

Maybe Nolan's been called out to the studio and didn't have time to deal with the mess. Maybe I can get this cleared up before he gets home. That would be the Optimal thing to do.

It feels wrong to go into Nolan's study without his permission. But with two quick steps it's done. Here the smoky scent of his Montes hangs like an invisible cloud. I spot the cigar stub sitting in a spray of ash on Nolan's big oak desk, next to the ashtray. Next to it, not *in* it – as though it's been knocked over and left like that. The feeling of utter wrongness chokes me.

Stop it. Stop it! Don't be such a child, Lola.

Nothing has been packed away in Nolan's study yet; he likes to keep his workspace *just so*. The walls are covered in shelves of books and awards and photographs taken on various filmsets. These things represent his life's work, his pride. On his desk there's a picture of me, too. None of my mother.

Lorelei herself has been AWOL for most of my life, so she doesn't get a spot on the desk. But she is in the framed *Nightjar* poster – the only movie she ever starred in. It's Nolan's most iconic film, shot in Lorelei's hometown of Harrow Lake, Indiana. *Nightjar* earned its place on the wall, even if Lorelei didn't.

I turn off the record player and the upbeat melody jolts to a stop. I can hear the desk phone now. It's lying on its side, a tone of quiet distress bleeding out of the receiver. I pick it up and am reaching for the switch hook to silence it when I see him. I freeze.

Nolan is slumped against a low bookcase, arms crossed over his stomach like he just decided to sit down and relax. For a second, I feel foolish for imagining anything was wrong. This is a joke, obviously. Even though Nolan never

21

jokes, not like this. My palms sting, my fingers curled too tight.

'Nolan?'

He doesn't answer. His eyes roll like he's struggling to focus, nostrils flaring. Pain – intense pain. I've seen that look before, I guess, but only on-screen or on-set, and never from him. He's faking – he must be. *Acting*. Except Nolan doesn't do that, either. Unless . . . is he doing this to teach me a lesson? To punish me for leaving the apartment? How am I supposed to react? What's the Optimal thing for me to do?

But no, the blood – it's all over his hands, leaking from between his fingers. His cellphone lies in a puddle of it on the floor next to him, the dark screen smeared with fumbled fingermarks. A whole lake of blood.

I'd better clean that up before Nolan sees it.

The thought floats into my head like a soap bubble, and I almost laugh. Because that's not an Optimal thought to have right now. Because . . .

Because, God, he's hurt. He's really hurt.

The truth of it hits me with such force, such certainty, that it slams against my chest. I stutter-step in my rush to get to him and my feet skid under me so that I land hard on my knees. I grab the edge of the desk to pull myself back up, but a sudden sound stops me. It's like fingers snapping again and again, only too quickly to be real. Like chattering teeth, but too loud – *snap, snap, snap, snap, SNAP*. The noise echoes through the apartment, then stops when it reaches the open doorway. My elbow hits the desk edge with a loud crack as I whirl to face it, pain lancing all the way to my shoulder. But there's nobody in the doorway, and the sound is gone. There's only a vacuum of empty space.

What was *that?*

I crawl to Nolan's side, waiting to hear footsteps, a door slamming, but there's only the thudding of my heart against my ribcage. Whatever made that chattering noise is gone now.

'Lola,' Nolan says, but it's more of a groan. I don't know what to do, where to start. I need to figure out why he's bleeding, but I can't bring myself to touch him. 'Lola, I . . . I need an amb–'

Nolan's muffled words kick my brain into action. I grab the phone and crouch next to him as I dial 911. I somehow sound calm as I give the operator as much information as I can, trying to drown out the *other* voice inside my head, the hissing static that keeps whispering that he's going to die, going to leave me all alone, going to disappear . . .

'There's already an ambulance on its way to you, Lola,' the operator says. 'We got a call from your dad a little while ago.'

Of course. Did I seriously think he just lay down and waited for me to come home? No. Even here, even now, Nolan has arranged everything.

'He's . . . he's bleeding a lot. I think he's been stabbed. There's so much blood!'

'It's all right, Lola. Now here's what I need you to do . . .'

Following her directions, I run and grab a towel from the bathroom, then force myself to hold it to his stomach. I don't want to face what's really covering my hands; what's making the phone too slippery to hold steady. I can't let Nolan see how scared I am.

If only we hadn't argued earlier. If only I hadn't left him . . . He shouldn't be lying here like this. It's my fault. It's all my fault.

A thousand years pass before footsteps pound up to the apartment door and I hear the clipped, efficient voices of the paramedics. Nolan grunts in pain, then falls still. Is he unconscious or . . .

'No, no, no, no, NO!' I repeat the word like its rhythm can take the place of both our heartbeats.

Things I learned about stab wounds while waiting to hear if Nolan was going to die

1. Plenty of people survive being stabbed. More than you think. As long as you miss the major arteries (carotid in the neck, or femoral in the groin), they'll probably survive if they get help quickly.*
2. Depending on where the person is stabbed (three times in the lower abdomen and once in the upper thigh, in Nolan's case), it can take hours for them to die – if they die, that is. Again, most don't.
3. If the stabbing victim loses more than forty per cent of the blood in their body, they will usually need immediate and aggressive resuscitation, and will definitely need a blood transfusion to save them. (Whose blood are they giving Nolan?)

* This is the only Optimal thing I can come up with. I'm not going to mention anything on this list to Nolan when he wakes up. I'll just find somewhere to bury it.

25

4. I remember reading a news article about four Russian teenagers who were abducted by Satan worshippers and each stabbed 666 times before being eaten: *666 times*. Would you even look human after being stabbed that many times? Probably not. Maybe it made them easier to eat. *Shit*. Why am I even thinking about this?

CHAPTER TWO

I sit in the waiting room at the hospital, tracing the veins in my arm with a black pen someone left next to a book of word puzzles. I start with the biggest veins. Three thick, angry lines thread up from inside my elbow and dive under the meaty base of my thumb. Next I draw over the smaller veins, weaving and connecting them, making dark cracks cover the surface of my fingers, knuckles, palm, all the way down my forearm. But then the lines start to swim, morphing into cracks in a parquet floor, filling with viscous red liquid . . .

Stop it!

Still, I don't stop drawing, carving the memory into my skin. The ink has reached my elbow by the time two shoes stop in my peripheral vision. I blink slowly. Brown shoes.

'Lola?'

I follow the line up from the boring shoes, past a badly fitting grey suit, over his mustard yellow tie – why always mustard? – to the thick black hair sprouting from Larry's collar. His tie has been loosened, his top shirt button opened as if to let all that body hair jostle its way out.

'How long have you been here?' Larry's words are clipped. His beady eyes dart around before falling on the fault lines covering half my arm. 'A while, I take it.'

The clock on the wall says it's a little after seven, but it could be morning or evening. People have rolled in and out of the waiting room in waves since I was ordered to stay put while Nolan recovered after surgery. At the moment, it's just me and some old lady asleep in the corner next to the muted TV – and Larry.

'Have you been here by yourself since last night? You should have called me.'

'Why?' Calling Larry was the last thing on my mind while I waited for the doctors to save Nolan's life. It's not like he could have helped.

A door thumps open somewhere. They wouldn't rush if it was bad news, would they? Are those good-news footsteps or bad? A woman in a white coat bustles past, and I exhale. It's strange how people just appear out of thin air here, inhabit your space without a word, then are gone again. The doors swing. No locks. Nothing to stop you if you wanted to run away. I read that Danish people leave a window open in the house where someone is dying so that their soul has a way to escape. Maybe that's why they don't lock the doors here – so many people dying all the time. The place would be packed with souls by now if they had no way out.

I should lock the doors so he can't leave me.

I make a weird, strangled sound.

'You're supposed to tell me if you're in trouble, or you need anything,' Larry says. 'You know that.' I don't *know that*, actually, but I can't handle a fight right now. 'I couldn't believe it when I got the call to say Nolan had been attacked. And I'd just left you to go inside the apartment by yourself –!'

'Well, you're here now,' I say. Larry lowers himself onto a squeaky plastic chair and leans towards me.

'So you just . . . found him like that? That's what happened, right?'

I nod, but it becomes a shudder as the image of Nolan lying there covered in his own blood flashes through my mind.

'You look . . .' Larry doesn't finish, but I can guess what he means. My hair hangs in clumps around my face, and my eyes itch. I've chewed my fingernails to the point that they sting, and my arms are covered with black pen. I've got quite the *Silent Hill* aesthetic going on.

Larry glances at the sleeping woman in the corner, then leans back and crosses his legs at the ankles. She's no one.

'You didn't speak with the police, did you?' Larry says.

'Well, yeah.' There were a lot of questions – I remember that – but not much of what I said. Nolan's lawyer was there for most of it, her expression as crisp as her Dior suit. She was probably the one who called Larry. I'll try not to hold that against her; it's what lawyers do. 'Is that a problem?'

'*Yes*, it's a problem,' Larry snaps, standing up again and starting to pace. 'They really shouldn't have done that –' Larry whirls on me suddenly, his gaze so intent I almost shrink back. But I don't. 'What did you tell them?'

I try to remember, but the conversation is hazy. So I make an educated guess. 'I told them I got back to the apartment and the door was open. Nolan was lying in his study. He said he needed an ambulance, then passed out. That's what happened.'

Larry lets out a sigh. 'OK. That's all right. No harm done. Though obviously you won't be able to go back to the Ivory while the police are there, and the media are bound to be hanging around outside,' he says. 'They'll be salivating over this. Probably praying Nolan will die, just for the headline.'

It occurs to me that he's not just his usual brand of tense – he's worried. Understandable, I suppose. Or is it? I watch him tapping one thick finger against his lips. Aside from me, Larry is the only other person with easy access to the apartment. And he said Nolan texted him to come get me, *but what if he didn't*? What if instead Larry went to see Nolan at the apartment after I left, and something happened between them? It wouldn't be the first time they've argued about me. What if this time it got out of hand and –

No. No way. No matter how much they butt heads, Larry would never actually hurt Nolan. They've known each other forever. They were 'frat bros', and all that bullshit. Besides, who'd take care of Larry's never-ending gambling debts if Nolan died?

If Nolan died.

I think I'm going to throw up. 'Do *you* think he's going to die?' My voice is small. Maybe that's why Larry ignores me.

'I'm not sure if Nolan spoke to you about this, but he left instructions in his will that –'

'He isn't *dead*,' I say.

Larry exhales loudly through his nose. 'As I was saying, if anything were to happen to him while you're still a minor, your grandmother would get custody of you. So you'll go there.'

'My grandmother?' I say. 'I don't have a grandmother.'

I don't have any relatives besides Nolan. Well, except Lorelei. And then I realize what's coming.

'I mean Lorelei's mother,' Larry says. 'She still lives in Harrow Lake.'

I was five when Lorelei packed up her shit and left. I have only random memories of her: the way she looked so serious as she put on her make-up, how she'd whisper bedtime stories so I had to edge closer to listen, the tune she used to hum when she washed my hair because it was the only thing that would keep me from squirming away.

Lorelei stuck around just long enough that I felt like my world emptied when she left. And then Nolan filled it all.

'You expect me to go to Lorelei's hometown? Like, just drop by for a nice, friendly visit? Are you serious?'

My response is automatic. Optimal. Nolan would never want me to visit Harrow Lake.

So why would he put that in his will?

There must not be anywhere else for me to go.

Larry watches me, unmoved. 'We're in a bit of a pinch right now, Lola.'

I slump back in my squeaky plastic seat. 'Is *she* there?' I ask.

'Lorelei?' he says. I'm sure he waits as long as he can before answering. 'No.'

The answer's a sucker punch. Double sucker punch, because I don't even know if I wanted the answer to be yes.

'But this doesn't make any sense . . . . Why didn't Nolan ever tell me about this?'

'That's between you and him. I've told you everything I know.' Larry cocks his head: *take it or leave it.* 'So the publicist is preparing a press statement, but I'm waiting on the official word on his condition before I give the go-ahead to release it. You need to be gone before the vultures start circling.'

I can't say I'm not a tiny bit curious about this grand-mother he just dangled in front of me. And I've always secretly wanted to visit Harrow Lake – it's a living snapshot of Nolan's past I never thought I'd be allowed to see.

'Jesus, Lola,' Larry says, his tone weary. 'What are we gonna do about all this . . . mess? I can't believe it all got so fucked up. I should've . . .' He shakes his head.

I stare at a spot on Larry's tie as though it might tell me exactly how our life became a bloody hurricane in one night. The spot looks like a burrito stain. It probably doesn't have the answers I want.

'All right. Harrow Lake it is,' I say, as though Larry has actually asked for my thoughts on the matter. 'That's obviously what Nolan would want us to do.'

'Good. That's good.' The tension under that ugly suit slackens. 'I'm not sure how long he'll be in here, but I'd bet it'll be weeks rather than days – probably with medical care at home after that. Unless Nolan says otherwise, you can come back as soon as he's up to receiving visitors. A couple of days, three days max –'

'Wait, you're not coming?' Whenever Nolan's away for work and can't take me with him, Larry stays with me. Always. Even if that means Nolan has to hire someone new to be his gopher on location.

'Nolan needs me here to handle things.' His mouth sets in a stoic line. 'So you'll be travelling solo this time. Your grandmother will take good care of you in Indiana.'

Larry probably thinks I'm nervous about being alone. And I am, a little. Last night, out on the streets of a city I sometimes call home, I could still feel Nolan's invisible thread wrapped around my wrist, trailing along the miles and miles of sidewalk behind me, tying me to him. But will that thread follow me all the way to Indiana? Or will it snap, leaving me on my own?

Free of him . . .

The thought is a silverfish, quick and slithery.

'The police might want to speak to you again,' Larry continues, 'but they can just wait until you get back. Like I said, you won't be gone long.'

'I'll need to grab some things from the apartment. Will the police let me back in?'

'No need. I packed a bag for you when I went to check on the CCTV footage,' Larry says, getting to his feet.

I hadn't even thought about that. Of course Nolan's attacker will have been caught on camera. 'Did you see who it was?'

Larry's eyes snap to mine, then away. 'There's nothing on the tape. Must've been a glitch in the system. Anyway, why don't I bring the car around?'

He's gone before I can answer. I sit there for a moment, rolling his words over in my head. How could the tape be blank? Was the person who attacked Nolan some kind of professional, who knew how to cover their tracks? Or . . .

Or was the tape blank because Larry wiped it? He has a key. Knows the security system. And he knew I was out of the apartment.

This thought digs its claws in a little too deep to shake off. *Could* Larry have hurt Nolan? The question hums under my skin, inside my head. I try to picture Larry doing it – pulling out a knife and . . .

I swallow hard. No, Larry wouldn't do that. Not to Nolan. Besides, he's the type to use his fists, if anything.

I go and find the room where Nolan is recovering. There are two security guards outside the door and they nod to let me know I can go in if I want to. But I don't. I press my hand up against the observation window, my fingertips turning bloodless against the glass.

Nolan's face is slack and tired against the hospital pillow. He never looks like that, not even when he's sleeping. With all those tubes and wires attached to him, he's so ordinary. Old. Broken.

No.

34

Nolan Nox can't be *reduced* like that. Like he's nothing.

I let my hand drop to my side, leaving behind a hazy imprint on the window.

'Tell him I was here,' I say to the handprint. It doesn't answer.

CHAPTER THREE

'Are you my grandmother?' I ask the man at the airport holding the sign with my name on it.

He doesn't laugh, just frowns. 'I'm Grant,' he says. No indication of whether this is his first or last name. 'You must be Lola. Your grandma asked me to collect you.'

He isn't thin, but he looks skeletal somehow, in a shirt and pants with suspenders, and a pair of well-worn but polished boots on his feet like a pilgrim. I guess he's around forty, with close-cropped hair that's just starting to thin and deep lines around his mouth.

'She didn't need to send someone,' I say, not moving. 'I can call a cab.'

The pickup parked behind him is exactly the kind of truck a serial killer would drive.

'No taxi cab'll go all the way out to Harrow Lake,' Grant says. 'I guess you could rent a car and drive there yourself, if Russell's Rentals is open. Want me to see?'

He smirks like he can tell I don't have a driver's licence. *'I don't need another damn thing to worry about,'* Nolan said. *'Besides, where would you go?'*

'Or you could walk,' Grant adds with a shrug. 'It'd only take you a day or two to get to Mrs McCabe's place.'

Moira McCabe.

That's the name Larry gave me before he waved me off with the packed suitcase and a promise to let me know as soon as there was any news about Nolan.

I've already called the hospital twice since the plane landed, using the crappy prepaid phone Larry handed me at JFK Airport along with one of Nolan's credit cards and my passport. I thought it was strange that Larry had my passport ready, as though he was expecting I'd need it – but then I remembered the move to Paris. I should be in France right now.

A white-hot rush of anger has me grinding my teeth. Larry knew about the move before me. I mean, of course he did – he must have made most of the arrangements. But the reminder that telling *me* ranked lower on Nolan's list of priorities than telling *Larry* feels like I've been shoved aside all over again.

Haven't you, though? Isn't that why you're in the middle of nowhere right now – so you're out of the way?

My thumb hovers over my phone screen. I want to call Nolan again, but so far my calls keep hitting a wall of hospital workers. *Nolan is in the best place . . . recovering as expected . . . needs his rest . . .* and on and on and on. Just vague reassurances they might be reading from a prepared list. (I know a list when I hear one.)

There's nothing I can do now except go with this stranger in front of me like a good little lamb. I text Larry a picture of Grant, just in case he is in fact a serial killer, then go over to the truck.

'Where shall I put my bag, Mr Grant?' I smile at him the same way I smile at Larry: functionally, a sequence of muscle contractions pulling my lips away from my teeth.

'I'll take that for you, sweetheart.' He heaves the suitcase into the back of the pickup and throws a tarp over it. 'And it's just Grant.'

By the time I climb up into the cab next to him, Grant's eyes have already crawled all the way up from my toenails to the roots of my hair. I stare at him until he turns away with a grin.

I blink awake to find the truck rumbling through a forest. Grant drives like looped footage: hands moving from ten-and-two to gear shift, then back. The last time I looked out the window it was at a long stretch of highway dotted with cars. Now there's only a dirt track that I can barely make out in the glow of the headlights. Is this what Harrow Lake looks like? Is that even where he's taking me? I picture a cabin in the woods full of hunting knives and snares, or some End of Days bunker with a drain in the floor.

I reach for the phone lying on the bench seat next to me.

'Hey there, sleepyhead,' Grant says, and I almost drop the phone. I'm pretty sure he's been keeping one eye on me this whole time.

'Where are we?'

'Almost there. The main road into town runs past the campsite on the west shore of the lake,' he says. 'It's easier to find. But that's mostly just for the out-of-towners. We're taking the back road.'

'Out-of-towners?'

'Sure. During the summer festival, plenty of folks come to visit the spot where *Nightjar* was filmed . . .'

I grew up with people whispering '*Nightjar*' whenever they saw Nolan in the street. I've watched his masterpiece hundreds of times. It brought my parents together, made stars of them both, although Lorelei never acted in another movie after it. She played the part of wife and mother for a while, I guess, then took off to become someone else.

'That won't do you much good now,' Grant says, gesturing towards the phone in my hand. 'Not in Harrow Lake. The signal won't reach down into the basin –'

'So how am I supposed to contact anyone? I need to be able to reach the hospital.'

'Your grandma has a landline at the house, I think.'

'You think?'

He chooses this moment to become a man of few words.

We circle the water's edge as the streetlights flicker to life. This is Harrow Lake – the town and the body of water it's named after.

Will Nolan be angry that I came here? Putting it in his will was one thing – a someday, never, not really, kind of promise – but if he truly wanted me to visit Harrow Lake, he would have brought me here himself. Shown off the town he created, more or less – the birthplace of his masterpiece.

Then again, if he's pissed, I can spin it, convince him that coming here is really just giving me the opportunity to learn more about his work. That would be the Optimal approach.

The lamp posts are elegantly curved and double-ended, the bulbs set in glass lanterns. They look like stiff old ladies carrying pails of light. I wave at them, but they don't wave back.

The lake itself is a dark, sleeping eye, glimpsed between rows of storefronts that reflect my tired face. It's large enough that the far side is invisible in the fading light as we crawl along Main Street in a line of cars. The quaint clapboard buildings have hand-painted signs above the doors advertising things like GARVIN'S GROCERIES, THE EASY DINER, ROAMER'S GUEST HOUSE and TAYLOR'S TACKLE & BAIT. I know these places. This is *Nightjar* in the flesh, living and breathing around me. Familiar and alien at the same time.

The glass-fronted interiors are still lit as a few people hang banners and colourful garlands. My heart falters for a second when I see my mother's face peering out from one of the windows. But it's only a picture of her – one of the *Nightjar* posters from the movie junket.

'Everyone's setting up for the parade next week,' Grant says, pointing at a swathe of bunting. 'It starts the week-long festival we hold each summer – and gives all those *Nightjar* fanatics a chance to come see where the movie was made without bothering us the rest of the year.' It doesn't sound like the festival is a highlight on his calendar.

'You should see about getting involved with the parade. All the local kids do. Talk to your grandma about it. I'm sure she'd be –'

'I'll be gone by then.'

Three days, max, Larry said.

Unless Nolan . . .

No. There is no 'unless'.

I catch a drift of some old music over the chug of the truck's engine. I'm not sure what the song is, but it's familiar. Goosebumps rise across my ink-stained forearm.

Tucked back behind the other stores, a lantern illuminates an old sign: BRYN'S MUSEUM & MEMORABILIA. Some-one steps into the circle of light beneath it. Probably the owner, about to lock up. Except there's something unsettling about the figure; something strange about the way it stands under that spotlight. So tall and thin it looks like it has been stretched on a rack.

'You all right there?' Grant's question snaps my gaze to him. When I look back at the museum, the figure is gone.

'I just . . . I thought I saw someone outside the museum, but they're gone now.'

'Shouldn't be anyone down here at this time,' Grant says. 'The museum closes at five except on Thursdays.'

I stare back at the spot beneath the flickering lantern, now just an empty patch of light.

The buildings fade to trees, and a short while later a house appears out of the darkness. The lit windows are small, and I can see the upstairs rooms are tucked into the eaves of the sharply slanted roof. No streetlights here. No other houses nearby to act as beacons of civilization. This is a place where the sun never quite chases away the shadows.

'Talk about *Cabin in the Woods*,' I say under my breath, not quite able to force myself to reach for the door handle. But the truck door swings open anyway. Grant stands outside with my bag in his hand.

'Did you say something?'

I slither out. The heat of Grant's hand rests at the small of my back, lingering there. Maybe I should tell *him* about the man at the movie premiere, and the smell of roasting meat. But I step away instead, taking the suitcase from him.

'See you around.' I leave him by the idling truck as I hurry up the porch steps and knock on my grandmother's door. It swings open, an eerie reminder of when I arrived at the apartment . . . was that only yesterday?

The inside of the house smells dead, like old wood and insect husks.

'Hello?' I call out to the dust, walking slowly across the bare floor of the hallway. 'Is anyone home?'

A stained-glass lamp casts warm colours on a side table, illuminating a vintage black phone with a rotary dial. Nolan has one just like it. Maybe I should call Larry. Maybe if I explain that I'm standing in a house straight out of one of Nolan's movies, he'll tell me to come home.

There's a hiss of air behind me. I turn and find a woman clutching her chest in an open doorway. She wears a long black dress and her white hair is pinched into a knot at the top of her skull, with a few ringlets left loose around a pan-white face. Her make-up is stark: heavy brown shadow fills her sunken eye sockets, her whisper-thin brows drawn down into a look of disappointed surprise. Plum-coloured lipstick bleeds out into the fine wrinkles crosshatching her skin. She's like a pickled doll.

'I . . . The door was open.' I assume she's my grandmother, and now I realize I have no idea what to call her. Grant referred to her as my *grandma*, but that feels weird. She's a stranger.

'I'm Moira McCabe. Are you . . . You must be . . . Lorelei's girl? My goodness, you've grown!' She holds out her hand.

I start to correct her, then stop. I'm so used to being *Nolan's* girl. I feel like I've walked onto the wrong movie set. I take her hand, but drop it when I feel how cold and papery her skin is.

'You've turned out such a pretty little thing. Let me look at you.' She runs a strand of my hair between her fingers. 'You're just like her.'

'Like Lorelei?' I say, barely resisting the urge to smack her hand away.

'Of course,' she says. When she smiles, her teeth are like yellowed fossils in her mouth. Maybe it's the lamplight. 'Folks must tell you that all the time.'

'Not really.'

'Oh, they will, sweetheart – once you learn how to make yourself up properly.'

Wow. 'I appreciate the tip,' I tell her flatly. Her smile doesn't falter. Maybe she thought she was being kind.

43

Lorelei *was* flawless when she went out in public – red sweetheart lips, smoky lines framing her bright blue eyes, and her hair in Greta Garbo waves hanging to her shoulders. I don't have Lorelei's blue eyes – mine are such a deep brown they look black, like Nolan's – but my hair is wavy like hers. Nolan won't let me cut it, even though it hangs all the way to my waist. And he doesn't like it when I wear make-up, either. *You're perfect as you are*, Nolan says. *It upsets me to think of something so perfect being ruined.*

'My name's Lola.' I glance pointedly at the hand still hovering near my face. It's like having a fly buzzing right next to my ear. She lets it drop to her side. 'I guess you're expecting me . . .' I suddenly have the awful feeling Larry didn't bother to call ahead, and she had no idea I was about to land on her doorstep. But then I remember Grant waiting for me at the airport. Of course she's expecting me.

'Please, call me Grandmother.'

Grandmother. It's formal, detached. The way you'd refer to an ancestor's portrait. It'll work.

'And don't just stand out there in the hallway – come in, won't you?' She disappears through the doorway. I hesitate just a moment before dropping my bag in the hall.

The living room is small, with wood-panelled walls and three chairs around a colourless rug and an empty wooden coffee table. No TV – naturally – but a Philco radio sits on a corner table, its speakers carved into the wood like Gothic church windows. Yet another piece that makes me think of Nolan.

It's only now, standing in this space that looks a century out of sync with the world, that I realize just how much I'm surrounded by technology at home. The TV, my e-reader, the laptop I borrow for schoolwork, the smart fridge – even the oven can cook a meal practically without human intervention. All I have here is the phone Larry gave me, and its panicked proclamation of NO SERVICE. No cellphone for Lola, just like always.

There are two photographs on the mantelpiece above an empty fireplace. One is a picture of Lorelei at around five or six years old. It's strange – I've never seen a picture of her that wasn't taken when she was at least eighteen, after she got the part in *Nightjar* and met Nolan.

The other picture shows her as a teenager with an older man. Her father, I guess, though there's not much of a family resemblance. He looks like a man who might've played football when he was younger: solid and strong, with well-weathered skin. He sits in a high-backed chair with Lorelei in his lap, focused on her rather than the camera.

I see the same chair now in the corner near the radio, a faint depression in the seat cushion. I'm tempted to touch it, see if it's still warm.

Then it hits me: I'm in her home. Lorelei lived *here*. Stood where I'm standing. I want to recoil, like I've just walked in on a house fire.

'I'm quite sure the doorjamb can hold itself up without your help,' my grandmother says lightly. I must look confused because she beckons me into the living room. She

45

sits in a rocking chair with a lamp shining behind her, making a halo of the hair she wasn't able to tease into her high bun. It would probably collapse like spun sugar if I touched it.

'Can I use the phone?' I say. 'I need to check in on Nolan.'

'You call your father by his first name?' Her smile is tight with disapproval.

'That's what he prefers, Grandmother.'

Her face softens. I make a note of that: 'Grandmother' is Optimal.

'Well, fathers and daughters always have a special bond, don't they?' She laughs girlishly, then pauses when I don't join in. I desperately want to end this conversation, but I have no idea what she wants me to say.

'So, is it all right if I use the phone?'

She makes an irritated sound, and waves in the direction of the hallway. 'Go on and make your call, dear.'

I almost walk right into Grant. My suitcase is in his hand.

'Shall I take your granddaughter's bag upstairs, Mrs McCabe?'

'I'll –' I begin, but my grandmother cuts me off.

'Yes. Thank you, Grant,' she says.

He steps aside just enough that I have to squeeze past him, chest to chest.

I leave them talking in hushed tones behind me. Normally, I'd linger to eavesdrop, but right now I'm more anxious to hear Nolan's voice. I pick up the phone and dial.

'Mr Nox woke up a short while ago,' a nurse tells me over the crackling line. 'Only for a few minutes, but the doctor spoke with him and said he's doing very well, exactly as she'd hoped after the surgery.'

'Can I speak with him?'

'He's sleeping right now – better if you call back in the morning.'

I hang up, and whatever dregs of energy I had left seep into the floorboards.

Someone is right behind me.

'Your room is upstairs – your mom's old room.' It's Grant.

'Nolan woke up,' I tell him. *He's going to be all right.* I don't say this part out loud. My voice might crack. That wouldn't be Optimal.

Grant's expression doesn't change. 'Second door on the right. Mrs McCabe turned in already, so you probably won't see her until breakfast. Is there anything you need before I head out?'

Wow. Way to express concern about my father's condition, Grant.

And nice of my grandmother to go to bed and leave me without a word. Is that normal? Or have I managed to upset her within ten minutes of meeting her?

'I guess she thought you'd be on the line awhile,' Grant says distractedly, busy raking his eyes over me like he might've missed something the first time. 'Damn, but you sure do look like Lorelei. *Mm-mm-mmm.* A real sweet little piece of –'

'You knew my mother?' I blurt. I shouldn't be surprised in a town this size. But I try to picture her standing next to Grant, and I can't.

47

'Oh yeah. I knew her, all right. Everyone in Harrow Lake knew sweet little Lorelei. You know, if she hadn't gotten her head turned by that fancy-pants movie guy, I could've been your daddy.' Grant's smile is a bear trap, quick and sharp. I'd like to scratch that look right off his face.

'I doubt that,' I tell him stiffly. He and Nolan are worlds – galaxies – apart.

But Grant just laughs, then shakes his head. 'Prickly like her, too. Be a doll and stay inside the house tonight, OK?' I cringe at his words. 'I wouldn't want you getting lost out in the woods. There's no moon tonight.'

'So?'

'So you never go into Harrow Lake woods on a moonless night, or the trees might mistake you for one of their own. With no moonlight, a girl like you could end up wandering for hours and see nothing but trees and trees and more trees.' He steps closer, and I force myself not to back away. 'They say if you lose your way out there you need to keep moving. Stand still even for a moment, and you'll feel your toenails sprouting long like talons, digging down into the earth, planting like roots. In the cold dark, your skin'll harden into bark, and your arms will twist towards the sky like you're reaching for a moon that ain't there.'

He reels this off like he's reciting a nursery rhyme.

'What a cute story,' I say.

I wonder whether Grant has children – whether he tells them terrifying tales about being claimed by the forest to keep them in their beds at night. Perhaps reading my thoughts, Grant smirks.

'I guess your mother didn't pass on the old tales to you. No doubt you'll pick 'em up while you're in town. But I wasn't kidding about not going out there at night – the woods is no place to be after dark. You never know what might happen.' He winks as if he's being friendly. 'Sleep tight, Lola.'

Sleep with one eye open, asshole.

After he leaves, I listen to the unfamiliar groans of the house around me, and the chug of Grant's truck fading to a sigh.

I lock the front door, taking one last look outside through its narrow window. There are only the dark woods out there, where you never know what might happen.

The walls of Lorelei's room are covered in a faded grey pattern like upside-down beetles, repeated over and over and over. It's almost hypnotic, though that could be because I'm so tired. One section of the wallpaper has started to peel away near the picture rail to reveal another layer of paper underneath. Only that one has exactly the same beetle-like pattern on it, which is odd. I climb up onto the bed to get a better look. Beneath the furling corner, the second layer of paper is also loose. I carefully peel it back. This room has been decorated and redecorated with the exact same wallpaper.

'Who does that?' I ask the wall.

I press the paper back into place. It's a little sticky with damp, but it holds, and I climb back down. Every item in this room, every piece of furniture, looks like it should be in a museum showing what life was like in 1920s, small-town Indiana. I knew this town would look like a relic on the outside – but I guess I thought it would be different inside. It's like I've imagined myself inside an ancestor's dollhouse.

The wall opposite the bed is lined with shelves. The highest shelf holds only an old carriage clock with hands left to die at ten after two – probably because it's too high to reach without a stepladder. What I didn't notice when I first walked in is that the other shelves hold dozens and dozens of walnut-looking things, all laid out in neat rows. But, as I pick one up to inspect it, I see it's not a nut; it's carved from wood and pitted, with a split running right around the middle. I squeeze the two halves apart, and it opens to reveal a hollow space.

I stifle a scream. A shiny black bug waggles its legs at me from inside the nutshell, and I almost drop it. But the bug isn't real, either – just a painted beetle with legs attached by wire hinges that allow them to dance whenever the shell moves. Even the slight motion of my hand sends those legs jittering against the inside of the shell. In that moment, I have the oddest sense of déjà vu. But maybe that's just because all bugs freak me out.

I set it back on the shelf, leaving it open, determined that it won't get the better of me. Then I force myself to open every single one. There's a ladybug, a beetle with emerald-green wings, then a brown one with orange stripes across its back. I go from shelf to shelf until I'm done. Dozens of bugs in all sorts of colours.

Did Lorelei collect them? If this was my room, the shelves would be full of books, not little toys. Maybe Lorelei was into bugs? I try to imagine her playing with them, but I can't picture it. I don't even remember the sound of her laugh. It's been a long time since I've wondered about Lorelei like this.

Forget her, Lola.

I refuse to get caught up with thoughts of Lorelei. I'm not a kid any more.

There's only the closet left for me to explore. It opens with a small iron key, the door swinging wide to reveal a rail filled with dresses. I assume they're Grandmother's – her winter clothes, or ones she doesn't wear often – but when I look closer, I see they aren't hers. They're Lorelei's.

Of course they're Lorelei's – I'm in her room, for God's sake.

Big surprise, they're cut in the rustic, late-twenties style. Muted fabrics with modest necklines and low waists. Plain, except for an occasional ribbon-trim or brightly coloured button. These aren't the clothes I remember Lorelei wearing when she lived with me and Nolan. Then I come to a section that isn't Lorelei's at all. It's Little Bird's.

Little Bird was the character my mother played in *Nightjar* – the beautiful, small-town girl who starts out as the local sweetheart, but soon becomes an object of superstition and fear when the town is cut off from the outside world and its residents begin to starve.

I've been half in love with Little Bird my whole life, memorizing her lines in the movie, copying the way she

51

talked and how she moved. Despite the way she dies in *Nightjar* (it *is* a horror movie), everyone loved her, Nolan especially. She was his first creation, after all. I actually think Little Bird was the person he really fell for, not my mother. Bright and happy and charming . . . his idea of the Optimal woman. Not someone who would walk out on her family without a word.

The Little Bird outfits are more colourful. The pleated green pinafore she wore in the opening scene. The sailor-style dress from the fairground. The pretty smocked primrose one with embroidered rosebuds that she wore at the Easy Diner. And more: a deep emerald-green one from the night of the storm; a royal-blue knit for when the townsfolk turned and chased her into the caves; and finally the plum-coloured frock from the final scene at the church ruins. Her death scene.

I run my fingertips across the different fabrics, feeling an electric tingle. These are unique. Pristine. *Optimal.* And as tangible a piece of Nolan's heart as I will ever find in the whole world. I almost can't bring myself to close the closet door.

I'm about to draw the curtains when a movement outside catches my eye. No, not a movement; whoever is out in the yard isn't moving at all. It's their *stillness* that makes them stand out. Someone petite – so not Grant. Maybe a teenager, or a slender woman.

I go cold. It's Lorelei. She saw me rifling through her things. Somehow, it's her.

Don't be ridiculous, Lola, Nolan's voice snaps in my head. *She's long gone, and good riddance.*

I glance at the closed closet door, then back to the window, hoping and not hoping that the figure will have vanished. But she's still there, facing the house, a dark silhouette in the weak moonlight. Then a faint giggle carries up on the breeze. It's a girl.

But what is she doing out there? Why would anyone be out in the woods so late at night? Grant's warning about the trees slithers through my mind and I feel like I should throw open the window and call out to her, but I hesitate, my heart racing.

It's just a girl. What are you afraid of?

The windowpane mists where my breath hits it. I wipe it with my palm. The girl outside waves up at me, mirroring the movement. Wait – is she mimicking me?

WTF?

I fumble with the window latch, but the hinges only move a couple of inches before getting stuck. The gap is just wide enough for me to talk to her without yelling and waking my grandmother. But the girl is gone. The yard is empty. Just the crooked shadows of the trees intrude beyond the boundary fence.

Where the hell did she go?

Is she out there in the dark woods, peering back at me?

You're behaving like a child, Nolan chides. I scowl at my reflection in the window. He's right. He usually is.

I draw the curtains, then crawl into bed fully clothed and lie there, counting the nutshells on the shelves. There are seventy-two.

With every whisper of breeze through the open window, the lace curtains cast twisting patterns onto the clock on the high shelf. They shift and change, tricking my tired eyes into seeing the hands twitch with movement: time struggling to move forward, and failing.

CHAPTER FOUR

I take a quick, cold shower the next morning (no choice on the temperature) and rush back to my room – Lorelei's room – wrapped in a towel. Kicking aside yesterday's dirty clothes, I look around for my suitcase. It's not here.

It was in here a second ago. I mean, I think it was. Wasn't it? I was so tired and weirded out last night, I can't remember if I saw it then. But Grant brought it up here. He told me which room I was staying in. So it *must* be in here.

The closet is too small to hold it, and when I drop down to check under the bed – carefully, in case there are spiders – all I find is dust. Wait – not just dust. There are short, deep scratches on the floorboards near each of the bedposts. Was Lorelei the sort of girl to run and jump into bed at night in case the boogeyman reached out from under it to grab her feet? Considering the shelves of bugs, I doubt she was.

She isn't worth even a moment's thought. Nolan's voice, his hand smoothing over my hair – a memory from when I was little. I'd asked him where she went, or something like that. The next time I brought up the subject of my mother, he didn't answer at all. Asking about Lorelei was never a good idea. Never Optimal.

I duck my head back out onto the landing.

'Grandmother?' I wait a beat, but there's no answer.

Maybe Grant left my bag in the downstairs hallway?

The thought of running around a stranger's house in a towel makes my teeth itch, but that only leaves me with yesterday's dirty clothes to wear. I pick up my jeans between finger and thumb. They smell of sleep and travel sweat. Gross. My eyes slide to the closet.

No. I can't be seen wearing my absentee mom's old clothes while Nolan lies attached to machines back in New York.

But . . . the clothes in that closet aren't *all* Lorelei's, are they?

A few minutes later, I follow a rhythmic thumping sound and find my grandmother kneading dough in the kitchen.

Baked goods cover almost every surface in the room – loaves of bread, pies and an unfrosted cake. The smell is cloyingly sweet.

In the doorway, I put my pointer fingers and thumbs together to make a square and look through it. The floor is a chequerboard of faded blue and white tiles. I don't think Nolan would like them. Too cheap.

My grandmother stands centre-frame at a wooden counter, an apron covering her dress, which is black, just like yesterday's. The sleeves are rolled back, and a few stray curls of her hair bounce every time she thumps the dough in front of her.

At first I think she's humming, but the low, keening sound she's making isn't any kind of tune. She's crying.

Shit.

I drop my finger-frame. Look down at my green dress with the pleated skirt. I shouldn't be wearing this. It was a terrible idea. I back away from the door and am about to tiptoe back upstairs when the movement catches my grandmother's eye. She looks up from her kneading and screams.

Her rolling pin falls from the counter with a clatter and she screams again, her hands quivering like moths in front of her. She looks like she's seen a ghost.

Oh God. It's not me she's seeing – it's Lorelei. Standing in the doorway wearing Little Bird's clothes, I must look the double of my mother. Judging by her reaction, Grandmother hasn't seen Lorelei in a while.

I take another step back. 'I'll go change.'

But the shock fading from her face now makes me hesitate. She shakes her head and finds her voice.

'Oh, Lor– Lola. You shouldn't startle me like that.'

Grandmother quickly dabs her sleeve to her face. She's wearing the same stark make-up as when I met her last night, only now it's smeared. Maybe I should say something. The moment stretches out too long.

'I see you found your mother's old movie things,' she says at last, gesturing to the dress.

'Yeah, I guess I should've asked first, but I couldn't find my –'

'Oh, no. It's fine.' She shakes her head again, thin-lipped. I can't tell if she's annoyed because I scared her or because I'm wearing this dress. Either way, there's not a lot I can do about it.

'What's all that for?' I gesture to the bread and pastries on the counter.

'Oh, it's for the Easy Diner. I bake for them.'

'Like as a job?'

Grandmother doesn't answer, but juts her chin at a plate of something sticky as she goes back to kneading.

'I made you breakfast,' she says. 'Two hours ago.' I don't miss the sharp note in her voice.

'What is it?'

'Canned peaches on toast. It was your mother's favourite.'

'Really?' I eye the glistening mess. 'I'm not much of a breakfast person. I usually just grab a coffee.'

'I see,' she says. 'That's fine.'

I'm quite certain it's not fine, but I'm not going to force down that nightmare on a plate just to try and win her over. I'll figure something out; learn what Optimal looks like to my grandmother.

'Do you know where Grant put my suitcase?' I say to her rigid back. 'It wasn't in my room. That's why I borrowed this dress – I didn't have anything else clean to wear.'

'Your . . .' She blinks at me. 'Oh, but you *should* wear your mother's old things – there's no point leaving them to gather dust in the closet. And that dress looks just delightful on you.'

'Yeah, I think I'd still like to have my own clothes, though.'

'Right. I see.' She strides from the kitchen without another word, not waiting for me to follow her. I stay in the kitchen and listen to her footsteps clacking up the stairs, then across the boards above my head. After some more clacking, she comes back.

'No sign of it, I'm afraid,' she announces, like it's nothing.

'What do you mean?'

'I mean,' Grandmother says, slowing her words, 'there's no sign of your bag.'

I wait for her to go on, to say that she will *of course* find it for me, but she doesn't. 'Seriously? A suitcase can't just disappear!'

'Well, there's no need to raise your voice. It can't have gone far.'

A wave of anger washes over me. 'But I need my stuff!'

'*Lola*.' She slaps a hand down on the counter and I jump. 'I'm sorry you don't have your things, but I'll ask Grant about it when he calls by later. He must have forgotten to take your bag out of his truck.' I'm about to insist that's not possible, that I carried it into the house myself, when I remember the girl I saw standing out in the yard last night. Could she have snuck into the house and stolen it?

Calm down. It's Nolan's voice, and hearing it slows my thundering heart a little. *It's only a bag and a few clothes. There's no need for hysterics.*

'When I went in your room just now, I noticed you've moved the jitterbugs,' Grandmother says, snatching me from my thoughts.

'The what?'

'The wooden bugs in your mother's room. Do be careful with them – Lorelei made them herself.'

'She made them? Like, from scratch?' That doesn't fit my memory of her. Lorelei was not crafty. She didn't do anything with her hands that made her seem *capable* in any tangible kind of way. But maybe this was something she left in Harrow Lake; she had a habit of leaving things behind.

'Oh, yes. Lorelei used dead wood from the forest. She carved and painted each one by hand. They were very precious to her. I would hate for any of them to get broken.'

'I will be very careful with Lorelei's bugs.'

My grandmother narrows her eyes at me. 'Are you being funny?'

I hear Nolan snort in disbelief. 'I doubt it.'

'Well, good. I can't abide young girls who think they're funny.' She has that in common with Nolan, then.

'As for your clothes,' she continues, brightening, 'there are plenty more dresses in the closet upstairs, so I'm sure you can make do.'

'I guess so,' I say.

'Good. That's settled. And I'm sorry you feel so upset about your bag,' she says, making it clear how petty she finds it. Grandmother reaches out to touch my hair again. 'Your mother was the same way. So . . . *sensitive*.'

'Do you ever see her?' I blurt, taking a step back. 'Lorelei?'

'See her? What on earth do you mean?' she says.

'I just thought maybe she came back here to visit . . .'

'No.' She stares at me like I'm being ridiculous.

'Where is Lorelei now?' I press.

'Perhaps you should ask your father,' she says with a lightness that feels forced. 'She was his wife, after all. Not that I ever thought they were a good match.'

So she blames Nolan for Lorelei leaving. Of course she does.

When Lorelei left, Nolan said he was glad to be rid of her, that she was bad for both of us. But I saw his lie for what it really was. He needed to convince himself, and me, that she hadn't really hurt us. That a woman who could abandon her family wasn't someone we needed in our lives.

He cleared out her closets. Burned every photograph of her. He told me to forget about her, that we *both* should. Maybe Nolan should have told Grandmother that as well.

'The last time I saw her was just after your grandfather's funeral. Goodness, was it really twelve years ago?' She toys with a lock of my hair, and I force myself to stay still. 'She came to say her goodbyes, I suppose. And then she was . . . gone.'

Her words remind me of what Nolan used to tell me when I asked about Lorelei after she moved out: *She left a note saying she was taking a trip to her hometown to say goodbye, then went God-knows-where to do whatever the hell she wanted. She isn't coming back.*

Something in his tone made me wonder whether deep down Nolan thought that she might actually come back and snatch me away in the night, leaving him alone.

'You know,' Grandmother says, snapping her fingers, 'Lorelei left some of her make-up here when she came to visit. I'm sure at least some of it will still be usable. I can find it for you, if you like?'

Lorelei never wore make-up around the house, but when she went out she wore it in perfect 1920s style. Maybe she thought people expected her to look like Little Bird. Or that they wouldn't recognize her if she didn't. She was stunning, though.

That crap isn't for you, Lola. I bite my lip, hearing Nolan's words so clearly he could be standing at my shoulder.

But the make-up would make me more *Nightjar*-authentic, I argue silently. More like Little Bird. No – a new and improved version. Little Bird 2.0.

'Sure,' I tell Grandmother. 'Why not?'

My borrowed green pinafore has a pleated skirt, with a waistline that sits low across my hips. This was what Little Bird wore in the opening scene of the movie.

I'm analysing my reflection in the mirror, trying to decide how I look in this outfit, this make-up, when a face appears behind me. I startle so badly I almost leap out of the damn dress.

'That's much better.' My grandmother sounds so pleased. 'You look just like Lorelei now.'

'I look like Little Bird.' I'm annoyed at her for creeping up on me, so it comes out snappy.

'Goodness me, this town was here long before that awful film, you know!'

I feel the shadow of Nolan's hand on my shoulder at her snippy words, fingers digging in as his knuckles whiten. 'Would this town *still* be here if it wasn't for that *"awful film"*?'

She stills. 'Don't get smart. All I meant was that you look like you belong here.'

I toy with the idea of telling her I'm not wearing any underwear, see if she still thinks I belong. But I fight the urge to needle my grandmother. For now, at least.

CHAPTER FIVE

Now that I'm made up like a Little Bird clone, my grandmother practically shoos me out of the house so she can finish her baking. Fine by me. I haven't even been here twenty-four hours, and my insides are getting clogged with dust and spiderwebs and Lorelei's lingering presence.

At least Grandmother was happy for me to go out and explore by myself, something Nolan would never agree to. Still, part of me worries that I'll return to the house and find something horrific has happened, just like at the apartment. That breaking Nolan's rules brings terrible consequences.

Stop it, Lola!

Thinking like that is not Optimal.

I follow a dirt track away from the house, looking for Nolan's *Nightjar* to emerge out of all these trees. The path winds between them, pitted with stones and fallen leaves, muddy enough to make a shitshow of my shoes.

I have a mental list of the *Nightjar* locations I want to see – the Easy Diner, the ruined church, the caves . . . but I'll need to see them in the order they appeared in *Nightjar*. When I tell Nolan about my visit to Harrow Lake – and he will expect me to, in great detail – he'll notice if I've taken the scenes out of order. That would *not* be Optimal.

I'm headed for Main Street, where the movie opens. And I'm wearing Little Bird's opening-scene outfit, so I'm on the right track.

It isn't long before I find it. Those elegant lamp posts curtsey in greeting along the roadside. The stores are all open, the sidewalks surprisingly busy for such a small town. But I remember what Grant said about them holding some kind of *Nightjar* festival in a few days, so maybe there are visitors mixed in with the locals. It's hard to tell since they all look like they're in *Nightjar* costumes.

I keep checking my phone, hoping Grant was exaggerating about the lack of signal in this town. He was not. My steps fall into the rhythm of the piano music piping through a sound system I can't see.

All the people bustling about the sidewalks stay in character, wishing me a good morning, doffing caps as I pass, playing the part with rose-tinted, old-timey civility. There's a sameness to them that's unnerving, and then I realize why: almost everyone's white. Another reminder of just how far I am from New York. I catch some people eyeing me curiously. Nolan has kept me well away from the public gaze, thank God (he only takes me to industry events or parties where there's a strict *no phones, no cameras, no social media* policy), but I look like Little Bird in this dress, so of course they stare.

That thought doesn't bother me like it should. Walking along this street feels like stepping inside someone else's daydream – as if I'm a different person here. No Larry to drag me back home. No Nolan waiting for me.

I'm completely alone.

My footsteps are suddenly too loud on the sidewalk. It feels wrong to be in this place that's so *Nolan* when he's not with me.

Nolan always prefers to use real locations to shoot his films. He likes the idea that he's layering one reality over another instead of just painting it onto plywood. He says it gives the story depth. It's hard to find places that look like authentic 1920s backdrops, but that's Nolan's thing – he is the King of Roaring Twenties Horror, after all.

I was nine the first time I was allowed to visit one of Nolan's filmsets. It took months of careful asking, showing the right kind of interest and smiling sweetly when he said no.

The movie was called *The Path from Innocence*, and the crew was shooting in a pine forest at night. They set up rigs to give the cameras enough light to record. I stayed absolutely silent while the cameras rolled or when Nolan was talking to his crew, watching the three actors limp dazedly between the trees, searching for invisible predators. In between takes, though, I asked him questions. How had he chosen the location? How long would the scene be after it was edited? Why were the cameras positioned at those exact angles? Not too many questions, but enough to show that I was thinking about his work. Optimal questions to make him proud of me.

The next time I asked to go on-set, he said yes. I stood next to Nolan as an actor walked into a snare and was whisked up into a tree by her neck, her broken string of pearls bouncing onto the ground beneath her like hailstones. She kicked her legs wildly, then less wildly, then not at all. I saw a guy get shot through the eye with a dart. I saw a woman with tight red pin curls soaked with blood and fleeing for her life. Then it was time to shoot a flashback of the redhead and her two friends as children playing patty-cake in the rain.

I went to watch the rigs that would make the rain turn to blood, and I overheard the casting people nearby talking about the kid who was meant to play Snare Woman as a girl; she'd dropped out without warning. They were making plans to call in another actor. I left the blood rig and went over to them; they should let me act in the movie, I said. It would be a surprise for Nolan. He would love it, I said.

Playing the part was easy. The script laid everything out – what to say, how to say it, and when. I didn't have to think about it at all. Just laughed and played patty-cake and screamed as I'd seen the others do during the run-through, getting drenched in my little blue dress and letting the fake blood make rats' tails of my hair and trickle into my eyes. I didn't even glance over at Nolan until he called 'cut'. Just knowing that I was a part of his work, the thing he took the most pride in, lit me up inside like I'd swallowed a firecracker.

When I did look at him, his expression was unreadable. But that was just Nolan. If he's working, he's one hundred per cent focused on his project. So it wasn't until we'd been home for a few hours that I noticed he was in a bad mood. He said nothing was wrong, but I could tell it was a lie. For five whole days, the weight of his silence was like the world collapsing on top of me.

'Why won't you look at me?' I asked him again on the sixth day. Desperation made me whine, which I knew he hated.

The seconds stretched to an impossible length as I counted each painful heartbeat, wondering whether my ribs would break under the impact.

'Why would I want to look at you?' he said at last.

I tried to come up with the right answer. He'd liked it when I showed I was *interested* in his work, but not when I became a part of it. Was he angry that I hadn't asked first? Or had I done a bad job? Oh God – had I ruined the movie?

I took too long deciding on my answer, and he let out a disappointed sigh.

'You're in the film. Soon everyone will be able to look at you – the whole world will look at this pretty little girl and think whatever they like about you. You can't control what they think, what they *do* with you in their minds. You're theirs now. Not mine. So why would *I* want to look at you?' He scrubbed a hand back through his hair. 'Lola, I couldn't bear for anyone to take you away from me. Can't you see that? It hurts me too much to think of losing you.'

It was like time froze. I understood. I saw what I'd done. It was supposed to just be me and Nolan. I had my own place in his life, somewhere nobody else was allowed. I didn't belong to anyone but him.

'I didn't mean it,' I whispered. 'Is it too late to cut me out of the film?'

He looked at me, finally. 'I already have.'

I didn't go on-set with him for a long time after that, and I've never tried to talk my way into the cast again. Now I know better.

The jaunty piano music still piping through the speakers pulls me along, dragging me back to Harrow Lake. I catch glimpses of myself reflected in the gleaming store windows along Main Street, passing by like Little Bird's shadow.

You're enjoying this, Nolan's shadow whispers in my ear. *You like dressing up like her. You're glad I'm not there.*

I stop and lean against one of the store sidings, pressing my fists into my stomach.

Stop it!

Three days, Larry said. That's all the time I have here. It isn't long, and I'm not going to waste any more time having imaginary conversations.

Striding towards the Easy Diner, I notice pre-lunch smells wafting out of the open door like they're being carried by the tune that guides my footsteps. But the song has changed, and my stomach lurches again as I recognize it: 'T'ain't No Sin'. I see Nolan slumped against the bookcase in his study, holding his insides together with his own hands. The scratch of a needle jumping . . .

There's a *shush* from behind me, but it's only a weeping willow tree, its leaves whispering in the breeze. There's that strange feeling of déjà vu again, like I felt when I saw the jitterbug in Lorelei's room – like I know this willow tree.

It stands in front of an old building, set back from Main Street. BRYN'S MUSEUM & MEMORABILIA. Where I saw that reedy figure last night. I walk closer.

The windows here are crusted with dirt, the paint on the door peeling like diseased skin. If not for the OPEN sign in the window, I wouldn't think anyone had been here in years.

This wasn't one of the locations used to film *Nightjar*, but something about how it's hidden away makes me want to go in. It feels like a secret. My *Nightjar* list can wait.

I enter the museum as the final notes of 'T'ain't No Sin' fade at my back.

CHAPTER SIX

Inside the museum, the air smells like paper and time.

An old man in a bow tie sits at the counter. His tawny skin is liver-spotted and sags at the jowls, making him appear delightfully morose. There's a massive *Nightjar* poster on the wall behind him, positioned so it looks like Lorelei is peering over his shoulder.

I wander around the lobby, bypassing the old man, the photographs, documents and old clothes, and head towards an intricate sketch of a pool inside a cave. The surface is dark, flat and glassy, with a faint circle of light shining on the centre. I wipe the dusty glass with my sleeve. There's something in the water, but I can't make it out. Is it . . . a face?

'Lola, isn't it?' I jump. The old man is right behind me. I'm amazed he was able to get so close without making a sound. 'I'm Mr Bryn – a friend of your grandmother's. I hear you're visiting her for a spell.'

Of course he already knows about me. So does everyone else in this town, I bet.

'Such a lovely picture, isn't it?'

Not really. 'Why is there a face in the water?'

Mr Bryn peers at the sketch. 'A face?'

'Does it have anything to do with the landslide?' I'm thinking about the disaster that struck Harrow Lake a century ago. Every blog, vlog, article and even a documentary about *Nightjar* included the tragedy as backstory to the movie – about the supposedly cursed ground and how dozens of the townspeople were buried alive. The fans lapped it up when *Nightjar* came out. It bugged the hell out of Nolan, who has no time for urban legends or curses or whatever.

'These old eyes aren't what they were, but I'm quite sure you're mistaken,' Mr Bryn says, cutting across my thoughts. 'Besides, Carter would never put such a thing up on display.'

I have no idea who Carter is, but the face is definitely there.

'How long will you be in town, did you say?' Mr Bryn asks.

'Only a couple of days,' I say. 'I'll go back as soon as my father is well enough.'

He grunts. 'I hope he recovers quickly.'

It takes me a moment to figure out he isn't so much wishing Nolan well as he's wishing me gone. 'Did you meet Nolan when he was here filming *Nightjar*?'

'No, I mostly kept out of the way while all that hoopla was going on. There's plenty of *Nightjar* crap in this place for you to look at, though, if that's what you want.' Mr Bryn turns away, so I almost miss what he says next. 'Guess it must be if you're all gussied up like that.'

He shuffles back to his seat behind the counter. I have most definitely been dismissed.

I study my reflection in the glass case. The dim light drains all the colour from my face. Would Nolan be pleased that I look so like Little Bird? Or would he only see Lorelei?

I focus on the sketch again. The pencil lines slash across it, again and again, tracing the image of the lake. I can hear the *wisp-wisp* of those strokes running over the paper.

My wrist is exposed where I've been rubbing my arms for warmth, and I notice the ink stains are still there. They're faint, like the lines of the sketch, but it feels as if the ink has sunk into me.

Blood in the cracks . . .

I pull my sleeve stiffly back into place. Time to explore the museum and its '*Nightjar* crap'.

The building is a series of rooms at odd levels, like it expanded and had extra nooks tacked on as Mr Bryn ran out of space. And it is *so* full – walls of glass cabinets and bookshelves turn the place into a maze. I keep going until a narrow corridor opens out into a room with a high ceiling and a mezzanine floor. One wall is covered entirely with framed photographs of *Nightjar* being filmed around town. I see several shots of Nolan: pointing across a clearing at two lighting techs setting up a rig; holding his arms out wide as he shouts instructions at someone I don't recognize; crouching by a camera guy as he captures a low-level shot of Lorelei's feet as she runs through the rain. It's a tight frame, but I can tell it's her. I recognize the shoes she wore in the scene. They're not unlike the ones I'm wearing now.

'You always put the right shoe on first,' I say to the picture. *Right shoe first, then you'll always put your best foot forward*, she used to say. I had completely forgotten that about Lorelei until now.

'Are you talking to us, or the wall?'

'What the –' I blurt out. Two girls perch on an antique desk hidden away in the corner. They're around my age, I think. The one who spoke is pale with wiry black hair cut at chin-level. She's wearing wool pants, a collarless shirt with suspenders, and scuffed lace-up shoes; I want to call her something cutesy like *ragamuffin*, but the sharpness in her blue eyes stops me. She's grinning at me, and I can see her slightly twisted upper canines. It gives her smile a feral edge that's weirdly appealing.

She's more bobcat than ragamuffin, I think. Not that I'd tell her that, either.

Her friend is a pretty black girl with deep brown eyes and skin, and braided hair held back from her face in a barrette. There's a pin on her dress that says *Easy Diner* with **FAYE** in bold letters underneath. She nudges the Bobcat next to her.

'You're the one from New York, aren't you? Nolan Nox's daughter,' Bobcat says, swinging her legs back and forth over the edge of the desk. I've spent my whole life watching people go wide-eyed and starstruck just saying Nolan's name, but she doesn't do that. Maybe that's why her friend is acting squirrelly, though.

'I'm Lola,' I say, then add, '. . . Nox.' I'm not used to talking to girls my age – or any age, really – and from the way she bites back a smirk, I guess I didn't quite nail the casual air I was going for. I feel irritated, like I've messed up my lines.

'Uh-huh.' There's an implied *obviously* in her tone. 'Are you staying in town long?'

'I don't think so.'

'I guess it depends how quickly your dad gets back on his feet, am I right?' She nods slowly, coaxing me to agree with her. 'So, what happened to him, exactly? Were you there?'

'Cora!' the girl called Faye whispers sharply. But the Bobcat – Cora, apparently – just shrugs.

'He's going to be fine,' I say, struggling to sound like the words aren't choking me. Because I don't *know* what happened. I don't know how Nolan is. I don't know when he will be allowed back home.

Is he going to die?

That's the question she really wants to ask. It's what everyone in this town – in the world – must be wondering. I swallow the knot in my throat and cut her a level glare. 'I'm sure you'll find out all the gory details in the news.'

Cora laughs and holds up her hands. 'Sorry, sorry. I'm being a ghoul.' She doesn't look particularly sorry, but she doesn't look like she's trying to be shitty, either. I just get a sense of . . . blunt curiosity, I guess. Her friend looks like she wants to crawl into a hole and die of embarrassment.

75

'Cora, we really should get to the diner,' her friend says. 'We'll be late. Again. And Mr Hadfield is already going to be mad at you for not wearing your uniform. *Again.*'

'If he's already mad, who cares if I'm late?' Cora slides from the desk and thrusts a hand into the space between us. 'I'm Cora, by the way.'

I wait a beat before clasping hands with her briefly.

'And this is Faye. Faye is too nice to enjoy horror movies, but she was terribly excited when she heard a celebrity was coming to town.' I'm not a celebrity, but I don't bother to correct her. Cora smiles crookedly when she hears her friend's exasperated sigh. 'And she hates getting into trouble, which really begs the question why she always waits for me when I'm always, always late.'

'Well, I won't then!' Faye snaps, hopping down from the desk. 'It was nice meeting you, Lola. Sorry about your dad.' She strides off, tossing over her shoulder, 'I'll tell Mr Hadfield you have cramps. But this is the last time!'

Cora turns to me. 'I might as well hang out here awhile. Hey, you must have a credit card, right, *Lola*?' she says, rolling my name around in her mouth like an ice chip. 'Wanna do something fun, like hire a limo and go cruising around in it? That's what folks do in New York, right?'

'Not really,' I say. I've been in limos dozens of times, but there's no need to tell Cora that.

'How about a nickel?'

I let out a startled laugh at the drastic downshift in her plans. 'No. But you won't get much limo for a nickel, anyway.'

I have my wallet, tucked into a pocket in my skirt next to my phone and one of Lorelei's beetles, but no change. It was impossible to resist taking a jitterbug after Grandmother got so weird about me touching them.

'Want to see something strange?' Cora says, gesturing to one of the cabinets. I'm not sure what to make of her yet, but I like that she's so obviously unimpressed by me – or my father.

Without waiting for my reply, Cora goes over to the cabinet. It's not a display inside, as I assumed, but an old-fashioned puppet. The details are hard to make out in the dim light, but it looks like the puppet's neck is broken. It's a sad-looking thing, trapped there in its cage. Maybe I should let it out.

'Just as well I know the secret trick,' Cora says, bypassing the nickel slot and hip-checking the side of it – once, twice. Immediately, there's a distorted wail, and a light flickers on inside. The puppet jerks up on its strings and I gasp. It's dressed in a miniature pinstripe suit with no features on its painted white face except for black pinprick eyes and a garish mouth that stretches in a grin from ear to ear as though the lips have been cut away. But it's the limbs that make me edge back. Stick-like, they bend so it sits on its haunches like an animal, its fingers long and sharp like claws.

I think I'll leave that thing where it is.

'What is it supposed to be?'

'Mister Jitters,' Cora says, then sings, '*He got trapped underground for a really long while, then he fed on the dead . . .*'

And got a brand-new smile, I finish silently, then frown. How weird that I know these lyrics. I mean, I do know the song – it was in *Nightjar*. But these aren't the words from Little Bird's song. There was no mention of any Mister Jitters in her version.

'Your mom changed the words when they put it in the movie,' Cora says.

I open my mouth to contradict her – I can't imagine Nolan wanting Lorelei to put her own stamp on his movie – but a sliver of doubt pins my tongue. Lorelei was the star of the film, and not only that: Nolan was falling in love with her. Maybe he did let her carve her name onto some small part of it.

He'd never let me do that.

I wince as a sour taste fills my mouth. I've bitten the inside of my cheek so hard it's bleeding.

Cora has gone back to making the puppet dance. 'Do you like him?'

'Mister Jitters?' This name, too, is oddly familiar. 'Why does it look like that?'

'He got trapped underground . . .'

'Jesus, forget I asked.'

Cora smirks as she concentrates on making the puppet dance. She's very good at it. If I couldn't see the strings and levers she's using to make it move, I'd almost believe Mister Jitters was alive.

'It's an old song,' she says eventually. 'Everything's old in this town, and everything has a story behind it.' She's focused on making the puppet prance around inside its

78

cage, her tone distracted. I feel uneasy watching her, like Mister Jitters might lunge at her through the glass. 'There are stories about your mom, too, you know.'

I go still. 'What kind of stories?'

Cora stops noodling with the puppet, and the broken-looking creature falls slack on its strings. The light above it goes out, and the music slows to a drone before stopping completely.

'About how she caught a monster's eye,' she says.

'Is that supposed to be a joke?' I say, a sickly feeling churning up my insides. She better not be talking about Nolan. It wouldn't be the first time I'd heard some asshole commenting about how much older he is than Lorelei. Like it even matters. She was an adult, too.

'It's not a joke, I swear. See, Mister Jitters isn't just a puppet. He was a guy who lived in a shack in the woods making moonshine during Prohibition. He used to sell it downriver in Drayton – or Drown Town as everyone calls it now, since it got wiped out in a flood. Anyway, Mister Jitters lived alone out in the woods with no family, no friends – kind of an outcast nobody wanted to know unless they were in the market to buy what he was selling, you know? He hid his moonshine in the underground tunnels that run all around the lake, but he got caught in a cave-in when the land shifted in 1928.

'Mister Jitters was trapped down there, yelling for someone to come dig him out, but nobody did. The folks in town could hear his screams, but they didn't want to risk any more landslides. Not for him.'

79

My breath quickens. I can imagine him perfectly – alone in the dark, the air getting thin as he pleads for someone to help him.

'He kept on hollering for days,' Cora goes on. 'They say he was hungry, screaming about how he was trapped with the rotting bodies of other townsfolk who'd been caught in the cave-in. But in the end he went quiet, and everyone assumed he'd died. That was until they finally started hauling up the corpses for burial, and they found big chunks of them were missing. And human teeth marks in what was left.'

I know this is nonsense and I should tell her so, but I'm a little curious to see how she's going to try to connect it to Lorelei. I keep my face blank, and Cora picks up her story again with a glint in her eye.

'Mister Jitters was alive, and still hungry. He'd escaped from the caves, but he'd gotten a taste for human meat, so he started hunting for people to drag back to his lair and eat. Only a few at first. Maybe one every few years. But lately it's been more and more. Now it seems like only a couple months go by before Mister Jitters comes back out to feed.'

'Now his hunger makes him shiver and shake,' I say softly. It's another line from the song, dredged from some dusty part of my memory. I feel like I want to scrape at it; that if I pick away the scab, it'll be there underneath, raw and real.

'You've heard of him?' Cora seems surprised.

'No. Yeah, maybe.'

80

'From your mom?'

'I'm not sure.' Maybe I read about him in a *Nightjar* fan forum or something. I know I've heard of Mister Jitters somehow. A long time ago. Could it have been Lorelei who told me?

'Even if he was real, Mister Jitters would be over a hundred by now. Not exactly a prime candidate for dragging people off and eating them.' I'm pleased by how unbothered I sound, even though I can barely tear my gaze from the puppet.

'Eating people turned Mister Jitters into a monster,' Cora says, her voice so low I'm not sure whether she really means for me to hear, 'but there was already a sickness in this town. That's why none of our dead folks are buried in Harrow Lake. They won't admit it, but people here know there's something rotting inside all of us, and they don't want that smell to bring Mister Jitters out to feed.'

Seriously? 'What does any of this have to do with Lorelei?'

'Your mother was obsessed with Mister Jitters,' Cora says, brightening as she shifts back to her story. 'Used to go into the caves looking for him. And Mister Jitters decided to let Lorelei live instead of eating her because she was halfway to becoming a monster, just like him.'

I don't like hearing Lorelei described this way, even if she did abandon me and Nolan. Still, I hide my unease from Cora. 'A monster, huh?' I say flatly. 'No way.'

'You don't understand,' Cora tells me. 'Don't you know how your mom got the part in *Nightjar*?'

Oh, FFS. 'There was no "casting couch" involved, if that's what you –'

'That's not what I meant,' Cora hurries on, probably sensing my fraying temper. 'But you know there was another actress who was supposed to play Little Bird first, right?'

I eye Cora warily. I do know this. Faith Knight was the actress originally cast in the role, and she came to Harrow Lake with Nolan and the crew from LA. The official line was that she quit a few days in because she was homesick, but Nolan once told me it was actually because Faith felt she was *too important* to sleep in a trailer like the rest of the cast and crew. I don't see how any of this explains Lorelei being a monster, though. 'So what?'

'*So* Faith Knight quit because she kept hearing noises outside her trailer.'

'What kind of noises?'

'Like fingers tapping against the metal side of the trailer, and teeth chattering outside her window. The sounds Mister Jitters makes, see? And on her last night in Harrow Lake, Faith looked out and saw someone standing there.' Cora raises one eyebrow and glances pointedly at the puppet in its glass case.

I fight the urge to slow-blink at her. 'You're suggesting she saw Mister Jitters?'

Cora nods. 'And she got so scared she left town the next morning. So your father held an open audition here to find a new Little Bird. Three local girls were in the running, and after they'd auditioned your dad told them to come back the next day for his decision.'

I nod, familiar with this part of the story. 'And he chose Lorelei.'

'He did. But the weird thing was that the other two girls never even showed up to hear the casting.'

'Because it was obvious Lorelei would get the part?'

Cora shakes her head. 'Because they'd both disappeared in the night. Two girls, living in two different houses, vanished without a trace. And they were never seen again.'

'Maybe they ran away together.'

'*Maybe*,' Cora says, but not like she's agreeing with me. I think I'm starting to see where she's going with this.

'Are you trying to say Lorelei got rid of her competition? Why would she need to do that?'

Cora shrugs. 'Everyone around here says she went to the caves and asked Mister Jitters to take the other Little Birds. See, *Nightjar* was her ticket out of this place, and I don't think she could risk anyone taking it from her.'

I see a flash of my mother in a scene from *Nightjar* where Little Bird enters the caves to escape the angry mob chasing her. I slow it down, imagine her calling out to a monster in that quiet blackness.

Stop it, Lola.

'That's horseshit,' I tell Cora.

'Maybe it is. Maybe those girls disappearing had nothing to do with your mother. Maybe it was just this place. But that's what everyone around here believes; your mother was only a step away from becoming a monster.' Cora shrugs. 'I thought you'd want to know, just in case you get a weird vibe from anyone. Harrow Lake might not be as friendly as you expected.'

Now I *do* roll my eyes. 'Sounds like the people in this town have some pretty messed-up ideas.'

'You don't know the half of it,' Cora says. The calmness of her voice makes me pause. There's a faraway look in her eyes as she stares at the glass case holding the puppet, and it pricks my skin with goosebumps. 'Harrow Lake never really recovered after the landslide swallowed half the town; it died, the way Drown Town did, even if nobody here will say it out loud. And dead things don't move on. They decay.' I try to read her expression to see what she's hoping to gain from this outpouring, but her gaze is bleak when she meets my eyes. 'I wouldn't stick around here too long if I were you.'

'Are you trying to freak me out so you can tell everyone what a wuss Nolan Nox's daughter is? Is that it – you want me to cry and run away because of some backwoods bullshit you just plucked out of your ass?'

'I wasn't trying to scare you,' Cora says, unfazed. 'I just figured you deserve to know what goes on in this town. You know, seeing as your mom clearly didn't tell you anything about it.'

Didn't she?

The puppet in the cabinet twitches, then stands up on its haunches again. Cora's hands aren't on the controls now. It looks like it just woke up.

'How did you do that?' I ask.

Cora looks to the cabinet, then back at me. 'Do what?'

84

The Mister Jitters puppet is advancing towards the glass. Its stick-like limbs move in sharp jerks. But the strings are slack; I can't see how she's doing it.

The puppet raises a hand to tap on the glass with its long, needle-like fingers.

'That!' I point at it, unable to tear my eyes away. The hair on my arms rises, as though those sharp fingers are touching me.

Tap-tap-tap-tap-TAP.

The sound grows louder, faster. I'm sure the glass is going to shatter.

'How the hell are you doing that? Stop it!'

'What can you see?' Cora says. There's something hungry about her, like a vulture. She steps towards me, but I back away.

Panic thrums beneath my skin, inside my skull. I have to get *out*.

'Lola, wait!' Cora calls after me. 'What did you see? *What did you see?*'

Things I know about monsters

1. They aren't real.
2. Where fictional monsters are concerned, there are many kinds. You have your mainstream monster breeds, which can either be friendly or not, depending on the writer's mood, like zombies, werewolves, vampires, etc. One-offs, like Slender Man, Pennywise, the Babadook, and so on. Then you have your alien monsters like the *Alien* aliens or the nocturnal creatures from *Pitch Black*, to more sentient killers, as in *Predator*. There are also monsters that exist only in small pockets, belonging to towns or cultures as part of their own mythology, like Mister Jitters. (Do people tell stories about him in other towns, or just in Harrow Lake? I miss Google.)
3. Not one monster has ever appeared in any of Nolan's films. He says you don't need monsters to create fear.
4. My mother believed in monsters. At least, I think she did. But what do I know about my mother, really?

CHAPTER SEVEN

By the time I reach the fairground, I've realized it must've been a prank. The puppet probably had some automatic setting that made it move on its own. That tapping sound could easily have been the old mechanism working, I guess. Or maybe Cora wasn't trying to screw with me at all, and I just overreacted. I wish I had the scene recorded so I could watch it over. Like Nolan says, the camera shows only the truth.

The sign above the fairground entrance reads NIGHTJAR TOWN FAIR, just like in the film. Nolan has said in interviews that the fairground was pretty much the only thing he had to build in Harrow Lake. And it's still here, a shrine.

The big town fair scene, the one everyone remembers, is near the end of the movie. All the townspeople have gone mad with hunger, and they're chasing Little Bird with knives and clubs, ready to punish her for bringing down a curse on the town with her 'flirtatious ways'. But Little Bird escapes through the underground gondola ride at the back of the fair, stumbling through tunnels in the dark until she finds the way out.

Should I go in? The Easy Diner should be next, if I'm going in order – that would be the Optimal thing to do. But it's way behind me now, somewhere in the centre of town. The fairground's right here. It wouldn't make sense to walk away now without going in.

As I cross the threshold, I have the strangest feeling – like I'm acting out something I saw in a dream. A sure sign I've watched *Nightjar* way too many times.

Beyond the gate, a breeze swirls leaves around the lot. It must be mid-morning by now, but the place looks abandoned. I step forward, half certain the iron gate will clang shut behind me, but it doesn't.

The rides are as well preserved as the rest of this town. A faint smell of sugar and candy apples even clings to the air, along with an undertone of gasoline and a sharp, metallic scent. I wander on past a Ferris wheel which looms like an enormous cobweb over one corner of the lot. Near it sits a carousel painted in pastel colours. There are no horses on the carousel, as you might expect – only dogs. Teeth bared and eyes gleaming, they chase each other in a weird parody of a hunt. That was Nolan's idea. He said the dogs' appearance in the early fairground scene foreshadowed the villagers turning into pack animals when they hunted Little Bird later in the movie. I'm not sure anyone really picked up on that, but I know Nolan likes that it's there. I like it, too.

I pass a covered whack-a-mole and a strength-tester game, then reach the wooden gate for the Rickety Railroad rollercoaster. I push it open, but hesitate.

The first and only time I ever went to a fair was on my fifth birthday. Nolan and Lorelei were both there along with a small cluster of pre-vetted kids belonging to Nolan's business friends. Nolan and Lorelei were fighting. I couldn't hear what about. Lorelei kept trying to smile, but Nolan has never been good at hiding his temper.

'You are not taking my daughter on a goddamn rollercoaster! Look at her – she's terrified!'

'Stop planting seeds of fear in her mind, Nolan,' Lorelei said. She spoke quietly, but Nolan brushed her aside and came over to me, picking me up and carrying me towards the park exit. I can still feel the absolute giddiness of being so high up on his shoulders, knowing I was totally safe with him holding me.

I cling to that feeling as I let the gate to the Rickety Railroad swing shut. There's another ride nearby called The Harrowing. It didn't feature in *Nightjar*, but it looks like some kind of ghost train. There are no carts waiting for riders, though. The empty rails lead through open doors into darkness. I guess it wouldn't hurt to take a quick look inside. I check that nobody is around, then climb up the steps and follow the track.

Trees are painted on to black walls, simulating a wood, with glow-in-the-dark paint highlighting where the 'moonlight' hits their branches. Aside from a few tiny specks of daylight coming through holes in the ceiling, the luminous paint is the only light in here. It's barely enough for me to make out the metallic sheen of the rails on the floor. I keep going, pushing open another set of doors and almost peeing myself when an owl drops from above my head and hoots loudly in my face. I shove the owl aside, letting it swing on its tether. It hoots manically for a few more seconds before it shuts off.

A faint tang of smoke hits me as I round a bend in the track. There's a mural painted on the wall facing me – a mural of flames. Torches, actually. They're held by the villagers of *Nightjar*, depicted during one of the later scenes in the movie when they went hunting for Little Bird. The fake smoke smells kind of meaty here. Maybe that's why the villagers look so hungry.

I'm about to move on when something brushes my cheek. I shriek and slap it away, but it's just cloth. Loose fabric hanging down from the ceiling. My swat has yanked a corner loose, and it falls crookedly aside. There's another part of the mural behind it.

Here the painted villagers are bigger, closer. Bared teeth, eyes narrowed in anger, and fists clenched around burning torches. But that isn't the worst part.

There's a space in it, right at the centre, where there are deep gouges like claw marks, leaving the pale wood exposed underneath. From the size and shape, it must have been the head and shoulders of a person.

I know this scene from the movie. Know who that person must be.

But why would someone do this to Little Bird? Why would they erase her from the scene?

Get rid of her . . .

I drop the hanging cloth and back away.

Who did that to my mother? Those marks in the wood weren't made lightly.

I wish I knew who made them – who hates her that much. It could be anyone in this town. Anyone, or everyone.

I emerge back into daylight, feeling disoriented. A poster on the side of a cotton-candy cart near the chain-link fence advertises next week's parade, and Lorelei's face beams out at me from the centre of it. She is *everywhere* in this town.

I glance back. There's nobody there, of course, only the exit door of The Harrowing hanging open as I left it. Still, I feel like I'm being watched. It's just this place, I guess. So many things here are just a little too familiar. It's making me feel off balance.

There's a flicker in my peripheral vision. Something is moving on the other side of the chain-link fence surrounding the fairground. Trees huddle in close to the perimeter, but there's no breeze to move them now.

There – again. Just a darting shadow, but I definitely saw it. I step towards the fence. A girl flits between the trees. Is that the same girl I saw in the woods outside Grandmother's house? It's impossible to tell as I didn't get a clear look at her, but something about this girl is definitely familiar. My skin prickles.

I look closer. Then someone appears on the other side of the fence, and I jerk back. It's Cora. She's smoking a cigarette.

'There you are,' she says cheerfully, like we've been playing hide-and-seek. 'I thought I saw you heading in there.'

'What do you want?' My tone is harsh, I know, but it doesn't faze Cora.

'I wanted to make sure you're all right. I mean, you left the museum in such a hurry . . . I guess I hit a raw nerve with all that Mister Jitters stuff.' She waves her hand. 'They're just stories.'

It's not an apology, but I wouldn't want one anyway. Nolan believes people hide what they really feel behind *sorry* and *thank you*.

Cora holds up her cigarette. 'Want a drag? Call it a peace offering. But watch out for the fence.'

'The fence?'

She stoops to pick up a stone and tosses it at the chain links between us. A shower of sparks sprays off where the stone hit and I jump back.

'The power stays on all the time when the fair is closed. It's meant to keep people out, but I guess it didn't stop you.' She gives me a look I think is meant to be stern. 'You know you're trespassing, right?'

'I didn't see any . . .' The words are still fresh on my tongue when I spot a big yellow hazard sign near the fairground entrance. 'Oh.'

'You'd better be careful nobody else catches you poking around in there,' Cora says. She holds out her peace offering again, steady-handed despite how close she is to the fence. This girl has nerve. I like that. But why is there even an electric fence here? It's not like someone could break in and steal the Ferris wheel. 'Thanks for the warning, but I'll pass on the cigarette.' I smile to let her know I'm not being salty. 'I guess I'm a little jumpy.'

'You really are,' Cora agrees. 'But you'll get used to the weird things that go on in this town.'

Three days, max. 'I won't be here long enough for that,' I admit.

Cora waves her hand in a *so what* gesture. 'This place will get to you, one way or another. It always does.' I'm not sure what that means, but before I can ask, her eyes go wide at the sight of something behind me.

She tosses her cigarette into the grass and quickly wafts away her last lungful of smoke. I turn to see what's spooked her, and bump into a chest.

'Whoa there,' the guy attached to it says.

He looks a little older than me. Square-jawed, broad-shouldered, and tanned, with hair just long enough to tie back. He's basically a poster boy for good, old-fashioned outdoor living. But it's his eyes that really stand out: they're a striking hazel. I'd suspect he wore coloured contacts if that didn't seem so unlikely in this time-capsule town. I stare. So does he.

'You shouldn't be in here,' he says. 'The fairground isn't open until after the summer parade next week. And you for sure shouldn't be getting up close to that fence – it's dangerous.' The guy freezes when he spots Cora inching away as though she might dissolve into the trees. 'Jesus, Cora! Shouldn't you be working your shift at the diner? And is that . . . have you been smoking again?'

Cora growls in irritation. 'Get lost, Carter. Hadfield sent me out to pick up some more bread rolls from Mrs McCabe's.' I'm surprised to hear her mention my grandmother until I remember all that food in the kitchen this morning, and that awful sickly smell. 'I just took a quick detour when I spotted Lola. Thought I ought to warn her about the fence before she went and got herself electrocuted.'

'Oh, sure. The way to the McCabe place doesn't bring you anywhere near the fairground. You need to keep this job, Cora. *We* need you to keep this job.'

All the fight goes out of Cora at these words, and it's almost distressing to watch.

'I should go,' I say, but Carter's hand is suddenly on my arm. I try to pull away, but he's too busy eyeing Cora to notice.

'Go back to work,' he says to her with a jerk of his chin, and she saunters off.

Still gripping my arm, Carter ushers me back along the main thoroughfare in the direction of the front gate. I dig in my heels, forcing him to stop.

'You know, I heard about this guy who came out of his house early one morning and found a girl in the middle of his lawn. Just sitting there, hunched over under a blanket with her back to him,' I say. 'He called out to her, "Hey, what are you doing on my lawn?" but she didn't answer. So he went over to her and grabbed her shoulder, because she's just a girl, right? What was she going to do about it? But then the girl turned around and it wasn't a girl at all, but a coyote someone had fixed to the guy's lawn on a rope. The coyote bit off two of his fingers.'

I look pointedly at where Carter's hand is clamped around my arm, and suddenly it's not anymore. I don't think he knows whether to laugh or call for help.

'I'll take better care where I lay my hands,' he says at last. 'Wouldn't want to tangle with a coyote.'

'Or with someone who'd leave one tied to your lawn.'

He laughs. 'You're kinda kooky, aren't you?' he says with a smile I don't return. 'I'm guessing you're Lola? I ran into Cora leaving the museum earlier and she told me she'd met you.'

'Are you her brother?'

He holds out his hand. 'Carter Lahey,' he says. His handshake is firm. 'Hey, I'm sorry to hustle you out, but it isn't exactly safe for you to be wandering around in here . . .'

'I was only taking a look.' I have every right to be here. Nolan brought the fair to Harrow Lake in the first place.

'You're staying with Mrs McCabe, right? My uncle told me you're visiting,' he says. 'Uncle Grant? You met him when you first got here. He's fixing one of the go-carts over there.' He gestures towards an empty go-cart track, but I don't see Grant.

'He works here?'

'So do I. At least until I can find something more permanent,' Carter says. 'There aren't a whole heap of jobs going around here. But it gets busy in town during festival week, so . . .'

He has Grant's habit of talking too much, if nothing else. So does Cora, now that I think about it.

'Do you know what happened to the mural inside The Harrowing?' I say. Carter follows my gaze to the door hanging open where I ran out.

95

'Oh, you mean the one with the torches? I guess you saw the part where your mom . . . yeah. I wouldn't read too much into that.' Carter's expression dips into something like sympathy, and I have to look away before I give in to the urge to punch him. 'It happened years ago. Would've had it redone, but my dad was the one who painted the mural and he's . . . not around anymore, so it just kinda got covered up. To be honest, I'd forgotten all about it.'

'Whatever. I just wondered.'

We're almost at the main entrance when I spot the girl again, up ahead. For a moment, I think it's Cora, but this girl isn't wearing a shirt and pants, but a dress like mine. She swings on the open gate like she's been waiting for me, but as soon as she spots us she hops down and takes off along the road, her hair whipping the air behind her. I scowl after her. There's something so familiar about her. Again I wonder if she's the same person I saw last night outside my window. I can't tell.

'Are you all right?' Carter says.

'I saw someone . . .' But the gate isn't swinging now. There's no sign of her.

Who the hell is she?

Maybe it's some *Nightjar* fan who's decided to follow me around while I'm here, but she's really starting to creep me out.

Carter scans the empty road, and suddenly I wish I'd kept my mouth shut.

'Anyway, I should go.' I hurry through the gate and past the sign for the NIGHTJAR TOWN FAIR without looking back. The gates shut with a clang behind me.

CHAPTER EIGHT

Cora is coming down the porch steps when I arrive back at Grandmother's house. She carries a large basket full of bread on one arm. It looks old-fashioned and uncomfortable, like most things in this town.

'He let you go, then?' Cora says, shifting the basket from one arm to the other. A batch loaf tumbles out as she does so, and Cora deftly snatches it up, brushes it off against her pant leg, and puts it back in the basket.

'Who let me go?'

'My brother,' she says with a wry smile. 'He talks more than I do once he gets going.'

I don't disagree. But my mind is getting tangled with everything I've seen and heard today: stories of monsters, dancing puppets, vandalized portraits of my mother, and the elusive girl I keep seeing. I feel like I know her.

You 'feel' it? Nolan snaps. *Only people who lack intelligence rely on feelings.*

'Cora, do you know a girl around our age who might be following me? I think I saw her outside my window last night, and again at the fairground.'

'What does she look like?'

I try to list only the facts I'm certain of, Nolan's words still ringing in my head. 'She wore a dress, and her hair was long. Fair hair and skin, I think.'

Cora raises one eyebrow. 'You saw her when you were looking out of your bedroom window, and again at the fairground? Let me guess – in the hall of mirrors.'

It takes me a second to realize what she's suggesting. 'It wasn't *me*,' I snap. 'The girl was *outside* my window. And then she was swinging on the fairground gate. I was not looking at my own damned reflection!'

She raises her free hand and laughs. 'Just a thought. In that case, you pretty much described half the girls in Harrow Lake when they're dressed for the festival. If you're worried about it –'

'I'm not worried,' I cut in, forcing an even tone. Raising my voice in front of a stranger is *not* Optimal. 'I'm not even sure it was the same girl I saw both times.'

'Well, OK. But if you see her following you again, don't keep it to yourself. People do some weird shit in this town.'

'Like dressing up in clothes from a century ago?' I deadpan. But Cora doesn't laugh; she's staring off down the lane.

'Everyone here's just so – I dunno. Maybe there's something bad in the water . . .' She musters a cardboard smile. 'Speaking of which, you should come down to the lake at sunset. I'll be there with my friends – Faye, who you met this morning at Mr Bryn's, and her sister, Jess. I've got a couple bottles of the red-eye my mom makes.

It tastes like ass, but it gets the job done. You can hang out with us, if you like.'

They always want something from you, Lola.

But I pause midway through shaking my head. I only have two more days in Harrow Lake, and Nolan isn't here to say no. What would it be like to hang out with other teenagers?

'I'll think about it,' I say.

'Perfect,' Cora says, apparently taking that as a yes. 'And don't tell your grandmother about the dropped loaf, will you? She'd tell Hadfield for sure, and I'm already on my final warning.'

She heaves the bread basket onto her hip and takes off without waiting for me to agree.

Cora and I now share a secret. I tuck away a smile before going back inside the house. Scribble a note about Cora's dropped bread and slide it neatly between a gap in my bedroom floorboards.

I keep my secrets safe.

The jitterbugs are all closed again. Grandmother must have done it. It's not enough that I'm stuck here with none of my own stuff – she needs to take away even the illusion that I have any privacy.

I check the room, looking for anything else that might've been moved or gone missing. Everything looks the same, but when I'm rifling through Lorelei's shoes at the bottom of the closet, I come across a yellow-edged copy of *Alice's Adventures in Wonderland*. Was this always here?

It's like finding an old friend. I open the cover and the smell of aged paper wafts out. I miss my own room, filled with *normal* bookcases and hundreds of books, floor to ceiling on each wall. Horror, mostly. Even though Nolan likes to speed-read them before I'm done and tell me all the points where the author went wrong.

At home, I read all the time, and watch movies over and over again. Getting lost for hours inside heads that aren't my own. Unless Nolan wants me to go with him to some event or party or whatever, where I get lost in my *own* head while I smile and say clever things to impress his rivals.

I'm thumbing through *Alice* when a scrap of paper flutters out from between the pages and lands at my feet. It's a note, in tiny, jumbled handwriting. A child's handwriting.

I told the teacher about Grant cheating in class today. Daddy says I'm not to tattle, or Mister Jitters will come get me.

I would know who wrote it even if I wasn't standing in her bedroom. Lorelei was the one who taught me about keeping secrets. When they get too big to hold in, the best thing to do is to write them on scraps of paper – just get them *out*. I hide them where nobody else will ever find them, so my secrets exist outside of me, and I don't have to carry the weight of them inside my head. I've been doing the same thing since I was old enough to write.

I run my finger over the words and think about Lorelei's father in the photograph above the fireplace. He looked so serious and grave. Why would he tell Lorelei a thing like that – that a monster would *get her*? Nolan would never say something like that to me. I put the secret back where I found it.

There is nothing else remarkable at all in Lorelei's old room, except for the shelves full of jitterbugs, and the wallpaper that has curled back on itself again high in the corner of the room. There's no ignoring it, so I climb onto the bed and try to flatten the slightly damp paper back into place, but just as I'm at full stretch, my ankle wobbles on the mattress and I lose my balance. My fingers close around the frayed edge of the paper as I fall, and with a swift tearing sound I land on the bed with the whole sheet of wallpaper draped over me.

'Damn it!'

I look up to inspect the damage. Maybe I can fix it before Grandmother sees. I really don't want to have to tell her I've torn down her ugly wallpaper.

The exposed underneath layer is just the same as the one I've torn down – that same deco-ish beetle pattern that makes my eyes blur.

Except now I can see that the pattern underneath *isn't* quite the same. Someone has drawn scratchy figures all over the beetle design. Crooked and stick-like with backward-bending legs . . . No, it's only one figure. Repeated over and over again.

Mister Jitters.

I edge away from the bed, trying to take in all the drawings. There are dozens of them just on the section I've exposed.

Mister Jitters will come get me . . .

I grope blindly for the door handle and catch one of the shelves behind me with my elbow. Pain lances up my arm. One of the nutshells now lies open on its side where I've knocked it. The little bug legs waggle in distress, making that skittering sound again. I snap the lid shut, but I can still hear it. If anything, it's louder. Covering the shell with my hand doesn't stifle it. I don't know what else to do.

The chattering doesn't stop; instead, it takes on an irregular extra rhythm, like a quarter-beat filling in the gaps, and then another. The noise is swelling. It can't be, but it is. It *is*.

I back away from the shelf until I bump against the door. It's not just coming from that one jitterbug. It's all of them now. They're all making that same chattering sound through their closed shells. It builds like rain beating against a window, like a hundred sets of teeth rattling. It's as if all those stick figures on the walls have woken up, their jerky, staccato footsteps dancing across the paper . . .

Tap-tap-tap-tap-TAP!

'Stop it!'

Covering my ears, I stumble out onto the landing. But the moment the door closes the sound stops. I wait a moment, watching dust motes winnow in the last rays of sun coming in through the window in the stairwell. Still nothing. I press my ear against the wooden door.

I try to conjure Nolan's voice telling me to calm down, that it was nothing – it wasn't real. For once, he's silent. I can't even picture his face for a second, and that's almost as terrifying as the sound I just heard.

Slowly, my hand shaking, I turn the doorknob. The jitterbugs are quiet. Everything is normal. Well, as normal as it was before. The torn wallpaper still lies draped across the bed.

What the hell just happened? Am I imagining things, or is someone screwing with me? Whatever the answer is, there's no way I can be in this house right now.

In the downstairs hallway, I pause as I pass the telephone. I so need to hear Nolan's steady voice right now. To have him tell me there's nothing to worry about, that he wants me to come home and not stay in this screwed-up place. I lift the receiver and listen for the dial tone. It doesn't come. Pressing the switch hook doesn't work: it's dead. I'm just replacing the receiver when a bony hand grabs my wrist.

I shriek, knocking the phone off its hook with a clatter.

'Clumsy girl!' Grandmother snaps. I jerk free of her hold.

'You scared me.' In the dim light of the hallway, she is barely more than a floating white head above the black vacuum of her dress.

'Who were you calling at this hour, anyway?'

'Nolan, of course. And it's only four o'clock!'

'*Nolan, of course,*' she mocks. 'And tomorrow it will be some other man, and another the day after. When will you stop parading yourself in front of them and embarrassing your father and me?'

'I ... *Embarrassing* ... ?' I have no idea what she's talking about. The only man I ever call is Nolan.

'You need to have some respect, Lorelei. For yourself, and for this family!'

Oh.

Ohhhh.

'But . . . Grandmother, I'm not Lorelei.' I watch as her eyes narrow to dark slits. 'You do know that, right?'

She steps away from me. Her hands wring together in front of her, two pale moths feeling their way blindly. 'I know that,' she says softly. 'Of course I do. It was just the shadows – too many shadows in this house . . .'

And with that she hurries up the stairs. A door slams a moment later, leaving me alone with only a dead phone for company.

Just before sunset, I head out to meet Cora. I cross the yard and hardly notice the figure standing outside until I practically walk into him. Jerking back with a yelp, I'm relieved to see it's just Grant. Then I notice the cage in his hand.

'You're in an awful hurry, sweetpea,' he says. All I can do is stare at the empty cage, my mouth gone dry. It takes him a moment to read my silence. 'I'm just setting some traps for your grandma.' Grant shifts, resting the wire trap next to his boot. He looks the part of the old-timey backwoods boy, leering at me and leaning on a tree stump.

'What exactly are you hoping to catch?' The cage is about the size of a large shoebox and, judging by the lack of blades or razor wire, isn't meant to kill its victims.

'Rats,' Grant says, and grins when I make a face. 'Your grandma's worried they'll get into her baking.' He shrugs.

'And a pal of mine gives the rats I catch to his dogs to play with. Keeps 'em keen.'

'Lovely,' I say, even as my mouth fills with a sour taste.

'I wanted to come visit, anyhow – to see how you're settling in. Carter was worried he didn't make a good first impression on you at the fairground earlier.'

'Oh, yes. I'd almost forgotten,' I say.

Grant snickers. 'Don't tell the boy that. I reckon it'd bruise his ego up good to hear you forgot you even met him.'

I frown, uncertain. Grant shakes his head like I'm missing something obvious.

'Carter falls in and out of love at least once a week. I reckon a sweet treat like you caught his attention all right.' Now he laughs loudly, like he's just cracked an amazing joke.

I can't handle this right now.

'I don't suppose you know what happened to my suitcase, do you?' I say.

Grant's brow furrows at my graceless shift in topic. 'Your suitcase?'

'You took it upstairs for me when I arrived, but I can't find it and Grandmother says she has no idea where it went. It has all my things in it, all my clothes, and I'm leaving soon.'

As soon as I can get out of this place, I'm gone.

'I took it upstairs? Well then, maybe your grandma moved it out of the way and forgot?' Grant says. 'Put it in one of the other rooms?'

'No. She looked for it. It's not there.'

His eyebrows crawl up his forehead, creasing it into deep ruts. 'I don't know what to tell you. I'm sure it'll turn up.'

For all I know, he's spent the last day wearing my underwear.

'Did you do something to upset her?' Grant asks suddenly.

'Who?'

'Your grandma.' I don't answer, but apparently I don't have to. 'Yeah, I thought so. She used to do that with Lorelei sometimes, you know – take away her stuff to teach her a lesson. You might try telling her you're sorry for whatever you did.'

I think of her weeping in the kitchen; throwing out the breakfast she made for me. Of the jitterbug I stole. My questions about Lorelei. The torn wallpaper I haven't even told her about yet. The way she acted just now while I was trying to make a call. There are a dozen little things I've done that have upset my grandmother since I arrived in Harrow Lake. Without even trying.

Still, it'd be really petty of her to hide my stuff just for being a tiny bit of an asshole. But then I think about how she called me Lorelei just now; maybe she thought she was punishing Lorelei and then completely forgot.

I hate this place.

'I'm going for a walk,' I tell Grant. 'Maybe I'll find my crap out in the woods.'

He barks out a laugh. 'You've got a dirty mouth on you, don't you?' Grant lays his trap down. 'Wait up, I'll keep you company.'

'No. You won't.' I don't like this man, and I don't care if he knows it.

Grant's lip curls, somewhere between annoyance and a leer. 'Just remember what I said,' he says. 'You never know what's out there.' He wets his lower lip with his tongue, then goes back to his rat trap.

I try not to run. Or vomit. Instead I force my footsteps into an easy rhythm until at last I'm shrouded by trees.

The setting sun dapples down through the tree canopy. I've never seen this before – the way the trees grow so that their leaves don't quite touch those of their neighbours, as though they each need their own personal space. From underneath, it looks like a negative of a cracked, arid landscape. I've read about this phenomenon, though; it's called crown shyness. It's something I think about whenever I'm in a crowded room. How I can be surrounded by people, yet completely detached.

It makes me think about the story Grant told me – about the woods on a moonless night, and how a person might find themselves lost there forever if they stay still a moment too long. I don't believe it, of course. It's just more small-town bullshit, like the Mister Jitters thing. But I can't help wondering if there will be a moon tonight. The knots in the tree trunks around me are like eyes watching, biding their time; the creak of branches swaying in the breeze like preparatory knuckle-cracking.

What made those jitterbugs rattle in Lorelei's room earlier? What made the Mister Jitters puppet dance?

Stop being ridiculous, Lola, Nolan tells me, and I nod once, firmly. I'm tired, that's all. And probably a little off balance after everything that happened with Nolan in the apartment. It's perfectly natural that my senses might get a little tricksy. That my thoughts might wander to shadowy corners.

It's not until the path veers uphill through a thin spread of trees that I know I'm lost. I was supposed to be heading down to the waterfront. My stomach flutters in panic as I slide my phone from my skirt pocket, checking if maybe there's a sliver of reception here.

Zero bars. I'll need to charge it as soon as I get my suitcase back, too. It's almost dead.

Should I stick to the path or not? Will it curve back down towards the lake or keep going up to higher ground? I guess it doesn't matter. Either I'll find my way to town or search for a signal up on the hillside.

The trees eventually thin out, and towering metal shapes loom against the spiky shadows of the treetops. I've somehow ended up between the fairground and the lakeshore. This isn't where I'm supposed to be, but at least I know where I am.

A scream echoes through the trees.

My heart pounds as I scour the shadows around me.

'Hello? Is someone there?' I call out. My voice is alien in the dark woods.

Some birds make screeching sounds, don't they? I'm almost convinced it was an owl or a hawk when the shriek comes again. Definitely not a bird. But it's also not quite the terrified scream I thought I heard before. By the time I've tracked the source, I'm at the waterfront and the scream has changed to laughter, with more than one voice joining in. Girls. Three or four, I'd guess. I'm so relieved when I recognize one of them.

Cora.

I'm close enough to see the light of a small bonfire flickering between the trees when I hear someone say Nolan's name. It's not Cora. The tone is too brash to be Faye. It must be Faye's sister then. Jess, wasn't it? She's talking loudly, her words slurring. I wait and listen, feeling that usual dark thrill of eavesdropping until I hear what they're saying.

'Did you see his latest one a couple of months ago? It was called something *Cage . . . Cygnet's Cage*? Yeah, that was it. God, it was so *gory.*'

I bristle a little at that. Sure, it was one of Nolan's bloodier films, but he makes horror movies – what does she expect?

'I thought it was his best one,' replies a voice that is definitely Cora. 'Apart from that ending – that was so . . . I dunno, out of sync with the rest of the story. It was just like . . . what was the point? You know?'

Even though *Cygnet's Cage* didn't do well at the box office, the critics raved about it. It's the story of this guy trying to make his name as a surrealist painter in 1920s London, when the art world was basically exploding with talent. Cygnet hires a struggling actress to model for him, but his frustration sends him to a dark place, and he locks the actress in a cage in his apartment, gradually carving off parts of her body and painting a series of canvasses showing her transformation until finally she dies. The movie ends with Cygnet becoming a massive success – obviously – and buying a mansion with its own aviary full of human-sized cages.

That isn't how it should've ended, though. It was supposed to end with the woman slipping out between the bars, mutilated and slick with blood, and getting her revenge on the artist by murdering him in front of a crowd at his exhibition's grand opening. I know this because *Cygnet* was based on something I wrote. Only a short story, but one I thought was good enough for me to leave a copy on Nolan's desk.

My story was told from the perspective of the actress, Evangeline, and I poured everything I had into her – I gave her a voice that was witty and sharp, even as the man reshaped her against her will. Evangeline was real to me – alive on the page. I was so excited for Nolan to see her.

He never mentioned the story to me, though. Over the next few weeks it nearly killed me not to ask if he'd read it. But when I heard he was working on a new project with a weirdly similar plot to my story – my story! – I thought I might explode with happiness. Until I heard about the changes he'd made.

For the first time in my life, I stormed into Nolan's study without knocking. I demanded to know why he'd changed it so the story was told from Cygnet's point of view – and without even telling me first.

'Oh, was it your story? I thought one of the scouts sent it.' Nolan's a good liar, so he obviously meant for me to see through it. 'As far as the POV goes, I think the world has seen more than enough angry women, don't you?'

I ignored that – had to, if I didn't want him to laugh and call me hysterical. 'But why did you change the ending?' I insisted, ignoring the warning look on his face. 'Cygnet wasn't supposed to get away with it!'

Nolan laughed at me. 'Get real, Lola. The ending you gave it was cliché – *weak*. Just another *Carrie* rip-off.'

Of course he was right. He's always right.

'My *Cygnet* shows that great art trumps morality,' Nolan said, and then he winked. Winking is such a strange thing: it brings you in on the joke, even when you *are* the joke. I hate winking. 'Honestly, Lola, don't be upset. You should be pleased that you played a small part in making such a great film. Isn't that what you've always wanted – to be a part of my work?'

I wasn't sure whether to be angry at him for twisting my words, or grateful that he'd shaped them into something better. Something that was *ours* . . . But I guess in the end it was really his.

That was the last story I wrote. The let-down was more than I could bear a second time.

I feel a little vindicated, maybe, as I listen to Cora's comments about the movie's ending. But that vindication brings with it a wash of guilt. Nolan is a genius. I shouldn't be listening to some random teenagers criticizing his choices.

'What's his daughter like?' the girl who must be Jess asks. I don't know why I care what the answer is, but I do.

'Lola?' Cora pauses before continuing, like she's really giving it some thought. 'You know, I like her. She seems like someone who'd be interesting to know.'

'Yeah, interesting,' Faye adds, but her tone says that's not the good thing Cora seems to think it is. 'She was dressed up to look just like her mom.'

I want to go over there and correct her. I'm *not* dressed like Lorelei – I'm dressed like Little Bird. There's a difference. For one thing, Nolan would never understand me wanting to look like my mother. But an homage to Little Bird? He'd get that.

I stay where I am, though. Hidden.

'I think she's just trying to fit in,' Cora says. 'She doesn't know fitting in around here is a bad thing.'

Her friends don't laugh or contradict her. I'm starting to think maybe Cora's right about there being something wrong with this town.

Did Nolan see that when he came here to make *Nightjar*? Is that what made this place so appealing to him? Or did he dismiss the whispers of monsters, woods that can claim a person, and 'something bad in the water' as pure superstitious nonsense?

Because that's exactly what he would call it: *pure superstitious nonsense*. But what about the tightness I feel in my gut? The prickle creeping over my skin, urging me even now to look behind me and check there's nothing – no one – lurking in these woods?

'Harrow Lake brings out the worst in people – like my mom,' Cora says. 'Like everyone in this damn town. Sooner or later, the bad comes out. That's why I'm getting the hell out of here first chance I get. I'll be gone before the bad gets its claws in too deep.'

'There's bad everywhere, Cora,' Faye says. 'Just look at what happened to Lola's dad. Can you imagine finding one of your folks stabbed like that? I hope you haven't been telling *her* all the stories about this place.' There's a pause. 'Jeez, Cora! She must be so freaked out already, especially with her dad in the hospital. What if he dies?'

What if he dies?

I can't listen to any more.

He's going to be fine.

I repeat this over and over as I hurry back through the trees, but it doesn't silence the whisper at the back of my mind. What if I'm really on my own? What will I do without him? I've only been away from him for one night, and already I'm losing my shit.

I need to speak to Nolan. Now.

The sycamore trees block out most of the sky, which is turning from blood orange to a deep blue. Phone in hand, I walk from one patch of twilight to the next. No signal. The woods look so different at this time of day than in the night-time scenes of *Nightjar*. It all looks familiar, yet not – like an old story I haven't heard in a long time. But there's no sign of a house or any other landmark I can use to get my bearings.

I'm lost. The thought slithers through my head, but I kick it out. I'm not lost, I'm just looking for a spot with a signal in this wilderness. There's still just enough daylight to see.

I hurry on in the direction my internal compass tells me Grandmother's house lies, but as the ground starts to even out near the brow of a ridge, I know I've gone off course – badly. This must be the rim of the basin Harrow Lake sits in, and that's nowhere near the house.

Damn it! What am I supposed to do?

Nolan?

Nothing.

Nolan!

All I can do is head downhill and hope I see something familiar again. I keep an eye on my phone, but it's as helpful as a brick right now. That is until I enter a clearing, and the signal finally creeps up to one bar. I let out a yell of triumph.

I flop down on the knotted roots of a squat, dead-looking oak tree sitting in the middle of the clearing. My phone pings with a bunch of messages, but they're only junk. Nothing from Nolan, or even Larry. How pathetic is it that I'm disappointed not to have a message from *Larry*?

I go to dial Nolan, then realize how pointless that would be. Even Nolan can't do anything about me being lost in the woods three states away, and I'd only stress him out. Not Optimal. Instead I call Grandmother's house and lean my head back against the oak tree while it rings, noticing the tiny dead-white acorn-looking things hanging from its branches. It looks like a stern glance would bring them all down. The phone is still ringing. Finally, it cuts out with a long *beeeeeep*, then goes quiet. I go to dial again and see EMERGENCY CALLS ONLY is back on the screen.

God, why did I come out here by myself? Why didn't I just join Cora and her friends?

It's fine. I'll sit here for a moment to calm down, then I'll chase down that crappy bar of signal and try my grandmother again. Easy. I'm sure she'll be able to find me. Maybe she'll send Grant out with a flashlight – even that sounds welcome at this point. I breathe in the smells of the forest: new growth, the crisp promise of night air, and a hint of healthy rot and sunshine. What all good girls are made of, or close enough.

I jerk upright when I feel the phone slip from my fingers. It clatters somewhere near my feet. I reach down, but it isn't where I expect it to be. I get up and trace a careful circle among the roots running like veins into the ground. There's no sign of my phone. But there's a hole, fist-sized and hidden between two gnarled roots. *No.*

I try to visualize putting my hand in there, to imagine it isn't full of slithering, crawling things. No way.

I once found a nest of spiders in the yard – we had a yard then, though I can't remember where – with the spiderlings just starting to hatch. They swarmed out, thousands of tiny black-and-yellow bodies rushing like a wave towards me. I screamed my head off. I don't know why I didn't just run away, but a moment later Nolan came racing from the house and stamped the spiders under his feet, yelling at Lorelei for just standing there.

'Why didn't you do something?' Nolan snapped. I remember being relieved that he was mad at Lorelei, not me.

'She needs to learn to not be scared,' she said in her calm, quiet voice.

I thought Nolan had killed all the spiders, but then later that night, when Lorelei was putting me to bed, she found one of them in my discarded clothes. She held my wrist so I couldn't wriggle away, and put the spider on my skin. I was afraid – terrified, actually – but more shocked at the firm way she held me. It was so unlike her, so determined.

'Don't be afraid,' she said. 'If you're scared of a thing, you give it power over you. And look how tiny this spider is, baby girl. You're so much bigger and stronger than it. See?'

I was too petrified to scream, too confused by what she said to do anything but bite the inside of my lip to stop it trembling. I felt the spider's legs moving over my skin, her tight grip on my wrist turning my hand cold.

Lorelei swept the spider off me and opened the bedroom window to release it. Still, I didn't move. Lorelei lifted me into bed, kissed my head and was about to leave, when she noticed my hand lying on the bedspread, skin blazing. The spider had bitten my palm.

'Good girl,' she said, stroking my hair. 'You didn't make a sound.'

Lorelei put some strong-smelling ointment on it and made me promise not to mention it to Nolan, but she'd already taught me to keep secrets by then. *Keep your secrets safe, Lola. If you don't, they can hurt you. If you feel like you need to tell someone, write it down instead. But keep it safe.* That was what Lorelei told me. After she left my room, I wrote down what had happened on a slip of paper, then taped it to the underside of my sock drawer.

I didn't tell Nolan about the spider, but I didn't have to. The next morning, my entire arm had swelled up like a balloon, the veins bulging red under the skin despite Lorelei's cream. Nolan was livid. The next place we moved to didn't have a yard, and Lorelei wasn't allowed to put me to bed after that.

I haven't thought about that spider's nest in years. Now the memory swarms, a wave of black and yellow. I wish I could scratch it out of my head.

The screen of my phone lights up from inside the hole. I have a new message. But the bright flash is gone before I can tell how deeply the phone has fallen. At least the case seems to have saved it from near-certain death. And – bonus! – it looks like it has found reception. *Ha.*

Folding back the sleeve of my dress, I ignore the sweat pricking my skin, take a deep breath, and reach inside.

'Don't bite,' I mutter.

The earth is dry. It leaves a powdery residue, coating my fingers like ash. The hole is probably full of crawling, wriggling things, but I can't see them, so maybe they aren't there. I edge my arm in deeper. Where is my damn phone? How far down can it be? I flatten my body to the ground to give myself a little more reach. Then I hear a noise. Rumbling, only less rhythmic than that, and faint. It's jarring. Like the sound a door makes as it opens late at night, slow and menacing – *Are you asleep?* – or the chattering of teeth.

I freeze. It's just like how the jitterbugs sounded in Lorelei's room earlier, their hundreds of legs tap-tap-tapping away inside their shells.

I need to grab my phone and get out of the woods. Out of this creepy-ass town.

Shoving my shoulder to the ground, I finally feel the smooth edge of the case against my fingertips. I coax it up the side of the hole. But when I wrap my fingers around it, there's something else there, too – something solid, rough. I shriek, yanking my arm out and stumbling back until I trip over my skirt and land hard on my ass.

My breath leaves me in sharp stabs. I pick up the phone, hand shaking. There are a few smudges of dirt on the screen, but it's what lies next to it that makes my lips part in surprise. That rough thing I grabbed was a nutshell – a jitterbug, exactly like the ones in Lorelei's room.

CHAPTER NINE

Up close, this jitterbug is slightly bigger than the rest – almost as big as my palm. But beneath the thin crust of soil, the hand-carved grooves covering the shell are identical. How is that even possible? Where did it come from? It's so totally out of place, like seeing Jigsaw from *Saw* wheeling his little tricycle across the set of *Love, Simon*.

'Oh, hey there.'

I stifle a scream as someone steps out of the trees. In the glow of the flashlight she's holding low so it won't blind me, I see a woman wearing a smart green uniform and a smile. She's in her late thirties, I guess, with blonde hair pulled back into a knot. Pretty, in a bland sort of way.

'I thought I saw someone over here. I'm Ranger Crane. You must be Moira McCabe's granddaughter, am I right?'

I can't answer. Her smile slips as she pans the light over me.

'Are you OK?'

I begin shaking my head, then feel Nolan standing reassuringly at my shoulder. I paste on a blasé expression. 'I'm fine,' I say. 'I just dropped my phone down a hole and there was a weird noise coming from underground, like something rattling. And I found this . . .'

'A noise? What kind of noise?'

Ranger Crane crouches next to me with her flashlight. It's a strange, bulky thing like a car battery with a handle on it, like something Jules Verne might dream up. She shines it down into the hole, her head bobbing left and right.

'I hope to heck the ground isn't shifting again,' she says. 'That's all we need.'

I want to tell her to stop, to keep her distance, but before I can utter a word the flashlight flickers once, twice, and goes out.

'Aw, dang it,' she says. I'm sweating now, despite the chill in the air.

Ranger Crane's face is lit up again, with a softer glow this time. She has a miniature flashlight on a silver chain around her neck. It's like something you might pick up at Radio Shack.

She sees me looking and gives a fake-stern glare. 'Don't go telling anyone you saw this. We're supposed to keep everything 1920s authentic while the *Nightjar* fans are in town for the festival. They'll come after me with pitchforks if they catch me wearing it.'

'Who will?' I say.

She laughs. 'The townsfolk. You know, like in your dad's movie.'

I know she's joking, but I can't bring myself to laugh. I open the jitterbug and hold it out for her to see.

'Do you know who this might belong to?' I don't know why I'm asking. I know the answer. Inside is a white beetle with a red pattern across its back, buggy black eyes catching the light as it wiggles its spiky legs. *Tap-tap-tap-tap-TAP*.

Ranger Crane peers at it.

'Is that a jitterbug? Haven't seen one of those in years . . .' She goes to take it, but I snatch it back and close the lid. Ranger Crane blinks in surprise. 'You found it up here? Someone probably hung it in the Bone Tree,' she says, looking up at the dead branches of the tree above us. 'Have you heard about the Bone Tree already? No? Folks usually just tie teeth up there, but I've known them to hang other things, too, if they had a special meaning.'

I watch the white acorns swaying in the breeze, and a part of what Ranger Crane just said slides into place. Those aren't acorns. There are teeth hanging from the branches – hundreds and hundreds of teeth.

'But . . . *why*?'

'Superstition, you know? *Don't let your bones go to ground until you're ready to go with 'em*, as they say. And, a hundred years ago, this was the tallest tree in Harrow Lake. Mister Jitters – you hear about him? Well, the kids think that when they lose a tooth, Mister Jitters'll catch a taste of their bones, and come out of the caves to hunt them down unless they hang the tooth from the Bone Tree.'

She laughs, but I don't find it funny. Her words remind me of what Cora said at the museum, about how dead people aren't buried in Harrow Lake.

'Of course, the kids who think they're tough come up here and dare each other to call his name. If they're really brave, they'll put their hand in among the roots of the tree – if they make it to a count of five, then Mister Jitters is sure to come. But I haven't heard of anyone making it to five yet. One did get the tip of his finger bitten off, but that was probably just some critter . . .'

I just put my hand in that hole. Was it five seconds? More? I don't know . . . it felt longer.

Mister Jitters is sure to come.

I've been raised on horror stories, but they've never made me recoil like this. I want to get away from this place, this woman, the faint rattle of teeth swaying in the dead branches above us. There are so many of them . . . so many people in this town who must believe, at least a little, that their monster is real.

Why did I have to drop my damn phone?

Ranger Crane puts her hand on my arm and shakes her head gently. 'It's just a story. Nonsense, really. But maybe you should put that back where you found it, all the same.'

'I didn't find it on the tree,' I say. 'It was in the ground.'

'It was . . . oh.' She forms her lips into a thin line for a moment. 'I guess that makes you a brave one.'

'I didn't know I wasn't supposed to put my hand in there.'

She taps a fingernail on the shell of the jitterbug. 'Maybe somebody left this as a gift for Mister Jitters.'

I don't care where the jitterbug came from anymore. 'Could you point me in the direction of my grandmother's house? I've gotten myself turned around in your well-signposted woods.' It comes out snappier than I intended, but I just want to get out of here.

She dusts off her knees. 'Sure. I'll walk you.'

We make our way through the trees, and I listen to the breathing of the cracked canopy above us and the regular *tap-tap-tap* as Ranger Crane's pendant swings back and forth against her chest.

'There's the McCabe place,' she says at last, just as a roof breaks through the trees up ahead.

'I'll be fine from here.' I go to leave her, but she stops me.

'You know, that sound you heard was probably just a rabbit that got startled by a big old hand shooting into its burrow. Or a squirrel, maybe.'

'Sure,' I say, but I can't imagine rabbits or squirrels or any other rodent chattering like that.

She nods efficiently. 'All righty. So it's nothing you need to go telling anyone else about, is it?'

Is she threatening me? I can't read this woman. When I don't answer, she hisses in a breath through her teeth.

'There's been talk around town that there are signs of another big landslide on the way – not signs with any basis in science, you understand, just folk tales and nonsense. Did you know that if you see a spiderweb spun with red thread, that means someone you know will be crushed to death?'

'I did not know that.'

Ranger Crane laughs at my dry tone. 'Yeah, apparently that's a thing. And there've been at least six red spiderweb sightings in the last couple of months, which of course must mean there's a landslide coming.' She rolls her eyes. 'I put it down to kids and red food dye myself. Oh, but there's also the screaming.'

'The screaming?'

'Mr Bryn keeps a cockerel. A couple of days ago it quit crowing at dawn, and now it makes this awful screaming sound like a baby crying right after sundown. Mr Bryn is convinced it's an omen.'

I imagine that old man from the museum worrying over his cockerel and stifle a laugh. Ranger Crane apparently reads something else into my silence.

'Hey, maybe I shouldn't be telling you all this. We get so caught up in our spooky stories here it's easy to forget how it might sound to an outsider . . .'

She keeps talking, but I'm thinking back to the Bone Tree hanging over me, its branches full of teeth. How could anyone grow up in a town like this and *not* believe in monsters?

'. . . the last thing you need right now,' Ranger Crane is saying. 'Still, maybe you should stay indoors when it's dark, all right? That's what I tell my two – not that they listen . . .'

She waits while I walk over to the front steps, then disappears back into the woods.

'I'm afraid Mr Nox is taking a nap right now. Any message?'

'Just . . . tell him I called again.'

CHAPTER TEN

I lie in bed, turning the jitterbug over in my hands. Thin starlight bleeds in through the curtains. There's no moon again tonight. No wonder Ranger Crane seemed so keen to get me out of the woods earlier. Maybe I was mere moments from becoming a part of the forest myself, and I never even knew it. I try to shake off the idea, but it lingers like it's sprouted roots.

Maybe I shouldn't have taken the jitterbug. If it was left as a gift for Mister Jitters – by Lorelei or whoever – then it probably wasn't a great idea to steal it from him. *Shit*.

I kick back the covers and lie there in Lorelei's cotton nightdress, hoping the whisper of a breeze from the open window will cool my damp skin. Grandmother must have pressed the wallpaper back into place while I was out, but now it's started to curl again at the corner. I shut my eyes. If I can't see it, it's not there. I recite lines of dialogue in my head – snippets from some of my favourite movies – and splice them together so they make new scenes. I do this whenever I can't sleep: I can watch Ellen Ripley blast Pennywise the clown out of an airlock. Pit

Child's Play's Chucky against the fiercest resurrectees from *Pet Sematary*. The jumbling of worlds eventually becomes a kind of white noise, forcing my mind to shut down and let me dream instead.

It's not working now, though. I can hear the faint rustling of the paper arching back from the wall. The whole sheet could peel away and land on me any second. Finally, I give up and open my eyes.

The wallpaper looks the same as before, peeling, but no more than it was. Just a corner of the sheet furled delicately back on itself.

Then I see it. The paper is moving. No – something *under* it is moving. The beetle-lines covering the wallpaper warp and shift, some *thing* making the paper bubble as it moves towards the peeling corner. I hear it, too. A rustling, snapping sound.

I should move, scuttle out of bed and get away from this place – or at least turn the light on – but I can't. Can't move, or make a sound.

A thin shadow crawls from between the sheets of wallpaper. Stretches, thin as a blade, until it's as long as my forearm. Then it bends and starts tapping at the wall around it. Like an antenna, or the leg of some giant insect.

Tap-tap-tap-tap-TAP . . .

I try to scream. It comes out as a moan, low in my throat. Then, as though drawn by the sound, another long shape emerges next to the first. Oh God. Oh *God*. They're not insect legs – they're fingers. Long, blade-thin fingers, dancing across the wall.

Mister Jitters.

I put my arm in that hole. I took his jitterbug.

A hand slides free of the wallpaper, dragging an arm behind it. Its long fingers still *tap-tap-tap* away. The wall bulges around what must be a shoulder, then a head. It swivels under the paper, and I see the outline of pinprick eye sockets, a mouth gaping as though it's about to speak.

With a violent effort, I sit bolt upright in bed, knocking something off the nightstand with a flailing arm. My hand shakes as I turn on the lamp and scramble out of bed, panting. But there's nothing on the wall; the paper lies flat.

It was just a nightmare. I was dreaming. My nightdress sticks to my skin with cold sweat.

The nutshell lies on the floor where I knocked it a moment ago. In the lamplight, the white beetle glitters, its legs dancing with a faint *tap-tap-tap-tap-TAP.*

'Where are the jitterbugs?' I ask my grandmother over breakfast. My breakfast takes the form of a milky cup of coffee, into which I stir too much sugar while she fusses over the stove.

'The jitterbugs?' she says without looking up.

'They're not in my room anymore.'

After another hour or so of lying in bed this morning, staring up at the unmoving wallpaper and feeling annoyed at myself for letting a bullshit story get to me enough that it infiltrated my dreams, I finally noticed that all the jitterbugs were gone. The shelves had been completely cleared – all except for the wooden carriage clock sitting on the highest shelf. Too high for my grandmother to reach, I imagine. The only jitterbug left is the one I found last night under the Bone Tree, now a hard lump in my pocket. After the dream I had, I should've thrown the damn thing away, but, when I took it from the drawer in the nightstand, it slid almost of its own accord into the pocket of my borrowed dress. Today it's the royal blue knit dress Little Bird wore when the townspeople chased her into the caves.

'Could the jitterbugs perhaps be in the same place you *didn't* put my bag?'

Now she turns around. She looks annoyed. 'What on earth are you talking about?'

'The jitterbugs. You moved them, didn't you? Like you moved my suitcase.'

For a second, I think she's going to give in and admit to hiding my stuff. But she just rubs her knuckles against her temples like I'm giving her a migraine.

'Will you please stop doing that?' she says.

I hadn't noticed how aggressively I was stirring my coffee. The spoon clatters against the edge of the cup. I set it down in the saucer.

'You're saying you didn't hide my suitcase just so I'd have to wear Lorelei's movie clothes? So I'd look more like her? Make it easier to pretend she didn't leave you without a backward glance?'

Something like pain flashes in her eyes, but only for a second.

'But it wasn't just me she left, was it?' she says crisply.

My fingers tighten around my cup. Grandmother glances at it, perhaps wondering if I'm going to throw scalding-hot coffee in her face.

The thought never crossed my mind, Grandmother.

'I haven't laid eyes on your suitcase, Lola,' she says. 'And I didn't move the jitterbugs. Honestly, it's as though you think I have nothing better to do than play silly games.' She takes off her apron and flings it on the counter. 'Now, if you'll excuse me, I'm going upstairs to lie down.'

'Wait,' I say as she moves to go. 'Why did Lorelei like them so much? The jitterbugs?'

For a moment I think she won't answer, but then her expression softens, becomes almost worried. 'It's the sound they make – Lorelei said it helped her sleep. She always was a fanciful girl, and never a good sleeper.'

'Do the jitterbugs have anything to do with Mister Jitters? That was who she drew all those pictures of, right?' Hidden beneath layers and layers of the same ugly wallpaper. Even though I'm awake now, with the sun sauntering in through the windows, I shiver at the memory of my dream.

Tap-tap-tap-tap-TAP . . .

I take the white jitterbug out of my pocket and lay it on the table in front of me.

Grandmother's hand shakes as she reaches for it. 'Where did you get that?'

I snatch the bug away from her. She can't have it. Her hand lands on my wrist instead. I try to pull free of her grip, but the claw is firm.

'Where did you get that jitterbug?' she repeats, sharper this time. I can tell she wants to rip it from my hand.

'I found it in the woods,' I say. 'Why?'

Grandmother drags me by my sleeve through to the living room. I'm too stunned to fight her. She taps the glass of one of the mantel photos with her fingernail. It's the one of Lorelei sitting with her father.

'That was her favourite. I thought she took it with her.'

She doesn't mean the picture itself. A jitterbug exactly like the one I'm holding rests in Lorelei's hand in the photo. It has the same white beetle sitting inside, the pattern on its back clearly visible, and the black eyes shining, almost alive. I run a finger over the smooth body of the bug. It's warm, like the heat of my flesh has seeped into it. 'You really think it's the same one?'

Grandmother doesn't answer at once.

'Her father made that jitterbug for her – it was the first one she had, before she learned to whittle them for herself. That one was always her favourite, seeing as it came from him. Lord, that man doted on Lorelei from the moment she was born.'

I study the two figures in the photograph. Teenage Lorelei is perched on one of her father's knees, his arm at her waist pulling her close. It hits me under the ribs: Nolan never sits with me like that. He doesn't make things for me – certainly not his movies. I would love it if he made me something, even something small . . . Hell, Nolan could make me a paper airplane and I'd treasure it.

But that's not Nolan. He doesn't do *gestures*. There's no point wishing for anything to be different.

'He spoiled that girl. And she broke his heart by taking off with the first man with a fat pocketbook.' My grandmother sneers. 'And doesn't your father just love lording *that* over everyone?'

The chair behind me creaks as she sinks down into it. Like the Mister Jitters puppet in the museum, collapsing as Cora grew tired of making it dance.

'What's that supposed to mean?'

Grandmother doesn't answer, just watches me with eyes like chips of ice.

I'm not embarrassed that Nolan's wealthy. I might have been born into it, but he certainly wasn't. I never met them, but I know Nolan's father died when Nolan was just a kid, and his mother raised him alone while working four different jobs to cover the rent. Whatever Nolan has now, he earned.

'Sure, Nolan has money,' I say, 'but he's generous with it. Last year he gave to a bunch of different charities . . .'

'Oh, yes. He's very *generous*. Sends his little cheques every month so he can pat himself on the back for *taking care of the old dear.* As if that makes up for the fact that he stole our daughter away and then couldn't keep her in line the way a husband should.'

'*Keep her in line?*'

Grandmother continues as though I haven't spoken. 'Do you know, he has his assistant call me – his assistant, mind, because he's too important to call me himself – once a year to *see how I am*?' She gives a snorting laugh. 'Checking whether I'm dead yet, he means.'

I didn't know any of this. On the one hand, it seems like such a kind thing for Nolan to do, but on the other . . . if he actually cares about her, then why hasn't he ever mentioned her to me? Why have I never met her before? For what possible reason would he maintain a secret connection to the mother of the woman who left him?

But Grandmother has no right to throw shade on Nolan, especially if what she's saying is true.

'You're lucky he bothers,' I say.

Lorelei certainly doesn't. The words hang in the air, unspoken.

Grandmother's chair rocks faster. I've upset her again. But I don't care. I don't *care*.

'I'm going out,' I tell her, and head for the door.

I've been walking for a long time, roughly following the lip of the basin the town sits in. The trees are thin here, the ground almost too rocky without proper hiking boots.

I'm looking for the Bone Tree again. Not to return Lorelei's jitterbug to Mister Jitters, although maybe I should. I want to try calling Nolan again, and I know there's at least *some* reception near that damn tree.

How often did Lorelei walk this same path from her home to the Bone Tree? Maybe I'm like one of the tree-people Grant told me about, my roots drawing some essence of Lorelei up through the soles of my shoes. And maybe this is the closest I'll ever get to my mother again. Walking in her footsteps.

'Lola, stop!'

Cora's brother, Carter, strides through the trees ahead of me. He's wearing the same wrinkled shirt and pants as before, his face flushed like he's been running.

I instinctively take a step back, seeing the notepad clutched in his hand. 'What do you want?'

He shakes his head. 'You shouldn't be up here. We're right next to the old quarry, and the hillside isn't stable. A couple of kids noticed signs of ground movement farther up the slope, so my mom asked me to come up here and take some notes. You really shouldn't wander alone out here when you don't know where you're going.'

You never know what might happen . . .

'I just came up here to see if there's any signal – to make a call,' I say. 'What kind of signs are you talking about anyway? With the ground movement? I thought you relied on screaming cockerels to let you know when there's a problem.'

Carter frowns for a second, then breaks out into a grin. 'Oh, you heard about Mr Bryn's rooster? Yeah, no. This is something a little more conventional: a couple of trees came down up the hill there.'

He's cute when he smiles like that, I realize. Cute enough that I don't bother to look where he's pointing.

I'm alone with a cute boy in the woods.

That thought is a little thrilling. I can't think of a time when I've been alone with a cute boy *anywhere*.

He's just pretending, Nolan warns me. *He wants something from you, Lola. They all do.*

'Did you get through to your dad?' Carter asks, as if reading my thoughts.

Phone call. Nolan. Hospital. All things I should be thinking about much more than how Carter's eyes are such a pretty hazel colour.

'I keep trying to reach Nolan at the hospital, but whenever I call they say he's asleep or with the doctor or not well enough to talk to me. And I'm supposed to be going home in a couple of days.' I'm saying too much, letting this strange boy see too much of me. It's not Optimal at all. I clamp my mouth shut.

'I heard about your dad,' Carter says gently. I shrug. 'And I'm sorry if I was snappy yesterday. I was just annoyed with Cora is all . . . But that's another story. Let me at least walk you back to your side of the lake, where the ground is more settled. I know a safe route.'

We follow an invisible path through the trees, occasional flashes of the lake to our left giving me some sense of my bearings. The sun is high above us, blade-like between the branches.

Carter is quiet. He moves in a way that says he's at home in these woods. Content. Every time we come to a rise or a boulder in the path, he leaps up onto it like he has too much leashed energy to just walk.

'So, you live near here?' I say to the back of his head.

'Right over there.' He points through the scrubby trees below us. 'It's the one with the red pickup out front.'

'You have your own place?' The house he indicated is more of a log cabin, and I can't imagine it's big enough for a whole family.

'Uh, no. My mom and Cora live there, too,' Carter says, then grins at me as my face burns. He must think I'm an asshole. 'Come on. Mrs McCabe won't be pleased if I let you get caught in a rockslide and go barrel-rolling down to the lake.'

'Oh, I'm not so sure about that. I don't think I'm her favourite person right now.' I'm probably not Carter's, either.

'What did you do to her?' he asks, half laughing.

I give that some thought. 'I asked too many questions.'

Carter snorts, but keeps moving. We clamber over tree roots and rocks, Carter pausing here and there to let me catch up, his hand held out for me to take if I need it. But I don't. Mine are clammy as hell from trekking through the woods.

We go on like this until my feet start to burn with the promise of blisters. I fall a few steps behind again, and on another rocky cluster manage to stand on the hem of Lorelei's skirt. The fabric tears. My phone clatters from my pocket, bouncing from stone to stone to a thorny-looking shrub a few feet away. I trudge after it. It's only as I reach down that I hear a noise – like twigs snapping, but more muffled.

'Lola, move!' Carter yells. I have only a moment to see him racing towards me before the ground disintegrates under my feet.

CHAPTER ELEVEN

I fall so fast I can't even scream. Daylight disappears before I hit icy water. Then I do scream, but too late. Water fills my mouth. I don't know which way is up. Whichever way I look, I see only black water. My mind conjures a pale, bony face surging towards me. The Mister Jitters puppet come to life, free of its glass cage.

It's not real. It's not real!

I kick until my back hits a hard barrier. Using the jagged stones as a guide, I try to figure out which way is air and life. Then I see it. A tiny speck of light shimmers above me. If I can just reach it . . .

I push away from the rocks, but something clasps around my forearm. The water swallows my scream.

Tearing free, I kick up towards the speck of light, praying that I'm heading for the surface, not deeper into what must be an underground lake. Just as my chest is about to explode, I burst to the surface, gasping in a great big lungful of air before choking and coughing up what I inhaled on the way down. I start to sink back under.

'Lola!'

My name sounds like it's coming from far away, but then an arm wraps around my waist, and I'm dragged backwards.

Mister Jitters! my panicked mind shrieks. *I woke a monster . . .*

I thrash against the arm pinning me, but it won't let go. My lungs are on fire. And then I'm on solid ground. I try to push him away, to lash out at the monster, but he's holding me too tightly.

'Let me go!'

My heel connects with some part of him and there's a hiss at my ear.

'Jesus, Lola! Cut it out, will you?'

Mister Jitters sounds so much like . . .

No, I think muddily, *that isn't Mister Jitters – it's Carter. It's Carter.*

I turn my head slowly, just to make sure, and his wet hair brushes my cheek. I spin clumsily in his grip and wrap my arms around his neck so tightly I must be cutting off his air supply, but he doesn't push me away.

A rough grey circle of sky hangs above us. Clouds move past the gap in the cavern ceiling. Carter doesn't let me go, not until we're all the way out of the water, and then he keeps an arm around me so I won't fall back in. He reaches up between us and there's a click as a dim glow cuts a sphere out of the blackness.

'You're OK,' he says. 'Just try to catch your breath.'

The light comes from a pendant around Carter's neck. It's just like the one Ranger Crane wears, but on a leather cord instead of a silver chain. The black pool glimmers, stretching out behind us, and threads into the crevices of the rock walls.

'Are you all right? Can you walk?' Carter asks.

'I'm fine,' I rasp.

'Why didn't you stick to the path like I told you?' he says, his voice echoing. 'And why were you fighting me? Are you so stubborn you'd rather drown than take my help?'

He's angry with me. I'm not really surprised after I kicked him. I can't believe I just freaked out like that. That for a split second, I actually believed in Cora's story about a monster living in the caves of Harrow Lake. I can't even blame it on a nightmare this time.

This is what happens when you wear the disaster dress, I tell myself. But this is not an Optimal thought.

'We could have died just now! We still might if I can't find a way out of here. Damn it!' Carter snaps.

'I didn't fall in on purpose.' I pull my arm free from where he's still gripping me and feel a sharp pain in my forearm. I poke at it. My fingers come away bloody.

'You're hurt.' Carter leans closer, bringing the flashlight pendant up to inspect the wound.

'It felt like something bit me.' I run my hands over myself, but can't feel any more cuts or scrapes. The hard lump of the jitterbug is right there in my pocket, though. I'm somehow not surprised it's still with me. 'Maybe it was Mister Jitters,' I say. A hysterical laugh bubbles right under the words.

'Is that who you thought I was?' Carter says as he checks the bite.

'Of course not. I'm not a child.'

Water droplets fall from the ceiling in a plinking rhythm. Drip, drip, drip. Like the jitterbugs, all chattering away in a mismatched rhythm in Lorelei's room. Or those long, tapping fingers burrowing out from between the layers of wallpaper in my dream.

'Do you hear that?' I whisper.

'Hear what?'

I don't answer. Carter must already think I'm a fool who stumbles into sinkholes and freaks out about made-up monsters. 'Can we just get out of here?' I say, shivering.

He points towards a faint glow in the corner of the cavern. 'Looks like there might be a way out through there. Come on, I'll take a look at your arm outside. You must have grazed it on the way down.'

We set off towards what turns out to be a very narrow gap in the rock. We squeeze through, Carter leading the way with his flashlight pendant, and the tunnel opens into a small chamber, the roof so low we both have to stoop. The glow is coming from a hole around knee-height, where delicious, glorious daylight bleeds in. But it's tiny – barely bigger than my clenched fist. There's no way either of us could fit through it.

'We're trapped,' I whisper.

He got trapped underground for a really long while . . .

But Carter is already pushing against the edges of the hole with his hands, shoving stones and dirt outward, slowly making it bigger. Once it's large enough to fit through, he gestures for me to go first, and I practically shove past him.

My wet clothes drag against dry dirt. I feel the darkness watching me as I scramble through.

And then I'm free, drinking in the cloud-filtered light. Carter clambers out of the hole behind me. His clothes are glued to his body and smeared with mud, just like my dress.

'Take a seat and I'll check your arm,' he says, pointing to a flat rock.

I sit, trembling, and roll my sleeve back to reveal a red gash a couple of inches above my wrist. I'm so glad Nolan's not here to see how freaked out I was.

What the hell am I thinking? I'm not *glad* he's not here!

I'd feel better if I could write this all down and hide it.

'That came in pretty handy,' I say between chattering teeth, tapping Carter's pendant with one finger.

'Oh, yeah. My mom gave it to me.'

It takes me a moment to connect the dots. 'Ranger Crane is your mom?'

'You've met her? Guess I shouldn't be surprised in this town. But yeah, I'm not supposed to wear the flashlight during festival week, seeing as it's not 1920s-authentic,' he says.

I picture Carter next to the woman I met by the Bone Tree, with her nice smile and the way she seemed completely at ease in the forest. I should have guessed they were related.

'She gave it to me when I decided to become a trainee ranger,' Carter adds.

'You're going to be a ranger like her?' I ask. I know what it means to have a parent you look up to, and to want to make them proud.

But Carter's face clouds over. 'That was the plan. But Mom didn't sign the endorsement for my application in time, so they turned me down.'

'That sucks. I bet she felt awful about it.'

'You'd think,' Carter says flatly. 'It doesn't matter. I can always try again next year.' His stiffness tells me it's a sore subject. He stands and brushes dirt from his damp knees. It doesn't really help. 'We'd better head back to my house.'

In spite of everything that's just happened and the fact I must now look like a drowned rat, my pulse quickens at his suggestion. 'Your house? Why?'

'Because there's something in that cut and I need tweezers to get it out. And we're right by my place.'

'Something *in it*?' I snatch my arm away and feel around the cut myself. It stings like hell, but I ignore the pain. He's right – there's something hard inside the wound. Something *in* me. 'Get it out. *Get it out!*'

He takes hold of me by my shoulders. 'It's OK,' he says. 'I'll take care of it . . .'

But I can't just leave it in there. I squeeze my flesh hard, forcing the lump up towards the cut. It hurts so much tears flood down my cheeks, but I need to finish this, get it out and –

Something white pokes through my skin. I dig it out with my nails. My hand is covered in my own blood, but I instantly feel better. Then I see what I'm holding between my thumb and index finger. A tooth.

There was a tooth in my arm.

CHAPTER TWELVE

'I'll grab my first aid kit,' Carter says, leading me inside his house. If I thought my grandmother's house was like a museum exhibit, Carter's makes me feel like a time traveller. The single-storey log cabin perches on the hillside, with a crooked chimney and myopic windows. I'm not even sure it has electricity. Walls, floors and ceilings are all bare timber, and the sparse furnishings look handmade with wood and raw animal hide. It's the kind of place New Yorkers go to escape the modern world for a weekend, not the kind of place I've ever imagined people *living*.

I follow him into a tiny room that turns out to be his bedroom. I almost back right out of there when I realize. But I'm being ridiculous. We're here for a first aid kit, that's all.

Carter's room isn't even half the size of my *bathroom* in New York. He keeps it neat, though. On the wall near the window is a mural carved right into the wooden panel, of birds nesting in a treetop, and there's another one of a coiled snake surrounded by leaves. They're simple and beautiful. I start to weave the story of the snake and the birds. *Don't linger too long in one place, or your hatchlings will get swallowed whole.*

Shit. I'm starting to sound like a local.

Our apartment in New York doesn't have any permanent marks like those murals. If you took out all of our things, it would be an empty shell. In a year's time, when we're in another city, or another country, nobody would be able to tell I had ever lived there.

Above Carter's bed there are several sheets of paper tacked to the wall. They're sketches, all done with light, swift strokes that make me imagine him rushing to capture the details and nuances before his subjects could vanish. The first is a drawing of the Ferris wheel in the fairground, and the next is an angled view of Main Street. The third shows the ruins of a church. I recognize it as the one in *Nightjar*, where Little Bird is murdered.

'I haven't seen the church yet,' I say.

'You won't, either,' Carter says. 'It's at the bottom of a sinkhole you can only reach by going through the caves, and the entrance was blocked off as soon as they finished filming.' I'm about to say it makes no sense for one of the key filming sites to be hidden away from *Nightjar* tourists when he puts his hands on my shoulders and says, 'Sit.'

I'm deliberately slow about it, but I sink into the chair next to the window. I shiver with cold, despite the blanket wrapped around me like a woollen toga. Only my hurt arm is exposed. It's the one with the faint ink tracks still showing on it. Carter must wonder what they mean, but he doesn't ask. He rolls back my sleeve. My breath catches at the sudden warmth of his hands.

Nolan would flip out if he knew how close Carter's lips were to my cheek right now, how I can feel his breath on my neck. *But he's not here to notice, is he?*

I jump as a squawk sounds from the corner of the room. There's a cage on top of Carter's dresser, with a small black bird in it. It squawks again, its beak too big for such a small creature.

Shrugging Carter off, I go over to it. I've never seen a wild bird this close before. Its feathers are pure black, sleek over the wings, and a little fluffy around its chest. Baby feathers, I guess. It's beautiful.

'You have a pet bird?'

'Well, she's not exactly a pet, but yeah. Her name is Caw,' Carter says. 'Short for Cora, if you ask my sister. She's a raven chick. Caw is, I mean. Not Cora.' He smiles. For the first time, I see his resemblance to Cora, too. His teeth are like hers, with those turned incisors. An imperfection, Nolan would say. It suits Carter. 'I always seem to find critters like her out in the woods. It drives my mom nuts.'

'Your mom's a ranger and she doesn't like animals?'

'Not in the house. You know, before I decided I wanted to be a ranger, I thought about becoming a vet,' Carter continues. 'But then I saw how long I'd need to study, and the college tuition fees . . . Hey, what are you doing?'

I didn't mean to reach out towards the cage. At least, I don't think I did. It just felt like I needed to let her out. But that's ridiculous; she's not mine to let go. 'I was . . . just going to pet her,' I say, not sounding at all sure of myself.

'Oh. Well, you probably shouldn't. She's not exactly tame, and she scares easy. I'm only keeping her until her wing heals.' Carter takes my hand and steers me firmly back towards the stool. 'Caw fell out of her nest,' he explains. 'If I put her outside before she's ready, she won't be able to fly, and something bigger and nastier will eat her.'

He leaves the room and comes back with a bowl of soapy-smelling liquid and a washcloth. I go to take them from him.

'You did the worst part. Just let me clean it up for you,' Carter says. I still don't let go of the cloth. He laughs. 'You really aren't used to letting someone help, are you?'

'Nobody but Nolan,' I say, but I let go. He gets to work, deftly washing away the blood and dirt from my arm.

'You two are close, then?' Carter asks.

I don't know how to explain my relationship with Nolan, how to frame it in a way Carter or anyone else would understand. A world with just two people can feel vast and tiny all at once.

'We're pretty close,' I say.

'That's good. I never really got along with my dad,' Carter says.

I note the past tense. 'Is he dead, or just not around?'

Carter doesn't look at me. 'Dead. It happened at the fairground a few years ago. Dad was in there working late and wild dogs got in, despite the electric fence.'

'Your dad was killed by *dogs*?' I picture the painted hounds of the carousel coming to life as though it's showing on an enormous theatre screen: an older version of Carter, stumbling between the metal carcasses of the fairground rides, a pack of foam-mouthed dogs circling him, herding him into a corner, their teeth snapping. Blood everywhere . . .

'That's awful,' I say, and I can't help thinking of Nolan lying in his study. 'Were you there when it happened?'

'Not until after. I found tracks leading into the cave entrance at the back of the lot –' Carter stops abruptly. 'Damn, I'm sorry. I shouldn't be saying all this, what with your dad being in the hospital and all.'

'It's fine,' I say. 'I'm fine.'

Carter is silent for a long moment, as though waiting for me to change my mind about that. 'What about your mom?' he says finally.

'What about her?' I say.

'You get along with her?'

'I haven't seen her since I was five. I barely know her.'

Carter nods, like he suspected as much. 'Do you think you might get to know her while you're here?'

'She isn't in Harrow Lake,' I say, confused.

'No, but you can learn a lot about a person from where they've been. The things they leave behind.'

His words cut into me. Lorelei left this town behind, but she left me, too. What does that say about me?

'I could help you with that,' he continues. 'Research your mom, I mean. I volunteer at the museum, going through old records and looking for things to put on display. I bet we could find out some interesting stuff about her.'

'Why would you do that?' I ask.

'Volunteer at the museum?'

'No,' I say. 'Why would you help me?'

Carter shrugs. 'To be friendly. Don't you have friends where you come from?'

Heat flushes my face. He shouldn't be asking me personal things like this. God, I shouldn't be alone with him. 'You mean in the modern world, where people live in real houses with electricity and indoor plumbing and – oh, I don't know, Wi-Fi?'

My words seem to echo in the silence that follows. Carter stares at me like he's debating whether to throw me out.

'Hold still while I finish this,' he says shortly, and focuses on the bloody cut on my arm.

The silence is awkward now, and it's my fault.

I just need to keep you out, I want to tell him. To explain, though I'm not sure it would even make sense out loud: *I need my walls*. But there's a tiny rebel part of me that wants Carter to look at me like he did a moment ago, so I start to list the things I could say to make him ask his questions again. None of them are Optimal.

'I had a friend once,' I try. 'It didn't work out.'

He's listening, but still not meeting my eye. 'Why not?'

'She wasn't real.' I can't help smiling as his movements stop and he looks up. 'Mary Ann was a ventriloquist's dummy.'

147

Carter's eyebrows shoot up in a way that makes me want to laugh.

'Nolan gave her to me when I was six. She was a prop from *Razorwire Rhapsody*,' I say. When Carter looks at me blankly, I add, 'The horror movie directed by Nikolai Brev?' There's not a hint of recognition on his face. 'Sylvina Lupa starred in it? Anyway, Nikolai Brev had a wager with Nolan about which of them would win the Saturn Award that year, and of course Nolan won, so he demanded Mary Ann as his prize.' It probably gave Nolan a kick to give her to me, knowing how it would needle Brev thinking of his rival's daughter playing dollies with a symbol of his best work.

'That dummy must have been worth a lot of money,' Carter says, and this startles me for a second. I've never considered that Mary Ann, as a movie prop, might be valuable. She was just a doll to me. A friend.

I breeze past his comment. 'She didn't have a name in the movie, so I named her.' I'd chosen the name from the book Lorelei had been reading to me before she walked out. *Alice's Adventures in Wonderland*. Mary Ann was just a side character, but I liked the name so it stuck with me. 'Mary Ann was more or less as big as me at the time, with big green eyes and long black lashes, and pouty red lips like she'd been drinking blood. She wore these shiny red Mary Janes I loved, and I insisted Nolan buy me a pair so we would match.' I smile at the memory. 'But then he got tired of seeing Mary Ann around the house. I guess it bothered him to watch me playing with her more than it ever bothered Brev. So he packed her away, and that was that.'

Except it wasn't. After searching for her (without much hope, seeing as I didn't dare go through Nolan's things without his permission), I went to bed and rage-cried until I finally fell asleep. Then I woke up with the surest sense that Mary Ann was there, sitting on my bed and whispering to me in the dark. Something I'd wished for so hard, it came true.

Mary Ann wasn't a dummy anymore – she looked and moved like a real girl. A child, like me. Her skin was smooth and lifelike, free of the grooves where hinges allowed her face to move. And that was how I saw her from then on, in the dark and quiet spaces where I knew Nolan wouldn't find out. Because even then I knew that seeing a girl who wasn't really there was definitely not Optimal.

'So . . . she was your imaginary friend?' Carter says.

'I guess. For, like, a year.' I should feel embarrassed admitting this truth to an almost-stranger, but it actually feels OK. Maybe it's the calm way Carter takes everything in his stride, or maybe it's just the little thrill of letting a glimmer of a secret out into the world. I've not spoken Mary Ann's name out loud since Nolan's warning to *quit acting out or there'll be consequences*. There could be consequences now, if Carter decided to use Mary Ann against me. I imagine him being interviewed on TV, calling me all kinds of horrible names and laughing, but that doesn't gel with the guy who nurses ravens back to health. The guy who is now carefully tending to a cut on a strange girl's arm, even after she's been rude to him.

'Where is she now?' he says.

'She got left behind during a house move.'

This is more or less true. I remember sitting in the back seat of Nolan's car, watching the house grow smaller as we rumbled down the driveway for the last time. Looking back to see Larry, always the last to leave, shoving something into a trash can in the front yard. Not just something – Mary Ann. The dummy version of her, anyway. I hadn't seen the puppet since Nolan took her from me.

I couldn't look away from the pale arm poking out of the trash. Couldn't unsee her hinged mouth falling open like she was calling for me to wait. Couldn't pretend it wasn't my friend that Larry was slamming the trash can lid down on over and over, trying to stomp her into the garbage.

As the car pulled out onto the road, I saw a final flash of Mary Ann's face webbed with cracks, a black void where one of her perfect white teeth now hung crooked. Then we turned a corner and she was gone. No matter how hard I wished to see the living-girl version of her in my new home, I never did. Larry had shattered that part of my imagination as surely as he'd smashed Mary Ann's beautifully carved face in. And he smiled as he did it.

I think that was when I started to truly, deeply hate him.

I swallow the stale, sour feeling that fills my mouth.

'It's not like I could've kept her forever, though,' I murmur.

'But why not make other friends?' Carter says. 'You know . . . ones you can keep?' He makes it sound like the easiest thing in the world.

'There's no point.'

'You don't see the point in having friends?'

'Not really. Where would they fit into my life? Nolan likes having me close by, even when he's working, and we move a lot. I don't get bored by myself. I have so many books and movies and games and . . . *stuff*, I could build a fort out of it. A real kick-ass fort.'

Now Carter laughs. Somehow this inane little slice of me has dissolved the tense atmosphere. Looks like I stumbled onto something Optimal after all.

'Do you ever write, Lola? Like, stories and stuff?' he says.

I lock eyes with Caw sitting quietly in her cage on the dresser, and think of *Cygnet*. 'No. Why?'

'It's just that I haven't been able to stop thinking about the story you told me at the fairground, about the coyote in girl's clothes. I guess that makes you a good storyteller.'

'You liked the coyote story?'

'I did,' he says. This pleases me way more than it should.

Why would you care what some boy thinks? Nolan asks accusingly, but I ignore him.

The grey clouds outside the window have knotted and clumped together, and they open up now as fat raindrops start falling against the glass. It's like being back inside that cave again, water dripping onto the underground lake in an echoing chatter. Did Lorelei ever hear that, when she ran through those caves as Little Bird? Did it remind her of her precious jitterbugs, too?

'So what would you normally be doing on a rainy summertime afternoon?' Carter says, tracking my gaze to the window.

'Normally?' It takes me a second to realize he means back in Manhattan. The truth is that I'm supposed to be in France by now, listening to Nolan stalking around the new apartment and being forced to watch *Saw* reruns with Larry (any of the bazillion *Saw* movies, which I loathe and Larry loves because he is a basic middle-aged white guy with an unhealthy yen for gore). 'Hanging out with all my friends, of course.'

'Well, I guess you'll have to make do with me,' Carter says.

He doesn't have to hold my wrist to keep me from squirming away now. I turn my hand so my palm rests flat against the inside of his arm, trying to make the movement seem natural. His skin there is soft. I trace my fingertips over it. Mark invisible lines to match the ones I drew on my own arm.

It's only now that I notice he's gone very, very still. When I lift my gaze to meet his, he lets out a shaky breath. I snatch my hand back. Feel my face turn beet-red. What was I thinking, pawing at this strange boy in his bedroom?

You obviously weren't *thinking*, Nolan snaps. Feeling his presence only makes me flush hotter. I start pulling down my sleeve, focusing hard on it. 'Are you done?'

'Oh . . . uh, yeah, almost,' Carter says. He sounds surprised.

What would have happened if I'd left my hand there a second longer? Would he have pulled away, or leaned closer? What would I have wanted?

'You know, I've been thinking about that tooth. It probably came from a deer or something. Maybe it fell in the sinkhole the same way you did.'

I'm sure he's just spewing words into the awkward space I've created, but that doesn't stop a grinning white face flashing through my mind, coming at me under the water.

The rain picks up its pace beyond the window, *plink-plink-plink*, like it's rapping on my skull. It grows louder, sharper, faster as it drills the warped windowpane, an almost insect-like chatter.

Tap-tap-tap-tap-TAP . . .

'Here, let me just finish up. I think you were lucky – this isn't like any kind of bite I've ever seen.' He wraps gauze around my arm. 'Your clothes are still soaked. I can lend you some of my sister's if you want . . .'

'No.'

'Oh . . . OK, no problem,' Carter says quickly. 'Or, uh, you could wear mine, I guess?'

'I'll change when I get back to my grandmother's.'

It's going to be hard enough explaining how I've ended up drenched and covered in mud; it would be even harder to come up with a reason why I was wearing a stranger's clothes.

'Look, have I done something to upset you?'

I want to glare at him, but I don't know why. Carter hasn't done anything wrong. I just feel weird and twitchy and I want to leave.

153

'Lola, I'm not trying to be an ass here, but you know it would be normal to say *thank you*, right?' he says. 'Thank you for offering me your clothes. Thank you for taking care of the cut on my arm. Thank you for jumping into a damn sinkhole after me.'

'I . . .'

Nolan believes *thank you* and *sorry* are empty words. *When I'm grateful, you'll know about it*, he always says. But Carter's been so nice to me. Maybe Nolan's wrong about some things.

'Thank you,' I tell Carter. I try to come up with something Optimal to add to it, to make him smile like he did before, but then I realize he already is. The *thank you* was enough.

'Any time.' He clears his throat, suddenly sheepish. 'Give me two seconds and I'll take you home.'

Home. Does Nolan think home is an empty word, too? Do *I*?

Things I know about teeth

1. A human adult has thirty-two teeth (if they haven't lost any): four canines, eight incisors, eight premolars and twelve molars.
2. I once saw a necklace in a museum made from two hundred human teeth. It was next to the skull of a man with incisors the same length as my pinkie finger.*
3. Tooth enamel is the hardest material in the human body.
4. Deer teeth don't have metal fillings.

---

* This would be an Optimal thing to tell Nolan, but there's no point because he was there with me at the time. He loved that exhibit. It inspired him to make his seventh blockbuster movie, *Rattus*, about a young scientist in Germany during the Weimar Republic who became convinced his incisors would grow right through his own skull if he didn't gnaw on human bones to grind them down.

CHAPTER THIRTEEN

I wait in the living room while Carter changes. Swaying back and forth in an old rocking chair, I think Nolan would appreciate the Norman Bates' mom vibe I have going on.

I feel better now. Calm enough to want to kick myself for losing my phone. I've only had it a couple of days, and now it's lying at the bottom of an underground pool.

Damn it.

The bare floors allow every little sound to travel, so I hear it when a door closes at the back of the house. Carter called out to see if his mom and sister were home when we arrived, and no one answered. But now slow footsteps carry from another room, followed by a clatter. Could it be Cora, home from working at the diner? Or maybe their mom?

I stop rocking and pad over to the door. The hallway is dim. I hope Carter will appear in his bedroom doorway, but I can hear him moving around in there as he changes. Another door stands ajar further along, and a woman's silhouette flits past it before disappearing from view. It's Ranger Crane.

I flatten myself behind the doorjamb. Hiding feels necessary. Maybe it's because of how we met up at the Bone Tree. Or because I'm in her house while her son is getting dressed in another room. Maybe it's because Carter was so relieved when he thought nobody was home.

Through a crack in the door I see Ranger Crane searching through the cupboard under the sink. With what sounds like a whispered prayer she holds up a glass bottle – there's no label on it, but the golden liquid inside it looks like whiskey. Her hands shake as she unscrews the cap. She takes a long drink straight from the bottle, then smacks it down on the counter and shoves it away like it's about to burst into flames. Her low moan is so desperately sad, I don't want to be anywhere near it. She's nothing like the ranger I met out in the woods.

The floorboards groan under my bare feet as I back away from the door. Ranger Crane doesn't turn around. I tiptoe back into the living room – except, when I close the door, I realize I'm in the wrong room. Boxes of papers are piled all around me, and a desk sits in the corner. Dust motes dance in the thin sunlight now sluicing through the single low window. This room feels like a tomb. I shouldn't be in here.

I'm reaching for the doorknob when I spot a black-and-white photograph on the desk, highlighted in the strip of sunlight from the window. It's a small picture, no bigger than my palm, and shows two teenage girls sitting on a tombstone. I think one of them is Cora for a moment, but that can't be right because the other girl is definitely Lorelei.

'Well, hello again.'

I whirl around. Ranger Crane leans in the doorway.

'I'm waiting for Carter –'

She silences me with a wave of her hand. 'Of course you are, sweetheart. Never even crossed my mind that you were in here stealing our junk.' Her smile is loose and not entirely friendly. 'Though, now that I think about it, your mother had a habit of taking what didn't belong to her. Maybe this little apple didn't fall too far from the tree.'

I can hardly be offended by her insinuation – I've stolen lots of things in the last few months. I have no idea if my mother used to steal, but I like the idea that this is something we share, a similarity between us that goes beyond our skin and our blood. But then Ranger Crane ruins it.

'I'm just teasing. Lorelei never took what didn't belong to her, unless you count guys with wandering eyes. I guess I should put a leash on Carter now that you're here.'

She laughs, but I don't like it.

'That's a good shot of us, isn't it?' Ranger Crane juts her chin towards the desk. She is the girl sitting with Lorelei, but her hair was much darker then.

'Were you two friends?' I ask, though I don't really need to. Like Nolan says, the camera only shows the truth – and Lorelei looks so happy.

She sighs. 'We were close. Until I started dating Theo, that is. Carter and Cora's father. That man was forever taking photographs. But this one . . .' She steps closer, uncomfortably close, and taps a fingernail against the glass covering the picture. 'When I saw it, I knew it was time for me and Lorelei to stop palling around, if you catch my drift.' There's a wistfulness to her smile that hints at regret. It's gone in a moment, turned sharp and bitter. 'Theo still kept a copy of the damn thing in here, though.'

A photograph made her decide to stop being my mother's friend? I don't immediately get what bothered her about the picture. Lorelei has her arm around Ranger Crane's shoulders, squeezing her tight and laughing. Ranger Crane is smiling too. But I can see it now, I think: the way the shot is angled so Ranger Crane is sidelined, with Lorelei front and centre. Ranger Crane might be in it, but Lorelei is the star. I guess Theo was one of those 'guys with wandering eyes'.

'She'd hate that you're here now,' Ranger Crane says, looming over me. The desk is at my back, so there's nowhere for me to go without shoving her out of my way.

'Why? Wouldn't my mother want me to visit her hometown?' But even as I say this, I think she's right. Before I came to Harrow Lake I had no idea how much of Lorelei would be on display here. She's everywhere. Lorelei is stitched into its fabric. And although I've been breathing in stories of her like air, Lorelei didn't want me in her life. The reminder stings, but it's what I need. Why should I care what Lorelei wants me to do?

Ranger Crane puts one hand on my shoulder, her thumb resting lightly against my throat. To an outsider it might look intimate. I brush her off, but Ranger Crane just smiles and backs up enough that I'm not choking on alcohol fumes.

'Lorelei hated this place,' she says. 'Swore she'd never come back after she took up with your father. And she never did, except for just after her old man died, and that was . . . well. She didn't leave a lot of happy memories in that house, that's for sure. You know, some people think this place changes people who stay too long, and not in a good way. Like there's something in the water here that feeds the badness deep down inside a person and makes it grow stronger. Sometimes . . . I think there's something to that.'

A shiver runs the length of my spine, like a claw.

'I thought your father was going to be good for her. Give her everything she wanted and keep her the heck away from Harrow Lake. But I guess those months he spent here were enough to turn him. In the end, he was just a different kind of bad.'

'*Don't* talk about Nolan that way. You don't know him.' My voice sounds steely and strong, but I don't feel it.

'You should leave before it gets you, too.' Ranger Crane leans in, and the whiskey smell hits me full force when she whispers, 'Maybe it's already too late.'

The sound of footsteps cuts her off, and as she turns I quickly slide the small picture frame into my skirt pocket. Ranger Crane leaves the room without looking back, and Carter appears in the doorway a moment later. It's unsettling how the ghost-pressure of Ranger Crane's thumb against my windpipe only eases when I see him.

'Everything OK?' Carter asks.

'Yeah,' I say. 'I'm ready to go now.'

CHAPTER FOURTEEN

Grandmother is in the hallway when I step through the door, the phone pressed to her ear and a distinct sourness puckering her lips. Perhaps that's what sends a surge of hope bursting through me. I run to her and practically snatch the phone.

'Nolan?' The line crackles in response. 'Nolan? Are you there?'

He knows.

There's no logic behind the thought, just an awful certainty that Nolan somehow knows what I've been doing in Harrow Lake. Saw me running around town dressed in clothes from Lorelei's closet. Visiting the film locations in the wrong outfits, in the wrong order. Going into strangers' bedrooms. Stealing photographs of my mother.

'*Lola?*' It isn't Nolan. It's Larry. The last sliver of hope fades away like wet cotton candy. Still, I'm relieved to hear a voice that's as familiar as my own.

'Is Nolan OK? Is he home yet?'

Larry clears his throat. 'Nolan is . . .' My world stops turning while he searches for the right words. 'He's not doing as well as expected. The doctors say he'll be fine, it'll just take longer, that's all. He's getting transferred to a private facility to recuperate before he goes home.'

'God, Larry! I thought you were trying to tell me Nolan was *dead*.'

Pick your words before dialling next time, asshole.

Larry goes quiet, probably counting to ten. 'He'll be at the facility for a while. I think it's a good idea for you to stay where you are until then.'

'Stay here? But you said it would only be three days! Where's Nolan? I want to speak to him.' My knuckles whiten where I grip the edge of the table the phone sits on.

'You'd only upset him if you spoke with him now. Lola, it's just a little while longer . . .'

'Larry, you always do this – always want to keep me out of the way! I need to come home.' There's silence on the other end, and I can imagine him covering the mouthpiece while he curses at me. 'Let me talk to Nolan. I haven't been able to reach him at all since I got here.'

'Soon,' he says, then rolls on before I can say a word. 'The police have arrested the man who attacked him. Some street junkie, apparently. They think he came in through a back entrance looking to rob the place.'

'Just some homeless guy?' The words taste wrong.

I may only have thought in abstract terms about who actually broke in and assaulted Nolan – it's hard to put a face to something like that – but a random stranger? How would he even get into the Ivory? And why was nothing stolen? Do the police even know what they're doing?

'Nolan ID'd him yesterday. This should all be wrapped up shortly, and then you can come back. It shouldn't take more than a few weeks.'

'*Weeks?*' My heart stutters to a stop. When I speak, my voice is barely a whisper. 'Doesn't Nolan want me back?'

'Of course he does,' Larry snaps. 'Do you seriously think he'd let you go? Look, Lola, I have a call coming in on the other line. Talk to you soon, OK?'

Larry hangs up without waiting for my reply. I just stand with the phone gripped tight in my hand, mouth hanging open. I should be relieved to hear they've caught the person who hurt Nolan, but it doesn't make me feel any better. The only thing that will at this point is getting on a plane back to New York and seeing Nolan for myself.

'Lola, is everything OK?' Grandmother says. I have the feeling she's repeating herself, that I didn't hear her the first time. I shake my head.

I can't stay here. Everything in this town feels skewed, even me.

Not that Nolan cares.

'Lola, you're welcome to stay here for as long as you like, and I'm sure your father will be just –' Grandmother starts, but I'm not listening. I race upstairs, with no thought beyond finding my damn suitcase and leaving this place.

There are two bedrooms besides mine, plus the bathroom, and my bag isn't in any of them. I feel wild, rifling through Grandmother's house. I don't give a shit that she's listening to me rush back and forth above her head.

Every room is the same: faded, dusty, lifeless. They practically scream at me: *There's nothing here!* This isn't a house for people to live in, only exist and wait. What is my grandmother waiting for?

I sink down onto the floor of Lorelei's room just as Grandmother appears in the doorway. She stands there in her black dress with her hands clasped in front of her. Why does she always dress like she's going to a funeral?

'Are you done tearing my house apart?' She sounds so patronizing I could scream. 'Honestly, getting upset isn't going to change anything. Go wash your face and I'll make us some tea.'

'Where the hell is my bag?'

'This again?' She throws up her hands like I'm some annoying kid nagging her for ice cream.

I just want to go home. Why can't she see that? I don't care about Lorelei, or whatever monsters exist in Harrow Lake. I want to go back to the apartment and wear my own clothes and be surrounded by my own stuff and breathe in the smell of Nolan's cigars and feel like the world is solid enough to hold my weight. I got so caught up chasing after the *idea* of Lorelei, and now it feels like I'm being punished for it.

'Come downstairs when you're done sulking,' my grandmother says.

I let my head fall back against the wall as her clipped footsteps disappear back downstairs.

Pull yourself together, Lola.

I raise my head, hold my shoulders back and try to summon Cersei Lannister, or Ellen Ripley, or the Queen of bloody Hearts. But I can't muster any of them.

I'm no Queen of Hearts. I'm Alice, thrown into a world I don't understand, chasing a rabbit I was never supposed to follow.

The bell above the door jangles in alarm when I stride into the museum the next morning, but Mr Bryn remains glued to his book. I have no time for his pettiness.

'Did Carter come through here?' I ask loudly. As long as I'm stuck in Harrow Lake, I might as well find out what I can about my mother. Figure out exactly who and where I came from. It feels like the Optimal thing to do – for me. And Carter said he would help me.

Mr Bryn eyes me suspiciously. 'What do you want with him?'

'I'm going to corrupt him with my big-city ways.' I smile, all forty-three muscles in my face contracting to expose my teeth.

Mr Bryn jerks his head towards one of the many archways leading off into the maze-like building. 'Record room,' he says, then returns to his book.

I take the same narrow corridor as the first time I visited, before I found Cora in the room with the Mister Jitters puppet.

'Hello?' I call, the sound deadened by the bodies of books surrounding me. I tread stealthily between the shelves, careful not to wake them. Then Carter's head appears between two bookcases, startling a laugh out of me.

'Lola?' he says. 'What are you doing here?' He steps back to allow me to enter the windowless room. A light flickers overhead.

'I decided to take you up on your offer, if it still stands,' I say. 'To help me research Lorelei?' I am Breezy Lola now. Breezy Lola does whatever the hell she wants, even if Nolan would hate it. Because as it turns out, he doesn't care.

'Ah, right!' Something inside me unknots as he smiles. 'I've actually made a start, just in case . . . It's not much yet, but then I wasn't sure if there was something specific about her you wanted to know,' he says.

I stay relaxed, even though my pulse is thrumming. 'Anything. Anything that'll tell me who Lorelei really is.' *And why she left me.*

I blink, see the pale face under the water. A tooth working its way out of my flesh.

She caught a monster's eye . . .

'You start that end, and I'll take this one,' Carter says, already getting to work.

There are alphabetized filing cabinets along one wall, so I start there. On a whim, I check for an entry on *Mister Jitters*, but there's nothing about him. There are several entries for McCabe, though. I pull out a slim folder with Lorelei's name on it. There are only a few newspaper clippings in it, announcing her landing the role in *Nightjar*.

I move on to a stack of boxes near the corner, and behind them – hidden until I step around the stack – is a corkboard covered in sketches. I recognize the style immediately; they're just like the ones in Carter's room, except these aren't of Ferris wheels. These are landscapes showing torrents of murky water with bodies floating in them, and another of the hillside, with sections caved inward in great black sinkholes just like the one I fell into. These sketches must be of the landslide, and all the people who died.

There's one I know immediately as the church from *Nightjar* where Little Bird is sacrificed, with its collapsed walls and gravestones littered around like torn fingernails. There are dozens of others showing a blanched white face with a garish, gaping grin.

Mister Jitters.

Carter appears next to me, holding a sheaf of papers. 'I never realized quite how much this room looks like a serial killer's lair.'

I gesture to the wall, my hand trembling. 'You drew all these?'

'Yeah. I did those –' he gestures to the floating bodies – 'because Mr Bryn thought it would be good to put up a feature about the landslide, and there are no photographs that we've been able to find, so . . .'

'And these?' I stare at the renderings of Mister Jitters. The monster stares back.

'Oh, yeah.' I glance at Carter and he shrugs awkwardly. 'I used the puppet in the museum as a model. Just for drawing practice.'

That rings false, but I let it slide. 'What about this one, with the face under the water?' The sketch I saw on my first visit to the museum sits discarded on a nearby stack of old newspapers. The image takes me back to the sinkhole, to not knowing which way was up or down. To that white speck looming towards me in the dark, and the feel of teeth against my skin. Under my skin.

'I didn't draw that,' Carter says. He peers at the sketch, then holds it up to the light and points at a scribble in the bottom corner: a date and two initials. *TL*. My brain automatically begins listing what those two letters could stand for:

Too Late.

Tricked Lola.

Took Lorelei.

'Those are my dad's initials,' Carter says. 'Theo Lahey. Dad mostly took photographs, but he sketched a little as well. He drew this a couple of weeks before he died.' Carter pins the sketch onto the corkboard. 'Wait here while I get one more box – I think I put it up on the mezzanine.'

Carter's footsteps echo away through the building. This room is so stuffy, the air stagnant. I don't see how Carter can bear to work in here.

I wander back over to Carter's sketches, despite a desperate urge to run away. Mister Jitters leers at me, gnashing those awful teeth. He seems angry at being trapped inside a paper prison. If I turned out the lights, would he crawl out of the sketches, a dozen versions of him crouching, insectile, filling the room?

Swallowing to ease my suddenly dry mouth, I reach for the sketch by Carter's father. The face in the water doesn't look like Mister Jitters – at least not any version of him I've seen before. In fact, it looks more like a woman's face. Strands of hair drift around her, but I get the sense that she isn't actually moving. She's peaceful.

I fold the sketch into my skirt pocket. The thought of Carter realizing I've taken it sends an old, familiar thrill through me: the prospect of being seen, not just for what I am in relation to Nolan, to Lorelei, to Hollywood and money and fame. Because I am none of those things. And I think I would like it if Carter saw me.

I look up at the sound of approaching footsteps. 'Hey, did you find . . .'

There's nobody there.

'Carter?'

Silence. But I'm sure I just heard someone outside the door. Slowly, I walk over and peer out into the murky corridor. It's empty. But when I turn the other way I see a dart of movement, as though someone just ducked around the corner.

'Hey!'

I hurry to the end of the row of shelves, sure I'll catch the girl who has been shadowing me ever since I arrived in Harrow Lake. But there's no one. Just another narrow corridor.

I spot an open door carved into the full bookcases lining it. A flickering, cold light shines from inside, and there's a faint thrumming sound, like an old plane propeller heard from far away. I walk into a tiny movie theatre. In the wavering light of the overhead projector, I make out four rows of stiff seats facing the screen. They are all empty.

'Carter?'

There's no answer. I'm about to leave the theatre when I recognize the movie showing on the screen. It's *Nightjar*, with some grainy effect that makes it look like it was shot on an old film reel. The movie has been cut into short clips and spliced back together into a montage. Nolan would be pissed. It's running backwards, with no sound beyond the rattle of the projector. Who set this up? Why?

Little Bird appears, her eyes glassy and unfocused, and the camera pans out to reveal the villagers feasting on her body – except their motions revive her, putting flesh back where it was torn away, and she sucks in her death cry. It cuts to the scene where she emerges, ragged and dirty, from the cave where she's been hiding. But she's walking backwards, her movements jarring and unnatural as she fades into the darkness of the cave mouth. Her eyes glint white against black on the screen, then she's gone.

Why would anyone recut *Nightjar* this way? The movie is creepy enough without turning it into this disjointed nightmare.

The villagers hold their lanterns high as they chase Lorelei through a tunnel in reverse. They're dressed just like the people I've seen on Main Street.

It moves on to a shot of the preacher walking backwards through the ruins of the church, and then the screen goes blank for a moment – the scenes aren't cut together right. When it comes back on, the shot shifts, seen from someone else's perspective as they look down at the leaf-laden ground in the woods. There's a pair of shoes, narrow with rounded toes. A girl appears, seen from behind now. She has long black hair and casts a slender shadow between the trees.

She reaches out to take someone's hand – one with long, needlelike fingers. And, as the girl's hand comes into focus, I see her skin is pale and cracked like dropped porcelain. The screen goes black again; another messy cut.

Mister Jitters wasn't in *Nightjar*. He wasn't. And there was no girl with long black hair, either . . . I stifle a shudder that I tell myself is just from the cold, and not because the girl looked so familiar, even though I only saw her from behind . . .

The video flares back to life, and now Little Bird rushes through the caves where the underground gondola ride runs, casting terrified glances over her shoulder as though she hears something coming in the darkness. There's no sign of Mister Jitters or the girl.

The scene folds in on itself, moving on, moving backwards, moving faster until my eyes blur and I close them for just a moment, blocking out everything but the rat-a-tat-tat of the projector vibrating inside my skull.

Then it stops. I blink, but the darkness is dense. Only a glimmer of near-light bleeds in under the closed door. I stagger up from my seat, shaking out limbs gone stiff and cold – when did I even sit down? – and grope my way to the door.

'Carter?' I call out. There's no answer. 'Mr Bryn?'

It's slightly brighter out in the book-lined corridor, even though the lights are off. Where the hell did Carter go? I hurry towards the front of the museum. I just want to get out of here.

The front desk is unattended when I reach it. No sign of Mr Bryn. The shelves and display cabinets cast long shadows. The walls inch closer.

'Hello? Is anyone here?'

My words flee through the hallways, stumbling and dying in the dark. 'Carter?'

How long have I been here? Why didn't Carter come find me?

Did I fall asleep?

No, it's this place, this town where time doesn't move forward like it's supposed to. Where stories get stuck in your head like a tooth burrowed deep in your flesh. I feel like Harrow Lake is working its way inside me.

I race for the front door, praying it's still open, almost tripping over some invisible obstacle in the dark.

I turn the door handle. Jump out of my skin at the loud *brrrrrrring* of the door chime. Thank God it's not locked. Why isn't it locked?

Outside, the town looks different. There are a few cars parked along Main Street, but it's dark now, and the storefronts are all asleep. There isn't a soul around. Only those bent old-lady streetlights burn through the darkness. Harrow Lake is a held breath.

I clutch my skirt to hurry down the steps and almost tear my dress when something crackles between my fingers. It's the sketch I stole from the record room, still tucked inside my pocket.

The shadow-form of the weeping willow looms up ahead. I walk faster, almost level with it. A breeze keeps catching in the willow's branches, drifting through them like thick fingers, making its leaves rustle and sway.

There's no breeze.

I ignore the thought and face front, straight towards Main Street. But I strangle a shriek when something tugs at my dress. I whip around – I've wandered close enough to the willow for its outer branches to catch my skirt. I back up a step, two. Someone is waiting in the hollow of the willow's branches, I'm sure of it.

'Who's there?'

No answer.

He's coming . . .

I picture Mister Jitters inside that stifled, hollow space. An enormous praying mantis, grinning his awful grin.

Impossible.

But when you're alone in the dark, impossible things grow bones and flesh.

Don't be ridiculous, Lola. I expect more from you. It's Nolan's voice now. God, how I wish it was real.

Except I'm not imagining the low sound coming from within the willow's overhang. Like a door creaking open . . .

I bolt, the chattering rhythm of my footsteps chasing me, only growing fainter when I reach the lane to Grandmother's house and the woods swallow the sound.

It's only as I'm going upstairs that I notice the picture is gone from my skirt pocket – as though long fingers reached out from the dark recess of the willow tree and plucked it out.

I took the sketch because I wanted Carter to see me.

I guess someone did. Just not him.

My cheeks are wet when I wake up, my chest aching with sobs. It's still dark. Maybe time really has stopped moving.

I hear nothing except for the creaks and groans I'm starting to get used to – just the old house stretching its spine. I can't remember what I was dreaming, but the feel of it lingers. It unravelled me. Like that movie at the museum, I've been torn apart and put back together out of sequence.

The wind shushes faintly through the trees outside. I slept with the window open, needing fresh air in this house that holds none. The moving patterns of the lace curtains project onto the ceiling, making shadow monsters. They hover above me, out of reach, shifting and dancing. It's impossible not to watch them.

I get up to close the window, hoping that will stop the shadow show playing out on my ceiling, and when I look out across the backyard I see her.

She's out there again.

I should go down there. I should scratch out her eyes and see how she likes watching me then.

She takes off – not into the trees like before, but towards the house. She moves out of sight and a door slams downstairs. I whirl around, ready to throw myself against my bedroom door to barricade it. But she's already inside. Facing me in the shadows of my room.

I stumble back onto the bed, a scream bitten off, tongue in my teeth. My spine presses hard against the cold wall. There are monsters at my back, too. Hidden in the wallpaper.

'Lola.'

I don't register the whisper until her face is lit by a sliver of moonlight filtering in between the curtains. I reach for my phone, but of course it's not there – it's at the bottom of a watery sinkhole. Instead I fumble for the switch to the bedside lamp.

My hand flies to my mouth when I see her. Her skin is a web of scars spreading down from her temple across her left cheek, down her neck to one pale hand. Her face is gaunt, her big green eyes steady as she watches me. And, when she grins, one white tooth hangs slanted from an otherwise perfect smile.

It's Mary Ann. This is impossible. She looks different, not the broken doll being pummelled into a trash can, and not the black-haired little girl my imagination summoned into being. This girl is a new creature – one who has crawled from some dark crack in my brain. She has grown with me, but into what, I'm not sure.

'Lola,' she whispers again, unfazed by the light. 'You've been crying. Were you dreaming about Lorelei again?'

I can only shake my head. This can't be happening.

Mary Ann tilts her head. The gesture reminds me of Caw in her cage in Carter's bedroom. 'Weren't you expecting me? You know *I'd* never abandon you, no matter what.'

She is the girl I saw outside my window my first night in Harrow Lake. The one I saw swinging from the gate at the fairground. It was her in the badly cut version of *Nightjar* at the museum. Coming back to me in glimpses. Finding me when I'm fractured.

Now it seems she's slithered out of the cracks.

'Scoot over,' she lisps, then proceeds to climb into bed next to me. I feel the mattress shift. The bedsprings squeal. I don't move. I can't remember what moving is.

Mary Ann turns off the light and tugs my arm until I lie next to her. Her skin is cool and smooth. I can see her face in profile, the marks from where Larry cracked her head turned into scars on her ashen skin. They look just like the fading ink marks on my forearm.

Blood in the cracks . . .

'What are you doing here?' I whisper. But she doesn't tell me. 'What do you want?'

'Just go to sleep, and no more bad dreams.'

I lie there in the dark for what feels like hours, listening to her steady breaths and the wind building up to a roar outside, until I finally figure out what this is. I'm dreaming, of course. Another dream. A very strange dream, but that's all it is. I try to force some of the tension from my stiff muscles, but I can't. Not when I feel her next to me; she feels so *real*.

Finally, I must fall asleep, because when I wake again she's gone. I can't hear the storm outside anymore. Just the breathless quiet.

CHAPTER FIFTEEN

My back aches after my restless night, and I try to stretch it out as I walk down the lane from the house. It's the official opening of the festival today, and I'm hoping I'll see Carter there. I want to know what the hell happened to him yesterday at the museum. If he hadn't just left me there, I never would've stumbled on that movie room. And maybe *then* I wouldn't have spent half the night dreaming up nightmare versions of imaginary girls.

The parade is in full swing when I reach Main Street. Old cars cruise by the people lining the sidewalk, early model Fords and Chevrolets and Durants, and other names I'm only familiar with because of Nolan's obsession with them.

The parade cars have been trimmed with garlands of fall leaves on their hoods and sills. People wander along behind them, dressed in thick woollen coats and hats that make no sense in the summer heat, but are true to *Nightjar*'s fall setting.

Behind the cars is a stream of scruffy-looking teens, made up like the savage townsfolk from the end of the film. They carry wooden bats and pitchforks, ready to corner Little Bird in the penultimate fairground scene. But they're all far too chipper, waving at friends in the crowd and twirling their weapons. Nolan would be appalled.

'Isn't this wonderful?' a woman next to me coos, then gasps when she takes in my Little Bird sailor dress. 'Oh my, you look so much like her, it's uncanny! Where did you get that adorable little number? It's looks *so* authentic!'

The woman has a southern accent and is wearing such an unflattering version of Little Bird's blue knit dress that I'm almost offended. But I just nod and ghost-smile, hoping she'll give up and talk to someone else.

I'm not that lucky.

'Your hair is too long, of course, and a little too dark. But even without the right make-up you're a dead ringer for her, sweetheart. Hey, I'd love to get your picture to post on my Facebook – I bet a ton of my friends would think I'd actually met the real Little Bird! Would you mind?'

'Yes,' I answer bluntly. She frowns, not sure if she's understood me correctly, so I clarify. 'No photographs.'

The woman's gaze sharpens as she studies me. 'No photographs? Wait, are you, like, *somebody*? Somebody famous, I mean?'

She starts rummaging frantically through her bag, presumably to find her phone so she can take my photo whether I want it or not. Panic tightens my chest. This is the point where Nolan steps in – or Larry, at the very least – and makes sure the woman can't get near me with her damn camera.

Get away from my daughter! Do you want to get hit with a lawsuit? Do you? Nolan roars beside me.

Should I run? Yell at her? What's the Optimal response? *Nolan! What do I do?*

No answer.

Shit!

She's fumbling with the screen, and before I'm really aware of it I smack the phone out of her hands. It clatters away along the sidewalk, lost among milling feet.

'Hey! If you've broken my phone, you're paying for it, honey . . .'

I'm already walking away. My heart thuds so loud I can barely hear the woman yelling and cursing at my back. Then the crowd swallows me, putting a nice thick blanket between us. Once I'm far enough away that I'm sure I'm out of sight, I choose another spot from which to view the parade, and find myself grinning. Maybe I shouldn't have done that, but it *felt* Optimal.

I scan the faces of the Harrow Lake locals in the procession, trying to see which one is officially playing Little Bird. And then I find her.

She struts ahead of the starving townsfolk, wearing a plum-coloured dress like Lorelei wore in her final scene, her hair in sleek blonde waves to her shoulders, with those perfectly painted lips and dark, smoky eyes.

I don't know her. But I do know the girl in the scruffy shirt next to her with a pickaxe held limply at her side. As though she feels my stare, Cora turns. She looks exactly as she normally does, except with a little dirt smeared on her

179

cheeks and an expression that tells me she's not thrilled to be taking part in the parade. She slips away from the procession and through the crowd to where I stand.

'I thought you were going to skip town before the parade?' she says, leaning in to be heard over the noise around us.

'Change of plan,' I reply tightly, my anger at Larry still simmering like hot bile.

'Well, I'm glad you managed to find your way here without getting lost again.' Cora raises an eyebrow. 'If my mom hadn't told me about finding you wandering in the woods the other night when you were *supposed* to come meet me and my friends at the lake, I might've been insulted. And you had Carter worried when you disappeared at the museum yesterday, but I said he'd probably bored you so much you caught the next flight back to New York.'

'Is he here?' I ask, scanning the faces around us. When I turn back to Cora, she's wearing a knowing smirk. 'What?'

'Carter will be here soon. Anyhow, I'm kinda glad I got to see you again. You remind me there really is a world outside Harrow Lake.'

I'm not so sure what kind of world she imagines when she looks at me, but I like that she doesn't see a scratched copy of my mother. I nod towards the girl dressed as Little Bird who is now clutching at her hair in mock terror as the parade drifts forward. From the way the hair slides back on her head, I guess she's wearing a wig.

'Who's that?'

Cora pulls a face. 'Oh, that's Marie Conner. She just took over playing Little Bird this year.'

'Have you ever done it?' I ask Cora.

'Me? Play Little Bird?' she scoffs. 'No way. Marie's sister, Gretchen, played Little Bird for three years until she disappeared last summer. Before that it was Maisie Parks, who was last seen swimming in the lake the spring before Gretchen took over. No, I don't think I'll be taking on that role any time soon. It doesn't exactly end well for anyone who . . .' Cora glances down at my dress and tries to stifle a wince.

'Are you saying girls who dress up like Little Bird have been disappearing for years, and nobody's done anything about it?' I ask, crossing my arms over my chest.

Cora sighs. 'Well, what would they do? The police would just say that Gretchen ran away, and Maisie, well, they'd just say she drowned. But, one way or another, people have been disappearing from Harrow Lake for a long time.'

'You mean since Lorelei asked Mister Jitters to take out the other Little Birds,' I say drily.

Cora shrugs. 'I can only tell you what I've heard. Maybe it wasn't your mom. Maybe it was just the disruption of the movie crew coming to town that made Mister Jitters . . . mad. I mean, you heard about that camera guy who went missing during filming, right? Sure, Moss *might* have just got lost in the caves. It could be a *coincidence* that people here with a connection to the movie seem to get picked off one by one. And maybe it means absolutely *nothing* that

Harrow Lake was the last place the original Little Bird was seen before she "moved away". But I don't like coincidences, and I have no interest in catching a monster's eye. I only do this –' she waves her pickaxe – 'because we have to keep the tourists happy. We'll *all* go hungry otherwise.'

Is Cora right about Lorelei disappearing *here*? Nolan told me he never saw her after she left to visit her hometown, but he always made it sound like this had just been a pit stop on her grand adventure. Or am I remembering wrong? Did she come here after telling Nolan she was leaving him or *before*? I was so little when she left and Nolan hates talking about it, so it's gotten muddled over the years.

Don't waste your time worrying about nonsense, comes Nolan's voice, but I barely hear him over a sudden throbbing headache. I try to will it gone as I study the faces in the crowd surrounding us. All smiling and having fun.

'So the police really have nothing to say about those girls disappearing?'

Cora shrugs. 'I guess they put out their bulletins and look through bank records or whatever, but eventually the cops just sigh and say, *Do you know how hard it is to find someone who doesn't want to be found?* They stop looking. Everyone stops looking.' Cora shoots me a tight smile. 'Anyway, I might not be Little Bird, but Pickaxe Villager Three will still get into trouble if someone spots me breaking character, so I'd better get back in line. Are you coming to the picnic?'

'I guess,' I say, still lost in my thoughts.

'Great. I'll see you there. And look . . . just ignore what I said, OK?' Cora bumps her shoulder against mine and smiles ruefully. 'Everyone else does.'

With that, she hurries back to her place and the procession moves on. Once the tail end of the parade passes, the tourists around me follow, as though joining the savages who are about to attack Little Bird.

I hang back when the procession reaches the museum, stopping to stare at the building. The place is deserted, with no banners or garlands to make it a part of the festivities. It sits apart, watching. I feel like a long, bony figure might emerge from the darkened doorway at any moment.

I speed up and join the last stragglers following the parade. They lead me to the fairground. The gates are open and inside it burns with light and music and the clank of machinery. The Ferris wheel turns at the far end of the lot. I recognize its eerie, sing-song tune. It's Lorelei's song from *Nightjar*. I shudder. For a moment, I wonder if the music is just inside my head.

I step through the iron gates for the second time. With today's sunshine brightening the muted pastel paintwork, the place is transformed, alive. Long tables line the main walkway, filled with people laughing and eating and enjoying themselves.

'Excuse me, Little Bird.'

A man I don't know squeezes my arm and steps around me. He's carrying a pitchfork, which he waggles at me faux-menacingly before breaking into a grin. He thinks I'm in costume.

'I'm not . . .' But he's already moved on, making a beeline for the buffet.

I spot Mr Bryn sitting with Grant at the nearest end, and farther along is the girl in the Little Bird wig next to Faye and a girl I'm guessing is her sister, Jess. Opposite them, among faces I don't recognize, Carter and Cora appear to be arguing again. I feel something like relief at seeing them: they're at least friendly, if not exactly friends. But as I look at Carter, I realize I'm still annoyed at him. Why *did* he leave me at the museum like that?

'Hey, glad to see you made it!' Ranger Crane appears next to me and squeezes my shoulder a little too hard.

'Yeah. Looks like I'll be in town a while longer,' I say, thinking about how she told me that Lorelei would hate me being here. Ranger Crane gives no indication she remembers that conversation now.

'That's great! Oh, here – have some cake. And you should come join me and the kids. I know they'd like that. They're such good kids. Terrific kids.'

Ranger Crane nods to where Carter and Cora appear to be solidly ignoring each other. She's back to smiling, energetic. *Chipper.* Is that because she's had a drink, or because she hasn't?

'Sure. Looks like fun.' I inspect the plate the woman just thrust into my hands and stop. The cake is red with pale pink frosting, and thick, gooey red jam oozes from the centre. It's disgusting.

'Don't you like red velvet?' she says.

'Yeah . . .' But this doesn't look like any red velvet cake I've ever eaten.

Very gingerly, I break off a tiny piece of the red sponge cake and inspect it before I put it in my mouth. I immediately want to spit it out again. It's far too sweet.

Ranger Crane beams, urging me to take another bite. 'I'll go grab another slice.'

She heads off towards the table where the cake is laid out on display and joins a line of people waiting to cut into it. It's a really long cake, with parts missing where slices have already been taken. It could almost be . . .

No. There's no way.

The cake has been made in the life-size shape of a woman – a woman who looks like Little Bird. Like Lorelei.

They are eating my mother.

I look away, but my gaze falls on Grant. He takes a huge bite of cake, then slowly licks the frosting from his fingers. Deep red jam oozes from it and drips onto the table, dribbling between the cracks in the wood. Everyone keeps stuffing it in their faces, that awful jazz melody tripping along with their voices, getting louder and louder as I stand there.

I cover my ears, and my plate hits the ground between my feet.

It's quiet. They're all staring at me. Carter gets up from the table, concerned.

The cake I just ate threatens to claw its way back up my throat. I want to heave it up, scrape it out. I want it *out* of me.

185

Carter calls after me as I run through the open gates, but I don't stop. I barely make it to the road before I double over and start retching onto the grass verge.

'Lola, what's wrong? Are you OK? Where did you disappear to yesterday? I looked everywhere . . .' Carter is next to me. I drag my sleeve across my mouth and shove him away.

'Leave me alone,' I snarl. Then I run.

I sprint all the way back to the house, not knowing whether Carter is following or if everyone is laughing at me. They can all go to hell.

'Nolan, I just need to talk to you. I need to know you're still there. Please . . .'

CHAPTER SIXTEEN

I storm upstairs, not caring if I wake Grandmother. Her door stays shut anyway.

I head to the bathroom. When I catch sight of myself in the mirror, my face is a tear-stained mess and there's a little bit of puke in my hair. Ugh. I'm almost done cleaning myself up when I hear a floorboard creak outside the door. Grandmother must need to use the bathroom.

'Just a minute,' I call out and quickly dry my hands. But, when I step out onto the landing, there's nobody there. 'Guess you didn't need to piss that badly,' I mutter. Then I see my bedroom door is open. I know it was closed when I came upstairs.

Is she seriously snooping *again*?

Except the lights are out. What would she be doing in there in the dark?

Her bedroom door is still shut, and now I hear the faint sound of her snoring. My skin prickles in warning. There's someone – or some*thing* – inside my room.

I toe off my shoes and stoop to pick one up. It's a shitty weapon, but the best I have to hand. I pad softly across the landing and flip on the light.

Mary Ann sits smiling at the foot of my bed. 'There you are,' she says.

I yelp and throw the shoe at her, but she just catches it and lays it neatly on the dresser.

'What are you . . . how . . . ?'

'I told you I wouldn't leave you,' Mary Ann says, and pats the seat in front of the dresser. 'Come on.'

I'm frozen in the doorway.

Mary Ann hums as she smooths her hair in the mirror, pulling it forward to hide the deepest cracks in her face. The tune is the one Lorelei used to sing from *Nightjar* – the same song I heard at the fairground. Cora's lyrics play over it in my head:

He got trapped underground for a really long while,
Then he fed on the dead and got a brand-new smile . . .

Mary Ann looks up and finds me still pinned to the spot. 'Do you have someplace else to be?'

And *that's* what saps the fear out of me, leaving me hollow. Because I'm in a stranger's bedroom, staring at a girl who can't possibly be here, and I have nowhere to run. No one to run to. Not in Harrow Lake.

Mary Ann reaches out and takes my hand. I *feel* her. Cold, smooth skin, but impossibly real. I let her draw me towards the mirror, sinking down into the seat facing it.

My face is pale, lips bloodless. I look like I've seen a ghost. Ha.

'Do you know where we should look next?' Mary Ann asks. Her loose tooth makes her lisp. *Nektht*.

'Look for what?' My voice is a whisper.

'For Lorelei, of course.'

We used to look for her all the time. After Lorelei left, I wasn't allowed to talk about her to Nolan, but with Mary Ann it was different. One night we tried to sneak out to look, but found ourselves foiled by locks and deadbolts, and Mary Ann suggested we set off fireworks from a window as a signal. Lorelei would see them and know we wanted her to come home.

We didn't have any fireworks, of course. So instead we burned snowflakes.

The snow wasn't actually snow at all, just paper patterns we cut from the pages of a manuscript in Nolan's study while he was out. We set them alight on the kitchen stove and sailed them out of a window, watching them spark and dance as they floated away into the night. Even though Lorelei never came back, for a little while it had seemed like she might.

Mary Ann narrows her eyes in the mirror. I have the uneasy feeling that she's reading my thoughts. I try not to look at her, as though that might make her disappear, but my gaze keeps sliding back to her face. The cracked skin. The broken smile.

'Nolan's ignoring you again, isn't he?' she says. I don't answer. 'Maybe he's mad. You know how he gets when he's mad.'

Mad that Lorelei left. Mad that I'm not her. Mad that he thinks I'll leave him one day, too. Wait . . . is that it?

I could leave Harrow Lake now, catch a flight and be back in New York in a few hours. But . . . but what if that just makes everything worse? What if he's angry that I came here? Or about having his filming schedule completely screwed up? Going back could be bad for his recovery.

Unless I can find a way to be the perfect daughter. Optimal.

There's a small cosmetics bag sitting on the dresser, filled with the make-up my grandmother dug out for me to use. Nolan loves Little Bird. He loved her before he loved Lorelei, or me. He *chose* her.

I pick up the kohl stick, lining and smudging my ink-black eyes. Little Bird's were blue, but it was impossible to tell in the black-and-white movie.

Mary Ann watches me, smiling as Little Bird comes to life in the mirror.

'You should cut your hair like hers, too,' she says.

She's right. I need to be perfect. I pick up the scissors.

Mary Ann and I spent part of the night in the woods, finding trees that looked like the ones in the *Nightjar* forest scenes, and I spoke Little Bird's lines and mimicked her movements as though they were my own.

Eventually, we went back to the house and I collapsed into bed. I didn't even care that Mary Ann sat watching me in the dark.

The whole thing seems surreal now, like a half-remembered dream. I don't know what I was even thinking, following Mary Ann into the woods.

She'd gone by the time I woke up. So now I set out alone to tick off another stop on my list: the Easy Diner. I'm wearing the right dress for it, the primrose smocked one with rosebuds embroidered onto the cotton. On Main Street I spot Carter coming towards me.

Oh God.

The entire town saw me drop that plate and run. Who knows how many of them watched while I heaved my guts up outside the fairground gates, but I know for sure Carter did.

I duck quickly inside the Easy Diner and I'm blindsided by the *Nightjar*-ness of the place.

Everything is chrome and red leather. The ceiling curves down like the inside of an old railway car. Behind the old man on the register is a cathedral-style radio like the one in Grandmother's house. There are booths along one wall, and above the third one is a black-and-white still of Little Bird sitting in that same booth, drinking a milkshake and side-eyeing the young guy next to her, wearing the exact dress I have on now. (By the end of the movie, he's one of the torch-wielding creeps who kills her. Naturally.)

The diner is busy. Upbeat jazz plays on the radio, but it's too quiet to tell which song it is. I'm still trying to figure it out when someone barges through the door behind me.

'So it *was* you I saw scurrying in here.' Carter is grinning. 'I thought I was hallucinating. Honestly, you could've walked right out of *Nightjar* looking like you do. Nice haircut.'

'I didn't scurry,' I tell him. 'I didn't see you.'

I pick up a menu from the counter, pretending to study it intently despite the CASH ONLY notice above the register. Carter takes a stool next to me and waits for me to put down the menu.

'Can I buy you a coffee or something?' he says.

'What do you want, Carter?' I say, wearily. Maybe he wasn't the one who spliced together that movie at the museum, but he left me.

Like Nolan did.

Like Lorelei did.

'A few things, actually.' He tries not to smile. 'To see if you're all right after you disappeared at the museum, and after what happened at the parade. To apologize on behalf of the folks here for not realizing how it would seem to you, seeing us all chow down on a cake made to look like your mom. And, last of all, I want a soda. How about you?'

'I want . . .' I begin. But what do I want? I want Nolan to call and yell at me to come home. I want the monsters I keep dreaming about to stay out of my head. And I want to know why Lorelei left me and never came back. 'Does your offer still stand – will you help me find out more about my mother? And I didn't disappear at the museum. You did.'

'*You* disappeared. *I* went to look for you. And of course I'll help,' Carter says. Even though he's trying to act prickly, I can tell he's relieved. Maybe he was expecting me to freak out again like at the picnic.

'Your mom and Lorelei were friends when they were our age,' I say.

'Yeah, I know.'

'I saw a photograph of them together. They were sitting on a tombstone.' There's no flicker of recognition on his face. Has he never seen the photograph I stole from his father's study? Or did he simply not notice the girl standing next to his mother?

'I thought it was strange they were in a graveyard, because Cora told me you don't bury dead people in town. But then I remembered the scene in *Nightjar* where Little Bird gets sacrificed on a tombstone, so I guess it must have been in the sinkhole where the church fell in. I really would love to see it.'

'They had to use scaffolding and cranes to get everything in and out for the film,' Carter says warily.

'But didn't you say there was another way in?' I insist.

He shifts in his seat. 'It's sealed off now.'

'You know a way in through the caves, though, don't you?' I guess, remembering the sketches I saw in his room. He didn't draw the church by copying movie stills. 'Or are you saying you've never been inside?' I make my voice low and teasing. 'Are you scared you'll wake Mister Jitters?'

Carter pauses a beat before answering. It's a very telling beat. 'It's off-limits. But I'll ask my mom if she knows anything about your mom that you might find interesting.' He slides down from his stool. 'And we can go through the archives at the museum again, if you like.'

'Sure,' I say flatly.

Carter frowns. 'Where *did* you go the other day at the museum? One minute you were there, and the next you'd vanished. I thought maybe you'd found something bad about your mom . . . or that I'd said something to upset you?'

The projection room, the spliced movie, Mary Ann. I could tell him that somehow she's woken up. But what if it's not this town that's to blame? What if it's something that's *in me*?

Your mother was obsessed with Mister Jitters . . .

I like that Carter just sees Lola, not the daughter of a film director. That he snaps at me for being rude, and smiles like a wolf when I say something Optimal.

'I'd forgotten I'd promised to pick up some groceries for my grandmother,' I say, and he nods like that makes perfect sense. For a moment, I hate him for not seeing through the lie. But, no matter how I feel, Carter is still a stranger. 'You don't need to worry about me.'

CHAPTER SEVENTEEN

It's late, and I'm standing somewhere cold and confined. The ground is hard under my bare feet, and I hear the *plink-plink* of water droplets somewhere nearby. It's freezing. Lorelei's thin cotton nightdress covers me, but that's all. My heart thuds, almost drowning out the sound.

What am I doing here? Have I been sleepwalking?

My head feels muddled, and I don't know how I got here. But there's something else with me in the dark. Not Mary Ann. Something . . . bad. I can feel it. It's coming for me.

I step backwards and the ground crunches under my bare foot, loose and brittle. I take another step, and the crunch is even louder this time. *Snap-snap-snap-snap-SNAP.* The sound swells – or the space around me shrinks until my eyes twist the darkness into chattering, lipless teeth.

Mister Jitters.

His cold touch traces the shape of my cheek. Drags slowly across my skin, down my shoulder, until it reaches the wound near my wrist. The finger slowly circles the cut – once, twice – then, with a sharp movement, it wiggles inside.

I jerk free, but fall into the gravel and start to sink. The ground is collapsing on top of me. I claw at it, trying to push myself back to my feet, but my hand lands on something hard and smooth, and I realize it's not gravel.

It's a pile of bones. A whole crater full of skulls and fleshless limbs.

I hear footsteps coming for me across the sea of bones.

And then I see it's not Mister Jitters at all – it's Nolan. He's walking towards me, but he hasn't seen me. I open my mouth to call out to him, but I choke, spitting and crunching fragments of teeth that aren't mine. They won't stop pouring into my mouth, rushing down my throat . . .

I gasp awake. My legs are tangled in the bedsheets and I'm shaking, but as the moonlit room comes into focus around me, I know where I am.

Lorelei's room.

'He's coming,' Mary Ann whispers from beside me. 'We have to go to the Bone Tree.'

'What?' I can't move. I think of that gnarled, dead tree, and the white jitterbug I found nestled between its roots.

'We need to go *now*. Mister Jitters is coming. I've seen him,' she hisses. 'He stares in through the keyhole when you're gone, and the jitterbugs all make that horrid sound. I heard them while you were dreaming.'

I might still be asleep. I used to drift out of my dreams like this sometimes when I was little, with Mary Ann whispering adventures in my ear, and we'd creep from room to room until Nolan started locking me in, worried I'd wander off and never come back.

'We need to go to the Bone Tree,' she says impatiently. She's not lisping the way she was earlier.

'Mister Jitters isn't real,' I say, as though I'm reciting something I've said a thousand times before. I imagine for a moment I see the stick-like figures bleeding through the top layer of the wallpaper, but it's just the beetle patterns and my eyes being tricky.

'He caught a taste of you and now he's coming. You have to hang your hair from the Bone Tree.'

'My hair?'

In the moonlight, I see Mary Ann hold up the hank of hair I cut off when I was trying to turn myself into Little Bird. I thought I'd thrown it in the trash.

'And my tooth fell out,' she says. Now I know why she sounds odd. She holds out the front tooth Larry knocked loose, a square white peg in the palm of her hand.

You're not real, I think.

But she grabs my hand, pushing the tooth into it. My stomach does a dry rinse.

'Mister Jitters knows you're looking for Lorelei,' Mary Ann whispers. 'He doesn't want you to find her.'

Stop wasting your time on this nonsense! Nolan snaps in my head, but it's becoming harder to focus on his voice.

'I don't think Mister Jitters really gets a say in what I do,' I tell her with a Little Bird smile – all surface, and sharp at the edges. But Mary Ann shakes her head slowly.

'Pretending won't work, Lola. He's already inside.'

CHAPTER EIGHTEEN

The knitted shawl I took from Lorelei's closet isn't warm enough in the night chill. Mary Ann's freshly strung tooth swings from her hand. The hank of my hair has been bound with yarn I found in the cross-stitch bag next to Grandmother's rocking chair, and sits like a dead rodent in my pocket.

I thought my head might feel clearer once I left the house, but Mary Ann followed me. Every little sound makes me jump.

Shards of starlight bounce from the polished bodywork of vintage cars, from the curved glass in the window of the Easy Diner, from the freshly swept sidewalk where dozens of Harrow Lake residents strolled just a short while ago. It's hard to picture them here now. The whole place feels forgotten.

I stop when I hear a clicking sound.

'Do you hear that?' Mary Ann's eyes show the whites all the way around the iris.

A voice whispers from the darkness:

'He got trapped underground for a really long while,
Then he fed on the dead and got a brand-new smile . . .'

The record plays through the hidden sound system, so softly it's like it's being whispered right in my ear. The fine hairs on my nape stand on end.

'Rat-a-tat-tat – such a terrifying sound!
With a jitter-jitter-jitter, he's stirring underground!
Tick-tock, tick-tock – better watch out, he's gonna
    snap-snap-snap your bones . . .'

The song stops as abruptly as it started. I hold my chest to keep my heart from ricocheting around my ribcage.

Now I can picture Lorelei singing it softly as she rinsed shampoo from my hair, covering my face so the suds wouldn't make me cry. The way her lips moved, the way she smelled. It's like having my skin peeled back.

Mary Ann tugs at my sleeve. 'We need to go faster.'

I nod. Maybe if I follow her to the Bone Tree like she wants, she'll leave me alone.

The empty street is more unnerving than if I was walking through a room full of serial killers.

We reach the high gates of the fairground. For a moment, I think I catch a few stray notes of Little Bird's song carrying on the breeze, and I lean in, straining to hear.

'Be careful!' Mary Ann points up to the sign: CAUTION! ELECTRIC FENCE.

Backing away a little shakily, I head on, keeping a safe distance from the chain links guiding us up the stony slope. The trees hang back from this part of the hill, so the light reaches me well enough. Finally, the almost-circle appears ahead. The Bone Tree looms up at its centre and my shadow stretches along the road to meet it. I catch a pebble with my toe, sending it clattering across the clearing. There's no wind to bother the trees.

A flicker of movement.

I freeze.

Is it Mister Jitters?

No.

Stop it, Lola. Get your head out of the clouds. Nolan's voice is harsh, reassuring.

'Lola?'

Thank God. 'Carter?'

He jogs over and a bird shrieks in the branches of the Bone Tree. It flies off in a rush of torn leaves and wings.

'What are you doing here?' I say, casting a glance towards Mary Ann – but she's vanished.

The moonlight pencils Carter in without colour. His hair falls around his face in a tangled mess.

'I got called out to deal with some kids trying to shut down the electric fence at the fairground,' he says. 'They usually try to climb over the gates, but tonight they went for the fence instead. It happens this time every year. Whoever plays Little Bird in the parade is supposed to write a message inside the entrance to the caves to stop Mister Jitters coming out to look for her.'

Even in the dark, I see his eyes cut to me quickly before he looks away.

'What kind of message?' I ask.

Carter clears his throat before muttering a response I don't hear.

'What?'

'*Lorelei is gone*,' he repeats, and it feels like he's punched me in the stomach. 'It doesn't mean anything. It's just some ass-backwards superstition. Probably based on half the folks in this town being jealous your mom found a way to leave this place behind. Anyway, they hardly ever make it past the fairground fence.'

'Shouldn't you let them in?'

His eyebrows shoot up. 'Why?'

In case it's true. The words stall before leaving my mouth, thank God. What if those missing Little Birds Cora told me about are the ones who didn't get to leave their message inside the caves?

I shrug. 'Seems like the kind of tradition this town would embrace.'

'I guess,' Carter says, pulling something from his pocket and letting it dangle in the space between us. 'In any case, I decided while I was out I should hang this for you.' Moonlight glints from the tethered tooth.

'Is that the tooth that was in my arm?' *He's already inside.*

'Yeah. I know it isn't technically *your* tooth, but it was inside you, so I figured better safe than sorry.'

'How . . . thoughtful?'

Carter laughs at my unappreciative tone. 'Hanging teeth from the Bone Tree is a tradition we definitely do embrace.'

I pat the pocket that holds my hair. 'I brought my hair to hang. I wasn't sure if it counted or not.'

'Can't hurt,' Carter says. 'I didn't know if you knew about the Bone Tree.'

'Your mom told me.' I step past him to the base of the trunk, where pale rocks nestle between the thickly gnarled roots, like they're held in a clenched fist. If I reach up as high as I can, my fingertips just skim the lowest branch.

Not high enough, I think. It needs to be out of Mister Jitters' reach.

'I've never climbed a tree before,' I say. I have no idea how it's done.

Moving like water, Carter is up in the branches in seconds. He offers me his hand. I hesitate only a moment before taking it. With my free hand, I grab hold of the lowest branch, but something moves under my feet and I slip. Only Carter's grip keeps me from falling. Then the *something* runs over my shoe. And another *something* scurries over to where I'm half dangling, followed by another and another. I kick one and it squeaks.

Rats.

As though that movement has woken the rest of the creatures nesting among the roots – *I put my hand in there!* – a swarm of black, furry bodies rushes out from the gaps.

'Jump!' Carter yells. Shrieking, I launch myself at him, feet sliding and scrabbling against tree bark until he catches me around my ribs and hauls me up onto the branch next to him. My hands clench in the fabric of Carter's shirt, and I feel his heart thudding against my fingers.

'Can't rats climb?' I say.

'Shh, don't give them ideas.' He snickers, and it cuts through some of the tension.

'Of course, if the rats *did* climb up here and eat us, the town would probably cover it up.'

'Oh, for sure. That would be bad for our tourist trade,' Carter agrees.

'So they'd burn whatever was left of us down to ash. Except they can't burn everything when they cremate you, did you know that? Nolan used to keep an urn on the mantel in one of our old apartments, one he'd bought at an auction with some random dude's ashes inside. I peeked in there one day when I was bored, and it wasn't just ashes – it was human gravel, and lots of teeth.' *Shut up, Lola!* But I can't. 'Teeth don't burn, you know. That means when the villagers burn whatever's left of us after the rats are done, they'll still have to deal with the teeth. Maybe they'll just hang them up here with all the rest.'

'You sure do have quite the imagination, Lola Nox,' Carter says, the warmth of his breath against my cheek making me aware of just how close we are.

Mary Ann appears on the branch next to me, staring down at the swarming blackness.

'Sometimes I wish I didn't,' I mutter.

It's impossible to make out the rats' shapes as they wriggle and squirm all over each other, but they don't leave the base of the Bone Tree.

'I guess we should hang your hair and this tooth while we're up here,' Carter says. Mary Ann watches me over his shoulder. I swallow thickly and nod.

Carter knots the gross old molar around a branch above our heads, then holds out his hand. I reach into my pocket for the lock of hair.

Mary Ann stares down at the ground. 'I dropped my tooth,' she says hollowly.

'Oh, no . . .'

'Are you OK?' Carter says. He looks concerned, like he's reading something in my face that I don't mean for him to see. 'It's just an old superstition, Lola. No need to be afraid of Mister Jitters . . . or rats, for that matter.'

The creatures seem to have scurried back into their holes now.

Carter touches my hand. 'Come on, we should get you back home before your grandma releases her flying monkeys.'

Mary Ann is gone.

Carter and I shuffle out along the branch and jump down, avoiding the roots in case we disturb the rats again. Almost as though we agreed it, neither of us speaks until we're on the rough track leading to my grandmother's house. I wait for Mary Ann to reappear, but she doesn't.

'I'd better not go any farther,' Carter says. Here, under the overhanging blanket of leaves and forest noises, his voice is quieter. 'Your grandma might look out.'

'All right.'

'Oh! I meant to tell you earlier – I found your phone. It was stuck in a bush near where you fell. It's at my house.'

'You did?' My only connection to my old life – to the world beyond Harrow Lake. The real world. And without even knowing how important it is, Carter has saved it for me. My voice is choked when I tell him, 'I thought I'd lost it.'

'Can you come over to my house tomorrow after I finish work so I can give it back? I don't think your grandma would like me stopping by.'

I remember how she flipped out when she thought I was Lorelei talking to a guy on the phone, and decide Carter's probably right.

'OK,' I say, but it's not enough, so I add, 'thank you.'

CHAPTER NINETEEN

'And where did you go so late last night? It was after midnight when I heard you come in,' Grandmother says across the breakfast table.

Mary Ann hasn't reappeared since she vanished at the Bone Tree last night. I don't know whether I should be glad she's gone, or worried.

Maybe she was never here in the first place.

I watch Grandmother eating her peaches on toast and try not to retch into my coffee: our new morning ritual.

'I . . .' How do I tell her I went to the Bone Tree? I'm amazed Grandmother's even talking to me. Nolan certainly wouldn't be. 'I went for a walk.'

'A walk? Alone?'

'Yeah. Well, I bumped into Carter. Why?'

Grandmother's tone becomes sharp. 'Just as I thought. I told Grant how it would be.'

'Grant?' What does he have to do with anything?

'I called him up last night and gave him what for about that nephew of his. When I heard you sneaking out in the middle of the night, I told Grant he was sure to be to blame.'

'To blame for what?'

She gives me a look that's pure exasperation. 'People talk, Lola. And no granddaughter of mine should be out tomcatting around with Billie Crane's boy,' she snaps. 'That woman has no respect for this town. Thinks she can act however she pleases, and hang the consequences. You know she was never actually married to the father of those kids, don't you?' My grandmother makes a disapproving sound in her throat. 'Not to mention the fact that Billie Crane's great-grandfather was one of the men who brought on the harrowing back in 1928.'

I blink. 'Are you . . . are you talking about the landslide?'

'Yes. Caused the deaths of ninety-nine innocent souls when their tunnels collapsed, and it made the whole hillside unstable. That's not even counting the flood it caused further downriver – a whole community of people was lost there: men, women, children, all found cold in their beds when the waters receded. So many dead. Those greedy fools mined too deep and almost buried us all.'

I notice she hasn't mentioned any bootleggers caught in the landslide.

'The quarry has nothing to do with Carter or his mom, though.'

'Quit arguing with me, girl!'

I glare at her in silence. I've had enough. If I'm stuck here, I'll do whatever the hell I want with my time.

Grandmother stirs her tea and it slops onto the saucer. She doesn't notice. 'Whatever they unleashed in that mine never went away.'

'What they *unleashed* . . . ?' My heart stutter-steps. *She means Mister Jitters.*

But her expression shifts, hardening. 'Don't start that nonsense again. Honestly, Lorelei, what would your father say?'

'Grandmother . . . I'm Lola, not Lorelei,' I say slowly.

'Don't you think I know that?' she snaps, as though it's the worst thing in the world. She slams her tea down on the counter and storms out. Her footsteps thud up the stairs and stop as her bedroom door bangs shut.

Her teacup has a hairline fracture running down the porcelain. I pick up the discarded spoon next to it and start to tap-tap-tap it against the crack. It spreads, growing deeper. I give it a final TAP and watch the cup split apart, tea spilling out across the counter and dribbling down onto the chequerboard floor.

I have to get out of here.

CHAPTER TWENTY

Grandmother is bustling about the kitchen when I get back an hour later. I went walking to try to clear my head, but I couldn't stop looking for sinkholes in the forest floor, and every snapped twig or rustle of leaves made me jump.

There's no sign of the smashed teacup now, and Grandmother doesn't mention our argument. She hands me an apron.

'Ever made cherry cobbler?' she asks. I shake my head, still frowning at the apron. 'Well, you might as well learn. Put that on, girl.'

I have nothing better to do until Carter finishes work, so I follow Grandmother's instructions without protest. I weigh ingredients using her ancient scales, stir fruit until it gets pulpy on the stove, and watch with some bewilderment as it all comes together into a sickly-sweet-smelling cobbler. When it's done, she dishes up two big bowls of it and sets them on the kitchen table. She takes off her apron so I copy her, and we both sit and eat in silence. It tastes exactly like it smells.

Grandmother smiles thinly. 'Not got much of a sweet tooth, have you?'

'It's very . . . sticky,' I say, distracted. Mary Ann has appeared behind her, sitting on the kitchen counter and staring out the window. Her fingers clutch the edge of the counter, knuckles white. It makes the cracks in her skin stand out starkly.

She's waiting for Mister Jitters to come.

'I suppose you're used to fancier food, living with your father,' Grandmother says drily, forcing my attention away from Mary Ann.

'Why are you letting me stay here?' The question is out before I can think better of it.

'You're my granddaughter.'

'Yes, *Lorelei's girl*. But you and Lorelei aren't close, so why would you want her daughter staying with you?'

Mary Ann's eyes snap to meet mine, her lips curving into the ghost of a smile.

Grandmother seems genuinely taken aback by the question. 'You think I didn't love my daughter?'

'Well, you say it in past tense, so . . .'

'That's what you do when someone you love is gone. I can't keep talking about her like she's coming back!'

I realize with a shock that she's on the verge of tears.

'Maybe she will,' I say.

My grandmother sways back in her seat. 'You really don't know, do you? I thought you were just being peculiar about it, but you really don't know.'

'Know what?' Mary Ann vanishes from her spot on the counter and reappears at my shoulder, like she's eager to hear the reply. My unease becomes a dread that coats my insides like cold tar.

Grandmother takes a deep breath. 'Your mother is gone. She's never coming back because she's *dead*. Lorelei is dead!'

What? No. Nolan would never keep that from me.

'Look at her – she's lying,' Mary Ann whispers.

Nolan has spent the last twelve years worrying Lorelei was going to come back for me. She can't be dead.

'Why are you saying all this? *Lying* to me?' I say. Grandmother reaches towards me. I stand, my chair screeching back across the floor. There's half a room between us, but it feels like nothing. It feels like everything.

'It happened after the last time you came here . . .'

'I haven't been here before, damn it! I'm not Lorelei!'

Now I see anger flash in Grandmother's eyes. 'I know exactly who you are. Hold your tongue. I meant when Lorelei came to see me after her father passed – and she brought you with her.'

'Lorelei didn't . . .'

Grandmother strides from the kitchen and returns with the photograph of five-year-old Lorelei from above the fireplace. Five-year-old Lorelei who, now I'm really looking, has black eyes, not blue. She's not Lorelei at all. 'Then how do you explain *this*?'

I look to Mary Ann to see if she will call her a liar again, but Mary Ann isn't there.

My heart thuds. Of course this place felt familiar. Like I'd seen it already, and not just the on-screen version in *Nightjar*.

'You see? This picture was taken that day. You were standing in the next room.'

Up close, I see what I missed before: the red patent Mary Janes I was obsessed with as a little girl; the cowlick parting it took me years to outgrow. A tiny mole near my left ear . . . Lorelei used to tell me that mole was a footprint left by a fairy that whispered happy dreams into my ear every night. How did I forget that?

How did I forget *Lorelei*?

'Of course, Lorelei was just *awful* to me when she brought you to stay – said some nasty, hurtful things – so I called your father and told him to come and collect his wife and girl. And he did. Lorelei was spitting feathers over that, too, as though I'd done something wrong by letting her husband know you were both here! Honestly, she was acting . . . well, she was acting unhinged, which is why, when Nolan called the next day, I think I already knew she'd done something foolish.'

Something foolish . . . ? 'What do you mean?'

'He found her in the bathtub. She'd taken some pills, he said.' Grandmother inhales shakily. 'Lorelei was always a troubled, impulsive girl.'

She's wrong. There's an itch at the back of my mind, something I can't quite put my finger on, but she aggravates it every time she speaks.

Nolan told me that when Lorelei left, he found a note saying she was going to visit her mother, and then planned to make a new life for herself somewhere else, without us. That she would see where the road took her, or some other hipster bullshit. But now I know that at least part of that was a lie: *she took me with her.* Did she plan to keep me with her in her new life? Did Grandmother calling Nolan put an end to that plan?

Would that have been enough to drive Lorelei to suicide? *No.*

'Why did Lorelei come back here?' I ask, noting how my grandmother's expression shutters immediately. 'What did she say to you?'

'She came to tell me how sorry she was to have missed her father's funeral,' she says. She's definitely lying now. I couldn't tell before, but I can now. Her hands shake as she knots them in the fabric of her skirt, and she won't look at me directly.

I wish I could remember being here.

'Why would she want to end her life?' I whisper, more to myself than Grandmother.

'How would I know?' I see something festering behind her eyes. Guilt? Shame? Over Lorelei's supposed suicide, or over *lying* about it? I'm not sure. 'I don't want to talk about this anymore.'

'But there was no funeral,' I press on. 'No news reports about her death.' I would have seen those. Would have heard whispers about it, even if Nolan for some reason chose not to tell me.

He didn't tell you because IT'S NOT TRUE.

But he's never mentioned me coming to Harrow Lake before, either . . .

'Your father was worried about there being a scandal. He thought you might get hounded by reporters and the

213

like. Of course I suspected it had something to do with the fact he had a new movie opening that month . . .'

I hold up my hand, halting her. This is too much to process. My every nerve ending prickles in anger, rejecting what my grandmother is saying.

'Then where is she buried?' My words fly like bullets. 'Look, whatever went on between you and Lorelei, that doesn't give you a free pass to pretend that she's *dead*. A famous actress can't just die without the world noticing.'

A lock of Grandmother's hair comes loose from her chignon, coiling at her throat like a silver adder.

'I don't know what he told the damn newspapers! Maybe he just told them what he told you – that she left him. I don't know!'

'Why didn't *you* tell anyone? Why doesn't everyone in Harrow Lake know that Lorelei's dead? It makes no sense!' I yell.

Grandmother's lips tremble as another strand of hair falls free. She's unravelling.

'Your . . . your mother was troubled, even from a young age, always talking about nonsense as though she believed it.'

Nonsense like Mister Jitters?

Nonsense like monsters and imaginary friends, Nolan whispers in my ear, but I ignore him.

I think of the drawings hidden under the wallpaper. Lorelei's father was the one who told her Mister Jitters would come for her. Does my grandmother know that?

'When she met Nolan and moved away, I thought it was over; I thought she'd outgrown her silliness. And perhaps she had, at least until . . . until her father passed. I was surprised when she didn't come home for the funeral, but then she showed up with you a few days later. It must've been too hard for her to come sooner. Fathers and daughters always share such a special bond, don't they?' She twists her hands in her apron, as though she's trying to throttle it.

'When she came back, she kept talking about that ridiculous story about the man in the caves, exactly like when she was a child. About how I should have believed her.' She shakes her head like she's trying to shrug away the memory. 'I'd *hoped* Nolan would pull her out of all that nonsense, but he didn't – or couldn't. She had some sort of breakdown, Nolan said. But how was I supposed to know what she would do? I didn't know. I didn't *know* . . .'

Grandmother's eyes are distant now. I'm starting to wonder if she even knows I'm still in the room when she continues, her voice barely a whisper. 'After she died, I didn't *want* anyone to know. Your grandfather was always so proud of his little girl; it would have been a black mark on his memory if people knew Lorelei had taken her own life.'

'You're telling me her death *embarrassed* you?' *What kind of mother is she?*

'I couldn't bear to have people look at me like it was somehow *my* fault. No matter what your father says, *it wasn't my fault*!' Grandmother reaches for me, and that's enough to send me running up the stairs to my room.

I slam the door behind me, setting off the white jitterbug.

'It can't be true,' I murmur, pacing. How could she say those things? Did Nolan tell her Lorelei was dead when she isn't? Nolan would need a damn good reason to lie about it. Everything he does has a damn good reason.

Maybe with Lorelei gone, he lashed out at the closest thing to her: her mother.

It's unlikely, but not impossible. And *not impossible* feels a lot better than *dead*.

The jitterbug chatters away on the bedside table where I left it. I'm about to go over and slam that, too, when I hear my grandmother coming up the stairs. I lean back against the door. It rattles as she tries the handle.

'I know it's hard for you to hear,' she says. 'And I wish I wasn't the one to tell you, but you can't keep searching for someone you'll never find.' A pause. 'Why would I lie, Lola? Tell me that.'

She lied about your suitcase, didn't she?

The door shudders again, but I'm stronger than she is. I wish there was a key so I could lock her out. But the keyhole is empty, has been empty since I arrived.

She stops rattling the handle and her footsteps retreat across the landing.

After a minute, I ease away from the door. I need to tell Nolan. There's no way he'll make me stay here if he knows about the messed-up shit Grandmother has been telling me.

I wait awhile before creeping back downstairs, my pulse keeping time with the rat-a-tat of the jitterbug now tucked safely in my pocket. I reach the hallway and take a deep breath before lifting the telephone receiver.

The phone is dead. There's no dial tone, not even the crackle that has by now become familiar. I press the switch hook a few times, hoping to jostle some life back into it, but there's no tone. It's still plugged into the wall. The phone is just dead.

'Damn it.'

Carter still has my cellphone. So without the landline, I'm completely cut off.

I need to get my phone back.

'Lola, wait up!'

Grant's truck pulls up next to me halfway to Carter's house.

'Where are you going?' Grant says. 'Need a ride?'

'No, I'm just out for a walk.' I don't want to be trapped in that truck with Grant again. I stride on.

A door slams, then heavy bootsteps hurry after me. I whirl around and I'm face to chest with Grant.

'Hey, what's the rush?' he says.

He's standing too close, one hand on my arm. His knuckles are grazed. I think of coyotes and bitten fingers, and step back before I can give in to the urge to snap one of them off.

'Why are you always running away, girl?'

I glare at him, and the grin falls from his face. 'How well did you really know Lorelei? Tell me the truth.'

'Pretty well, back in the day,' Grant says slowly, like he's debating whether lying might be safer now. 'Why?'

'Did she ever seem suicidal to you? When she came back here after her dad died, maybe?'

'What? *Suicidal?*' Now he recoils. But he's thinking about it. 'Are you saying she's dead? Is that what you're telling me?'

The idea shocks Grant, I can tell. But I don't know how to answer him. If Lorelei is dead, then why would Nolan be so protective of me?

Is it protection, though? Or control? Does he control you because he couldn't control her?

Shut up!

No. If Lorelei was dead, Nolan wouldn't have lied to me about it. So she must be alive. She *must* be. But I can't prove that any more than my grandmother can show me a body.

'I don't think she's dead,' I say. 'It's just that someone told me it was possible – that she might have hurt herself after she last visited here.'

Grant exhales slowly, like he's relieved. 'No way. That's not Lorelei. She could be a little reckless at times, but she wouldn't have done that. She only ever wanted to get out of this town. Much as it pains me to admit it, your father gave her what she wanted – a kid, and a different life, away from here.'

'Then why would she leave us? Leave *me*?' I grab hold of his arm now. Grant is starting to look worried.

'I don't know.'

'Why did she come back here?'

'I don't know!' Grant yanks free of my grip. There's a red crescent on his wrist where one of my nails has left a mark. It's an echo of the spot on my own arm where a tooth burrowed into my flesh. He rubs it, irritation plain on his face. 'All I know is Lorelei was glad to be leaving Harrow Lake. I caught her down at the fairground as she was on her way to see your grandma – she was hacking away at that mural inside The Harrowing with a chisel.'

I see a flash of that scarred wood, the deep gouges in it like claw marks. And now it's not some faceless stranger attacking my mother. It's Lorelei. But why?

Grant seems to sense the questions running through my mind. 'I asked her why the hell she'd wanna scratch up a picture of herself, and she turned to me with this great big smile and said, *Grant, I'm getting out of this place once and for all, and I'm not leaving any piece of me behind.* She was so happy to finally be free. I got the idea that maybe things weren't quite so peachy with your father, but that didn't give me any cause to think she'd . . . No. Lorelei was never as fragile as your grandma thought. She was a woman with dreams in her eyes, not nightmares.'

'Then why do people in this town say she was obsessed with a monster?'

'I know you've heard the stories about this town,' Grant says, 'about what's in those caves. But Lorelei liked going in there. She wasn't scared of the dark or anything like that. Me and Theo used to tease her about it, actually; sometimes we'd put on masks and hide out in the woods to try and frighten her, but she'd just laugh and say we wouldn't know a monster if one bit us on the butt.'

He smiles faintly, and for a second I think I might be seeing some genuine fondness breaking through the smarm.

'She had a way of getting caught up in things, though. Nonsense things. Like if she heard a story, or something caught her attention, she wouldn't talk about anything else.' He scuffs his toe in the dirt. 'Maybe that's why she came back here that day – she wanted to know for sure how much of it was real, and what was just in her head.'

'You mean Mister Jitters?'

Grant runs a hand through his thinning hair. 'Maybe that was just what she told me, to tease me back. Or maybe she really thought there was something living in those caves . . . I don't know. It certainly wasn't *me* she came back for. But I can tell you one thing for sure: that day, she didn't act like someone who'd given up on life.'

I sag, weighed down with so many unanswered questions. My grandmother believes Lorelei killed herself. Grant thinks she came back looking for a monster. Cora said the monster took her. And Nolan . . . what does Nolan believe? And why didn't he tell me I'd been to Harrow Lake before?

What else has he been lying to me about?

I cut away from the road and follow the slanting afternoon light through the trees towards Carter's house. I barely notice the woods thinning around me until I reach the clearing that overlooks the distant fairground. A faint rattle makes me look up. The Bone Tree looms over me, its branches dressed in teeth. I back away. Better not wake the rats.

I whirl at the sound of fast approaching footsteps and scream when a girl crashes into me. We fall among the gnarled roots of the Bone Tree. Her face is a mess of tears and snot and her red hair tangles around her head. It takes me a moment to recognize her without the blonde Little Bird wig.

'Marie?' She seems even more startled at hearing me say her name.

'Oh my God, you're Lorelei!' The girl whimpers as she scrambles away from me and to her feet.

'I'm not Lorelei,' I snap, dusting myself off and feeling some fresh bruises forming on my legs. 'Why the hell were you –'

'Did he send you?'

'What? Who?'

'He sent you, didn't he?' Marie is still backing away from me, her fingers knotted in her hair like she might pull it out. Her eyes are huge with fear. 'Every night since the parade, I've heard him at my window – that awful sound that gets inside your head and won't leave! He's coming for me, isn't he? He's going to take me!'

'Mister Jitters?' My voice is breathless, my heart hammering like a fist against cage bars. Her response is to burst into tears again. I reach out to touch her shoulder, but she jerks away. 'Did you see him?'

'I tried to leave the message, but I couldn't get in!' Marie wails. She's talking about the caves, I realize – the message for Mister Jitters Carter told me about. To remind him she's not the girl he's looking for. The one who got away.

But did *Lorelei get away?*

'Please don't let him take me,' Marie pleads, clutching my wrist. Her fingers dig in painfully where the tooth came out. 'Lorelei, please . . .'

'I'm not Lorelei!' I snatch my hand away. She stumbles backwards like I've shoved her. 'Look, it's OK, you don't have to be scared . . .'

She bolts from the clearing. I stand there for a moment, then chase after her. It's easy to follow her frightened sobbing at first, but she's quicker than me and soon the sound is so faint I'm not sure I'm going the right way.

'Marie?' No answer. I stop and listen, but hear nothing above the usual restless sounds of the forest. 'Marie!'

A scream breaks through the trees. I run towards it, yelling her name. She's still screaming – a terrible, haunting shriek, like it's being torn out of her body.

Then it stops. The forest holds its breath. There's no sound at all.

'MARIE!'

I run between the trees, but there's no sign of her. I can't see anywhere she might have fallen. No blood or claw marks. She's just *gone*.

Then I hear it: chattering. It swells from the forest. Wraps around me like fog.

Mister Jitters is coming.

I run.

CHAPTER TWENTY-ONE

The chattering follows me as I sprint for Carter's house. I stumble a couple of times on the uneven ground, but don't even pause to brush the grit from my palms. In minutes, I'm hammering on his front door. I try to steady my ragged breathing and listen for the sound behind me, but it's gone now.

Ranger Crane opens the door.

'Hey, Lola. What can I do for you?'

For a second, I don't know what to say. Then it spills out in a torrent.

'It's Marie Conner – the girl who was Little Bird in the parade – I think she's hurt . . .' *Or worse.* 'But I couldn't find her!'

Ranger Crane's smile drops. 'Where did you see her?'

'In the woods near the Bone Tree – I heard her scream, but then she was just . . . gone.'

Carter and Cora appear in the hallway behind their mother.

'What do you mean, you couldn't find her?' Carter says over her shoulder. 'Where did she go if she was hurt?'

'I don't know,' I snap. 'She was there one second and gone the next.'

Ranger Crane's eyes narrow. 'Do you think she might be playing a prank on you, Lola?'

'What? No! You didn't see her – she was scared. I think . . . I think someone might've been chasing her.' I will her to understand without my having to say his name. All three of them exchange a look. Finally, Ranger Crane nods like they've reached some silent agreement.

'I'll go take a look,' she says. 'There might be a . . . another sinkhole.'

'I'll come with you,' Carter says, and the two of them rush past me.

I watch them from the doorstep and jump when Cora puts a hand on my shoulder.

'Jeez, you're shaking!' she says. 'You look like you're about to pass out.'

The adrenaline is beginning to subside now. I feel hollow and useless.

She didn't fall into a sinkhole. That sound I heard – it was him.

I should've done something to help her.

'I know what you need,' Cora says, snapping her fingers. 'Wait here.'

Cora stands at the edge of the quarry near the house and spits into it. I'm propped against a tree, my ass getting damp with dew as early evening settles over Harrow Lake. We've drunk almost a full bottle of her mother's home brew between us – what Cora calls 'red-eye'. She's wobbling a little, but she's managed not to fall so far.

'They won't find Marie, you know,' she slurs.

The cold, leaden feeling in my gut says she's right. I told Cora what Marie said in the woods, but I haven't told her about Lorelei, or what Grandmother and Grant said, or about Mary Ann or Mister Jitters. I don't want to listen to any more of Cora's theories about my mother right now. 'Do you know her well?' I ask.

Cora shrugs. 'Everyone knows everyone in a town this size. What you mean is do I *like* her.' I don't contradict her. 'The answer is no. Marie has always been kind of a try-hard. But that doesn't mean I'd want anything bad to happen to her.'

'But it has,' I say bleakly. 'Like it did to the other Little Birds.'

Cora frowns, then drinks some more red-eye. 'I've decided I'm not going to get stuck here like everyone else. I've got a plan. I'll be one of those roving reporters – you know the ones they send out to cover the big news stories like assassinations, coronations, wars? I want to go out there and really see some shit. I mean, if I stay here, all I have to look forward to is getting snatched, or spending the next ten years turning into my mom.' She staggers over and slumps down by my feet. 'What about you?'

'Me?' I blink.

'Yeah. Are you going to be a movie director like your dad?'

Am I going to be ... Ha! What would Nolan do if I tried to carve out my own piece of real estate in *his* world?

Nothing good, certainly. But what does he expect me to do if not that? What's left for me?

I will make my own world. Dozens of worlds. Hundreds.

The idea is small and new, but it glitters. I take the red-eye from Cora and let it add fuel to that spark.

'I'm going to be a writer,' I tell her.

'What kind of writer?' Cora asks, and I grin.

'The kind with good stories and bad habits.' We *cheers* to that, taking a mouthful of red-eye each. 'And I'll choose a new name, so no one will know who I am, and see that name printed on the cover of a book. *Ten* books. I'll find a little house somewhere and paint it primrose yellow. Adopt a cat that spits and hisses and runs away for days at a time, but always comes home in the end.'

The liquor must be burning through my brain cells right now, but at least my hands aren't shaking anymore. When I hand the red-eye back to Cora, she's smiling.

'I think you should call it Cora,' she says. 'Cora the cat.'

I roll the idea around, then nod firmly. 'All right. I will.'

'Good. I like the idea that one day there'll be a hissing, spitting Cora somewhere outside of Harrow Lake.' She takes another long pull from the bottle.

'You really hate it here, don't you?' I ask.

'Do you blame me?'

Marie's terrified face flashes through my mind. 'No.' I reach for the bottle in Cora's hand.

She looks out across the water, where moving glints show the cars chugging along Main Street in the distance. 'I'd tear Harrow Lake up by the roots if I could.'

'Then why don't you?'

'Because that desire probably comes from the badness this town put in me.'

She's not laughing anymore. There's a fierceness in her eyes that makes me feel hopeful for her.

'Carter says I should wait until I graduate before I leave town,' she continues. 'But I don't see the point in waiting. If I stay here, I'll only end up getting stuck, like him. Carter will never leave. He'll just get some girl pregnant and marry her – convince himself he's found *true love* and all that bull, when really he'd be out of this town in a heartbeat if only he could figure out how to ignore Mom's guilt trips. He's got less sense than that bird in his bedroom.'

Behind us, someone clears their throat. Cora and I both jump. 'Ravens are very smart, actually,' Carter says.

He leans against a tree only a few yards away from us. I don't know how long he's been there, but he's easy to miss in the fading light. Cora sighs.

'No sign of Marie, then?'

Carter shakes his head wearily. 'Nothing. Marie's parents said she was due home hours ago. They're falling apart right now.'

'Have they called the police?' I ask.

'Yeah,' he confirms. 'For all the good it'll do. They'll put up posters, hold a search when she doesn't show up in a day or two. It was the same when Marie's sister Gretchen went missing last year. The police will probably just think Marie ran away, too.'

I remember Cora telling me about Gretchen at the parade. Now her parents have lost two daughters. How can a family survive something like that?

Carter nudges the empty red-eye bottle with his toe. 'Mom'll be looking for this when she gets back,' he says to Cora. 'You might wanna rearrange her stash so she won't notice.'

Cora springs to her feet, the wobble gone. 'I'll see you later, Lola.'

She disappears around the side of the house.

'So what has Cora been filling your head with?' Carter says. 'Besides booze, I mean. Which she knows she shouldn't touch.'

'She'll turn into a coyote,' I tell him, 'if you try too hard to pin her down.'

'I know.' Carter offers me his hand. I take it, and get clumsily to my feet. 'But she'll have a better shot at the life she wants if she finishes school before taking off.'

'If she gets a chance to finish school,' I mutter, thinking about Marie. About Lorelei, too, and things left unfinished.

Where are you, Lorelei?

'I graduated, and so will Cora,' he says, stepping out of the shadows so I see his determined expression.

'I –' I almost choke when I see his face properly. I didn't get a good look at Carter before, but now I see the corner of his mouth is swollen, his lip split with a purple bruise set around the cut. 'What happened to you?'

'I fell down the stairs,' he says.

'Your house doesn't have any stairs!'

Carter gives a bitter laugh. 'Or Wi-Fi, as you pointed out. It does have indoor plumbing, though, so we aren't quite the cave dwellers you seem to think we are.'

That was what I said to him just days ago, but my words sound so much harsher when he repeats them back to me. Why was I so mean to him? I don't remember now.

'Look, Lola, maybe you should be getting back to your grandma's house.'

'Probably.' I can't stop staring at his bruises. He opens his mouth to say something, then changes his mind. 'What?'

'Have you told your grandma there's something going on between us?' he says. I'm surprised by the question, but even more by the edge of annoyance in his voice.

'You mean like we're . . .' I struggle for the right word. 'I, uh . . . no.'

'OK. Sorry, I should've figured you wouldn't. And it's hardly important right now.' Carter rakes a hand over his hair, pulling a few strands loose of the tie. 'But I guess she doesn't want us to hang out anymore, so I gave your phone to Uncle Grant to pass back to you.'

'You did?' Damn it. Grant probably had it rattling around in his truck while he played his space-invasion games, and he never said a word.

'Yeah. He made it clear I was to stay away from you.'

'He what? Oh – *oh*.' I raise a hand and let it hover near the swelling at the corner of Carter's mouth, remembering Grant's grazed knuckles earlier. 'He seriously did this? What the hell is wrong with people in this town? *Sure, let's just beat up our kids and scare them to death with monsters!* Nothing screwed up about that at all!'

'Hey,' Carter says, shoving his hands deep into his pockets and hunching in on himself. There's none of that live-wire energy about him now. 'It's not a big deal. And we're not all the same in Harrow Lake, you know.'

He looks so down, and I'm only making it worse.

'I should go,' I tell Carter. 'I'm "stirring up trouble", as Grandmother would say.' *Just like Lorelei.*

'Wait – don't leave.' He catches my hand. His skin is so warm and rough. Would it be so bad to lose myself for a little while with him? What would it be like to just brush my lips against his, our bodies fitting together like two puzzle pieces?

I have too many puzzle pieces to sort through already.

'Hey, are you OK?' he says, and, although it's not the time to bring this up, with a girl missing, for the first time in a long while I don't want to bury my secrets, and I don't want to lie.

'My grandmother told me Lorelei is dead.'

'*What?*' He opens his mouth again to speak, then closes it. 'But . . . when?'

This is news to Carter. I'm so relieved he wasn't hiding this from me all this time, whether it's true or not.

'Years ago, according to Grandmother,' I say. 'But I don't believe her. She told me Lorelei took an overdose, and she and Nolan kept it secret to avoid a scandal. But I've been thinking about it, about why Nolan wouldn't tell *me* that – I mean, it's not as though I'd go calling all the major news outlets, is it? And Lorelei's my mother, for God's sake. It *can't* be true. After all, it was never reported by the media, and I never saw any rumours about it on the *Nightjar* fan sites, and they gossip about *everything*. I just can't see how it could be true.'

'Then she's alive,' Carter says firmly. 'And you want to find her.'

'Either way, I want to know what the hell happened to her.'

If Grant was right, last time Lorelei was here she wanted to find out for sure if Mister Jitters was real. What if Lorelei disappeared because she found exactly what she was looking for?

Nonsense, Nolan whispers to me. But I can't just shake off the idea without seeing for myself. If I want to figure out what happened to her, where she went, then I have to begin somewhere. What if I find him? That's a terrifying prospect.

What if I don't?

I don't know how to tell Carter any of this. That my mother's obsession has become mine, just like her jitterbugs and her dresses.

Carter puts a hand on my arm. My pulse quickens as I think about the first time Carter and I were alone like this – in his room, where pencil sketches cover the walls. That one sketch in particular showing a ruined church lit from above, as though it sat at the base of a sinkhole. There was another just like it in the museum. He tried to brush that off as nothing, too.

'You've been in the caves, haven't you? Even though it's not allowed?'

Carter fidgets with the leather strap of the flashlight pendant hanging at his throat. His brow furrows like he's concentrating on something unpleasant. 'Nobody goes into the caves, Lola. They're dangerous.' And now I know what he looks like when he lies.

'I want to go.' If I just see the caves, taste the air inside, I'll know if that's where she went – and why. 'I don't care about that ridiculous monster story, Carter. I just want to see for myself.'

He's wavering. I need to tip the balance. What is Carter's brand of Optimal? If it was Cora, I doubt I'd even need to convince her. But Carter isn't out to burn the world; he wants to fix it.

I'll play the bird with a broken wing if it will convince him.

'Won't you help me, Carter? I don't think I can do this by myself.' I look down, wring my hands. Glance up at him through my lashes. Hate myself a little.

'All right,' he says on cue. I'm almost disappointed by how quickly he gives in. 'But it's gotta be our secret, OK?'

'I know how to keep a secret,' I say.

Grandmother is dozing in her rocking chair when I get back to the house. I spot my phone propped next to the photo of me above the fireplace, like an offering. I go over and snatch it up. The screen is dark, powerless.

I lean against the windowsill facing my grandmother and follow the shallow rise and fall of her chest. Like this, she seems so frail. Like Nolan in the hospital. It would be very easy to grab the cushion she's been sewing and hold it to her face, nice and tight, until she went limp. She must feel me watching because she wakes with a start.

'How long have you had this?' I say, clutching my dead phone.

Grandmother blinks rapidly, not fully awake yet. 'How long . . . oh, yes. Grant brought it by earlier. I put it on the mantel so you'd see it. But the house phone is working now, if you want to use that.'

She looks so muddled, so tired.

'I heard a girl from town is missing. Are you all right?' she says. 'After what we talked about?'

These are exactly the right things to ask. Grandmotherly. *Optimal*. I'm immediately suspicious.

'I need to know what really happened,' I say. 'Why Lorelei brought me here. What happened to her. If she was hurt, or if something *else* happened to her. Do you know what I'm talking about?' She won't look at me now. She thought I was done with my questions.

'Did she actually believe Mister Jitters was real?' I try again, but I get nothing. 'Why won't you tell me what really happ–'

'HE NEVER TOUCHED HER!'

I back up so fast my spine hits the mantel. One of the photographs clatters as it topples over, but I can't tear my gaze away from my grandmother. Her knuckles are white around the arms of her rocking chair, her eyes stark as a rearing horse's. I don't know what to do. I don't know who this woman is in front of me.

'LORELEI WAS A LIAR! A ROTTEN, LYING LITTLE BITCH, JUST LIKE YOU, AND I'M GLAD SHE'S DEAD!'

A fleck of spit hits my cheek. I'm scared she's about to launch herself at me, but it's as though someone has cut her strings. She collapses into the rocking chair, swaying back and forth, the screeching of the floorboards beneath it the only sound for a long moment. Two black kohl lines run down her cheeks, and she doesn't even move to wipe them away. Then she starts to hum.

It's that song again. Lorelei's song.

'Nolan? Where are you? Are you even getting these messages?'

CHAPTER TWENTY-TWO

I go to meet Carter at the fairground after sunset. I almost hope he won't show up, but he's there waiting for me in the shadow of the gates.

'Hey.' The night casts harsh shadows over his face. 'I almost didn't see you there.'

'That's night-time for you.' I manage to speak without my voice trembling. 'Any news on Marie?'

'No.' He sighs. 'But you never know, maybe tomorrow . . .' The sentence hangs in the air, unfinished and convincing no one. He uses a large bunch of keys to unlock the gates. There are no lights on inside, and I think for a second we won't be able to do this, but then I see the leather cord around Carter's neck, the flashlight tucked into the collar of his shirt. 'Are you ready?'

'Where exactly is the cave entrance?' I ask, instead of telling him no, I'm not ready at all.

'The easiest way to get in,' Carter tells me, 'is through the abandoned gondola ride.'

With the dark silhouettes of the fairground rides now looming over me, this place feels dangerous, like anything might be waiting for us in the shadows. One of the painted hounds on the carousel seems to breathe when we walk by, and I look into its lidless, glaring eyes. 'We can't turn the light on until we're in the caves,' Carter says. 'Just in case anyone spots us. But once we're inside it's not far to the church sinkhole.'

I definitely should not be doing this.

Something brushes against my hand and I jump, then realize it was just Carter trying to take it in his.

'Nervous?' he says.

'Thought you were a spider.'

Carter snickers. 'Gee, thanks.'

My mouth is dry, in direct contrast with the line of sweat working its way down my back.

Carter puts his hands on my shoulders and turns me towards the rock face rising at the back of the fairground lot. 'There.' He whispers, even though there's nobody around. His hands run down my arms and squeeze.

'I can't see anything . . .' But as I'm saying this the moonlight shines down onto a wooden facade set back into the rock. It's hand-painted, like the rest of the signage in the fairground, but this one reads THE GONDOLIER.

Lorelei has been here. Stood where I'm standing now. Did Marie get this far when she tried to get into the cave to write her message for Mister Jitters? Am I walking in her footsteps, as well as Lorelei's?

'It was never actually used as a ride,' Carter says, right next to my ear. 'The cave was already here, so your dad put up this frontage and built the fairground around it.'

Classic Nolan.

'You said you know a way in?'

Carter pulls the edge of the facade from the rock wall, making a gap just wide enough for us to slip through.

'They padlocked the door on it,' he says as I slide past him into total darkness. 'But they forgot to secure the hinges.'

There's a smile in his words as he turns on his pendant light. It doesn't illuminate very far – just enough for me to see we're standing in a tunnel, rock on either side, on a path running deep into the hillside. It's too narrow to walk side by side. But as Carter turns, the light catches the wall nearest to us, and I see writing on it – three lines, all written by different hands.

Lorelei is gone.

Lorelei is gone.

LORELEI IS GONE.

Hand shaking, I touch my fingers to the letters. They feel damp and cold.

Maybe I should write the message, too, so I don't disappear like Marie . . .

Water droplets patter down from above our heads, falling in a persistent, irregular rhythm. It echoes around us, like snapping, chattering teeth.

It's just the water, I tell myself. *Just the water.*

Carter starts to lead the way, but I'm the one who wants this – who needs to see what exactly is down here, in the dark.

'Give me the light,' I say. He hesitates a moment before unfastening it from around his neck. I hold it out ahead of me. Light bounces off the damp walls, that noise enveloping us in shifting waves as the size of the tunnel expands and contracts. The air tastes old and rotten.

'Watch the path here – keep to the right,' Carter says.

Now a channel of water fills most of the path. That's where the sound is coming from – droplets hitting the surface. I pan the light upward, almost dropping it at the sight of enormous teeth jutting down from the cavern ceiling. The light shakes in my hand, and I force myself to steady it.

'Stalactites,' Carter says.

I've only ever seen them in pictures: rock formations created by rainwater coursing over the limestone for thousands of years. This place isn't just old, it's ancient. I think of what Cora said about Harrow Lake being dead, decaying. Standing here now, I believe her.

'You're shivering,' Carter says. 'Do you want to go back? The church isn't far, but if you don't like it in here . . .'

'I'm not going back,' I say, letting my determination ring out through the cave. 'I want to see the church.' I need answers – about where Lorelei went, what she saw. About what darkness lies beneath this town's surface.

Still, my hands shake. *It's the cold*, I think. *Just the cold*. There's no reason to feel grateful when Carter takes my free hand in his. But I do.

The path grows even narrower, and I stumble twice, my shoes getting soaked. Numbness has crept into my feet by the time we've entered a seventh or eighth chamber in the cave system. The noise of the caves beats on my nerve endings as my teeth chatter, like I'm trying to play a duet. With every step, I expect to feel the brush of razor-thin fingers on my neck.

'This is it,' Carter says, taking back the pendant and turning it off as we step out of the tunnel into a vast space.

The moon shines down like a spotlight, showing me a space maybe fifty feet across. The sides of the sinkhole rise up at a steep angle, and I see why it might be easier to rappel in from above. But at the centre of this sunken stadium is a familiar scene: rough-hewn stone blocks lying where they've fallen, and one wall still somehow standing, albeit at an angle. Its three arched windows are as empty as button eyes. And there are gravestones – lots and lots of gravestones. These must have been set upright to film the church scene in *Nightjar*. I guess there was never a reason to knock them back over.

I hear water running nearby, but it's different from the noise we left behind in the caves. I step out of the shadows to stand in the silvery light shining through the church's vacant middle window. Adrenaline pounds through me. This is the place. This is where they killed her. Little Bird, I mean. Of course.

There would have been a camera somewhere up there in the empty window, back when Nolan and Lorelei were here with the rest of the crew. I see her standing exactly where I stand, her face stark in the silvery light before she ducks into the shadows to spy on the bloodthirsty townspeople. It was the last shot of her before she was dragged to the tombstone they used as an altar, and killed.

'It's not the same in daylight,' Carter says. 'You see too much. Cigarette ends, bottle caps – you know, signs that other people have been here, even if it was years ago. But at night it's easy to imagine we're the first people to ever find this place.'

He moves to stand on the far side of a stone plinth. It's the altar. This is where Lorelei posed with her arm around a young Ranger Crane. Where Little Bird was torn apart in a frenzy of blood and fingers and teeth.

'Why was the church never rebuilt?' I ask. 'Somewhere else, I mean?' From what I've seen, everything else in Harrow Lake was returned to how it was before the landslide, the pretence of *nothing happened* set hard and fast over the town. Why would the church be the one thing left to crumble?

'Maybe the people here thought they were beyond saving,' Carter says. I guess he's joking, but it's hard to say for sure. 'I think the church was a ruin even before it slid into the sinkhole. Have you noticed none of the graves have dates on them? That's weird, isn't it? I've never found a record showing when the church was built, or even that it was in use at any time during Harrow Lake's history.'

'What does that mean?' I ask, scanning the stones around us. He's right. Although the markings are faint and worn, I can see there are no dates on any of them.

'I think the church predates the town.'

'But that would mean someone built it in the middle of a forest, miles from the nearest town. Why would anyone do that?'

'It's just a theory,' Carter says hesitantly, 'but I think people might've tried to settle here before, then realized it was a really bad idea.'

A chill runs through me as I get the same sense I had in the tunnels – that whatever evil there is in Harrow Lake has been growing here for a long, long time.

We shouldn't be here.

The cave we've just emerged from is no more than a crack in the darkness.

'That cameraman went missing down here,' I say, thinking aloud.

It was a very meta way to die – Optimal, even: to become a story while making one.

'Yeah, I think so,' Carter says. 'Your dad had the electric fence put in around the fairground after that – he must've wanted to make sure no one else wandered in and got hurt.'

It's more likely Nolan put up the fence in case the cameraman vanishing meant someone was trying to sabotage the film, but I don't say that to Carter.

The altar is like a sarcophagus. One corner has crumbled, and the stone platform lies crooked. But it's surprisingly warm with the residue of the sun's heat. Warm, like a living thing. As if Lorelei just got up and left a moment ago. I lie back on it, taking her place.

There ought to be stars, I'm sure, but only the moonlight reaches us.

'Hey, I meant to tell you – Caw flew away,' Carter says, sounding almost proud.

I'm barely listening. 'She did?'

'Yeah. She's one tough little bird.'

'Good. I'm glad.'

I let my arms hang to the sides, feeling the hand-stitched waistline of my dress tug over my hips, my lack of underwear underneath.

'Is this right?' I ask. 'Is this how she looked in the altar scene?'

'Little Bird?'

I nod, pleased that he knew I didn't mean Lorelei. Pleased he knows there's a difference.

'You know what,' Carter says after a moment, 'I have a confession to make.'

My insides tighten, waiting for the punch. 'What?'

'I've never seen *Nightjar*.' Carter winces as I'm struck speechless for a moment.

'You've never seen the movie that was made in your hometown?'

He shoves his hands into his pockets. 'I'm just not really a horror movie fan.'

His answer brings a smile to my face. Is this what it feels like to share secrets? I feel one welling up inside me in response.

'I have a confession, too. You know I told you about the imaginary friend I had when I was little?' I almost stumble over the words, they come so quickly. 'Mary Ann? She's back.'

'What do you mean?'

'I mean she's back. I've seen her. In my room. Out there. I don't know what she wants.'

'Are you being serious right now?' Carter reaches out like he's going to take my hand, then thinks better of it. 'Lola, has this happened before? I mean, since she went away when you were little?'

He's acting like I'm a skittish animal he has backed into a corner. He doesn't believe me.

'Forget about it,' I say. 'It was just a joke.'

I move to slide down from the altar, but Carter steps forward, boxing me in. His stomach presses against my legs, and the backs of my knees scrape against the stone.

'You're hurting me,' I say, and Carter backs away.

'I didn't mean to,' he says. 'I'm sorry. Please don't shut me out. I want to help –'

But my words echo through my head like a tidal surge – *you're hurting me . . .*

Nolan, don't! You're hurting me!

What the hell? I've never said those words. Nolan has never, not once, laid a finger on me – yet I can hear them in my mind as clearly as if someone is screaming them in my ear.

'Lola?' Carter reaches out towards me, but I swat his hand away. 'Lola, what's wrong?'

I don't answer. There's something in the blackness . . . stars? Just two specks of white light in the sky beyond Carter's silhouette. Glinting like needlepoints. No, not in the sky. It isn't the sky at all, but the black entrance of the cave. Those twin sparks of light recede, stepping back out of sight. I could be watching the video from the museum again, the one with the cut scenes from *Nightjar* running in reverse, and Lorelei's haunted expression as she retreats into darkness. But this is no movie.

Those aren't stars. They're eyes.

Tiny, pinprick eyes just like the Mister Jitters puppet.

He was watching us.

I shove Carter away from me and scream. I scream and scream, and I can't stop.

Carter drags me back through the caves. 'Come on, Lola! Talk to me. Please?'

But I can't think clearly, can't speak. I try not to breathe in the darkness.

God, those eyes . . .

I stay quiet the whole way back to Grandmother's house, and Carter gives up trying to coax me to talk. I leave him at the gate.

'I'll come see you in the morning, OK?' he says. 'Lola?'

But then my head clears, and I see what I need to do. I can't stay here any longer. I can't take another day of this. I need to get out. Harrow Lake is doing something to me, changing me. I was fine before I came to this town. Before the constant reminders of her everywhere. Of the monster she was obsessed with. Of her and Nolan and their life that didn't include me. Of all the secrets buried here. I have enough of my own. The one I let slip out made Carter look at me differently. And then the monster came.

'Will you take me to the airport?'

Carter blinks in surprise. 'What, now?'

'Yes. Please.'

He takes a deep breath. 'I guess I could. But wouldn't you rather wait until tomorrow? Maybe talk to your grandmother, check out flight times, that kind of thing?'

I don't want to push him into a no.

'You're right,' I say, and force a smile. 'First thing in the morning then?'

I watch him walk back along the lane, hoping this isn't the last I'll see of him. Grandmother's snores rumble from upstairs when I go inside. I should try to sleep as well, but I'm too wired now that I have a plan to get out of here.

In my room, I find the photo I stashed in the closet, next to Lorelei's copy of *Alice*. I take it to the living room and set the frame in the centre of the mantel, next to my handwritten note. Maybe my grandmother will hate the picture because Ranger Crane is in it, but I hope not; this is the only photo I've seen in this house where Lorelei is smiling. The only photo of her that seems real. Lorelei and her friend, before that friend abandoned her. With a pang, I wonder if Cora will think that about me – that I've abandoned her. I hope not.

I tip back and forth in the rocker, back and forth. Maybe I drift off for a few minutes. When I open my eyes, the overhead light flickers with a sound like moth wings. But that's not what woke me.

The white jitterbug sits open in front of the old radio, its legs tap-tap-tapping away at the inside of its shell. I must have put it there, though I don't remember. I close the shell and slip it into my pocket, where it chatters away softly beneath the folds of my skirt.

It's Lorelei's favourite. I'll take it with me when I leave Harrow Lake.

But as I look up, I see Mary Ann standing in the yard outside the window. She doesn't move, but I feel her gaze on me. She wants me to follow her. I don't know how I know that, but I do.

It's still dark; Carter won't be here for a while yet. I yawn sleepily and follow Mary Ann into the pre-dawn shadows.

CHAPTER TWENTY-THREE

I smell it as soon as I open the door to the apartment: emptiness. Unless you've lived in a lot of different places, you probably won't know what emptiness smells like. Stagnant air, ghost-scents of the last inhabitants, and some underlying sourness that you can only replicate if you lie face down on an old rug and breathe deeply.

All the time I was in Harrow Lake I didn't picture returning to the apartment like this. That it would be so still, so . . . hollow. I focus on the dim hallway, afraid I'll throw up if I see any trace of Nolan's blood webbing through the gaps in the parquet floor. I know Larry will have had the place cleaned, but knowing that and trusting it are two different things.

I wish I wasn't crossing this threshold alone.

I shut the door behind me, listening for the snap of the lock.

Déjà vu washes over me in an icy wave. Through the open living-room door ahead of me, I see that everything's wrong. The furniture, the pictures on the walls, the TV . . . it's all gone. There are no crates and boxes stacked in the corners of the room as they were the last time I was here, when Nolan dropped his *Didn't I tell you about Paris?* bomb. And we argued, and I left, and then I came home and found him lying there, and I had his blood all over me, under my fingernails . . .

Now the place is empty. Empty, except for the hall phone next to me and its blinking red light. Weird – there's only one message. I push the button to start it rolling.

It isn't from Grandmother, which I was half expecting. Or from Cora. Or Carter, who I should've stolen at least one kiss from – should've pretended for just a little while that I was the girl he's looking for, and he might be the boy to make me feel free with my feet on the ground. It would've been a pretty lie.

There's no sound at all for at least three beats after the *beep*, and then just static. A bad connection. Then the sound shifts, becoming a voice that's no more than a whisper.

> '*Rat-a-tat-tat – such a terrifying sound!*
> *With a jitter-jitter-jitter, he's stirring underground!*
> *Tick-tock, tick-tock – better watch out, he's gonna*
> *snap-snap-snap your bones . . .*'

It's Lorelei's song. Her voice.

The entire world shrinks, piling down, down on my back until I curl in on myself. Cheek against a polished tile floor. Lungs crushed against the cage of my ribs. I blink once, twice. Even the floor is wrong, I realize. The hallway of our apartment has a parquet floor, not tiled. But it *is* our apartment – a past apartment, a home that's no longer our home.

'Lola?'

Mary Ann blinks her wide green eyes at me and holds out her hand, the little girl she used to be. I take it, and the weight lifts from me like it was never there at all.

The walls are the deep green of a forest – Nolan's choice of decor when we lived in Chicago for one summer many years ago. Still holding my hand, Mary Ann puts a finger to her lips. Then I hear it: there are voices nearby. Nolan's voice, and Larry's. Together we creep towards the carved oak door to Nolan's study (no puzzle door here, but still ornate) and peep in at the keyhole.

The first thing I see is Nolan. Not the ashen Nolan I left sleeping at the hospital; this Nolan is from a long time ago, his hair darker than it is now. Fewer lines on his face. He sits perfectly framed at his desk, head in his hands, eyes fixed on a spot on the floor in front him. Then he's obscured as Larry walks between Nolan and the door. Larry leans against the corner of the liquor cabinet. Completely relaxed.

'She said she was going to leave me . . .' Nolan says, almost whispering. Larry makes an exasperated sound in response.

'This isn't your fault, Nolan. You did your best for her, but she never appreciated you. Always one eye on the door, that one.'

I tense, expecting one or both of them to look at the door and see me spying on them, but they don't turn my way. I shouldn't be eavesdropping on them.

'What the hell am I going to do?' Nolan says. I get the feeling he isn't really asking, but Larry answers anyway.

'I told you, I've taken care of it. She wanted to go to Harrow Lake so badly, well . . . that's where she's gone. That's all you know, isn't it?'

It's a pointed question, but Nolan doesn't answer immediately.

'But her mother . . .'

'Has also been taken care of. And will *continue* to be taken care of as long as she doesn't make a fuss. Like I told you, I've handled it.'

Finally, Nolan looks up. His eyes are bloodshot, as if he hasn't slept in weeks. 'What do I tell Lola? How exactly are you going to handle *that*?'

Larry gives a flat laugh. 'Maybe she'd be better off with her mother.'

'What?' Nolan snaps. 'What the hell is that supposed to mean?'

Larry stops pacing. 'It was a *joke*. Look, don't worry about Lola. She's a kid. Tell her Lorelei left, and won't be coming back. That's the truth, isn't it?'

'But what about what she saw?'

Larry sits in the chair in front of Nolan's desk, and I see the hairy backs of his hands resting on his thighs.

'She saw you arguing with Lorelei. That's all.'

'But . . .'

'Look, you're worrying too much. I get it, you have *Red Sheba* coming out in a few weeks, and work on the new movie starting right after that – this is all too much stress on top of everything else you have going on. But that's why you have me, isn't it?'

Nolan stares at Larry, and it's not a friendly stare. I would shrink under it. Larry just pulls a chequebook from his pocket and slides it across the desk to Nolan.

'I take good care of you, and you take good care of me. Like old pals should. Isn't that right?'

With an angry motion, Nolan snatches the chequebook and scribbles out a cheque before hurling the whole thing back at Larry.

'We *never* talk about this again,' Nolan barks, getting up from the desk.

My heart leaps into my throat as he strides right towards the door where I'm hiding. Mary Ann pulls me over to the coat closet in the hallway, and we both slip inside just as the study door opens.

We huddle together in the dark, the rustle of coats and umbrellas shrouding us while Nolan's footsteps thump around the apartment. I wonder if he's looking for me. If he is, I should get out of here quickly before he finds me and realizes I've been hiding – and eavesdropping. How many times has he told me not to do that – that spying on *him* is not Optimal?

But as I try to push my way back through the coats, I can't seem to find the door. There's so much fabric jostling around me. It's like the coats are multiplying.

No matter which direction I turn, I can't find the door. I get tangled in a waxy-smelling raincoat as panic sets in.

'Nolan?' I shout, but there's no answer. '*Larry?*'

Nothing. Not for a long moment. And then the first bars of a song hum to life somewhere in the apartment. It bleeds in through the cracks around the closet door.

'T'ain't No Sin.'

The sound seeps in through my pores, threading a tapestry under my skin – over the secrets stitched quietly there, over and over again. God, I hate this song. I've always hated it. It was playing so loud the day Lorelei left, too; turned all the way up to cover their arguing. Larry was right about that, I remember now – they did argue. This song always makes me feel jumpy and strange.

There's something else ... It nags at the back of my mind, just like when Grandmother lies to me. I need to scratch it, make it bleed out its secrets. But how am I supposed to do that with this damned song playing?

I hate it!

As the track fades into that loaded pause before the next begins, the itchy static grows louder. Morphs into the tap-tap-tap of sharp fingers. It's the crackle of dead air, the needle jumping at the end of the song. But it's the sound a monster makes when it claws its way out of the wallpaper, too. The sound of something waiting in the dark.

'Mary Ann?'

No answer.

Wait – I think there's another door at the back of this closet. Maybe I can get out that way ...

I roll my head towards the ceiling, where I know there's a chain hanging down that will turn on the light. But it's too high, too far. I see a silhouette up there, black on black, in the corner of the closet. Too tall to be real, too big to actually be in this tight space. His bony limbs bend at inhuman angles. My heart bangs out a rhythm: *who is that, who is that, who the hell is that??*

But I know. I know who he is, even as his snapping, juddering sound goes on and on. It's Mister Jitters.

He moves closer, a blade of shadow reaching down towards me. I huddle back into the shroud of coats, but there are too many, and I'm tangled in them, stuck.

'Lola! He's here!' Mary Ann has seen him, too. I reach blindly for her, but find only fabric.

A scream tries to punch its way out of me, but there's a band around my chest, pinning me in place, choking me. I try to raise my arms, but they're just as powerless.

My eyes are the only things I can control. I shut them tight.

Mister Jitters drags one stiff, cold finger across my collarbone, stopping at my throat. He presses against the pulse point hammering there like he's testing how hard he can push, how much I can bear. I try to kick my legs, to lift my arms and shove him away, but my muscles only spasm pathetically.

The closet is too full of his noise; that terrible rattle fills every secret place it can crawl into. It chokes me. Drowns me. Breaking me apart from the inside out.

Then it's gone. The weight lifts and I fall from the coat closet onto the hallway floor. I heave in enough air to burst my lungs, to scream for eons.

I look back through the open door behind me, but it's just a closet now. No more than four or five coats hang inside it. Nothing else. Nobody there.

Mister Jitters is gone. And so is Mary Ann.

CHAPTER TWENTY-FOUR

No, no, no, no, NO . . .

My heart pounds as I blink awake, grey light coming through the lace curtains of Lorelei's room. Except I'm not in Lorelei's room. Those aren't lace curtains. Tree branches shiver above me, their little white acorns swaying in the breeze.

I'm lying beneath the Bone Tree.

I try to scramble up, but my right foot won't move. With a wave of horror, I realize I've fallen asleep here. And, judging by how light it is, I've been here far too long.

The Harrow Lake woods have claimed me. My roots will hold me here forever.

No. No!

But wasn't there a full moon last night? I yank at my foot and it moves. My shoe is just wedged beneath a gnarled tree root. I twist it until it comes free, and stagger back from the Bone Tree, heart thudding in my chest.

What am I doing here? I was at the apartment . . . no, that was a dream. I was waiting for Carter to come pick me up to take me to the airport, then Mary Ann . . .

That's all I remember. I was sleepwalking again, following Mary Ann. Whether the conversation I overheard between Nolan and Larry was a dream or a memory or some confusion of both, I can't shake the certainty that Mister Jitters took Mary Ann. That was real. And now I'm alone in the woods.

Shit! Am I too late? Have I missed Carter? I have no idea what time it is. I turn to hurry away from the Bone Tree, but trip on all the damned roots. Something flies from my pocket as I land hard on my knees, coming to rest in front of me. It's the white jitterbug, lying open. Not just open, but *open*.

The inner base of the shell where the jitterbug sits has sprung up to reveal a tiny compartment hidden underneath. Carved into the moving base are the words:

KEEP YOUR SECRETS SAFE

Lorelei used to say that to me. She would repeat it every time I wrote a new secret on a slip of paper. And there's a slip of paper nestled within the hidden compartment. Hand trembling, I pluck it out and read it.

I can't bear to have that monster touch me again. Why won't he let me go? Please, just make it stop.

I drop the note. The breeze catches it, swirls it away.

That was Lorelei's handwriting. And not childish, little-girl handwriting. She must have been a teenager when she wrote it.

Before she met Nolan? How long? How much did she tell him about Mister Jitters? I need to get out of Harrow Lake and talk to Nolan.

I pick up the white jitterbug and hurry back to Grandmother's house.

She isn't standing over the stove as usual when I get there. The kitchen is empty, the stove cold and lifeless. She isn't in any of the other downstairs rooms. Upstairs, her bedroom door is closed. I knock – lightly at first, then louder. She doesn't answer, so I try the handle. The door swings open with a squawk. Her bed is made. Nothing's out of place about the room except that Grandmother isn't in it. I close the door and lean against it.

Where the hell is she? I check the yard just to make sure, but my grandmother is gone. This is the first time I can remember her leaving the house since I arrived in Harrow Lake.

Screw this. I only need to grab the few things I have with me, and then I'll see where Carter is. Back in the house, I storm upstairs. Slam the door to Lorelei's room with a satisfyingly loud crack. It sets off the jitterbugs, their legs tippy-tapping, snickering inside their shells . . .

They're back. The jitterbugs are all back, all sitting on their shelves, shells open and facing me. They're watching me.

Go to hell!

I snap each of them shut, one by one. I channel Nolan's icy brand of anger; between the two of us, we could obliterate this town. Wipe its secrets off the face of the earth and never have to think about Lorelei or monsters again. I'll tell him that Larry has been keeping my messages from him, sending me here when I just wanted to stay with Nolan. Getting me out of the way, like Larry always does. *Handling* me. Nolan will go ballistic. Larry will be no more than a smudge on his shoe when he's done. I remember Nolan doing that once – punching Larry in the eye so it was left swollen and purple.

Why did he do that? The memory is blurry and old, but then it comes to me. Nolan was a wreck, unshaven and stinking, a whiskey glass in his hand, and Larry yelled at him, 'Are you going to let that bitch ruin you?' and then Nolan's fist flew and Larry sprawled on the hardwood floor . . .

The image is so shocking, I wonder if I've made it up. That shabby drunk is so unlike the Nolan I know.

I squeeze my hands against my temples, just like my grandmother did. Maybe if I squeeze hard enough, the pieces will all fall into place.

I'm reaching for some fresh clothes from the closet when a floorboard squeaks near the bed. The jitterbugs' noise has stopped, like it was never there. Maybe they're listening.

Under the bed, the space is dark, mostly hidden by the quilt I've left hanging over the side. Anything could be hiding under there.

I slide into a crouch. I'm sure I hear breathing. Just like in that closet.

This is the point in any horror film where the girl should run, but never does.

So I run. Straight down the stairs and out the front door. But as I near the gate, I see a face in the upstairs window – the window of Lorelei's room.

I trip, skinning my knee in the dirt. Who was that? Grandmother? I get up and run back across the yard.

Footsteps scurry over the landing above my head as I enter the front door. I'm up the stairs in a beat. 'Where are you? Grandmother? Mary Ann?'

There's a faint scuttling noise, like someone running upstairs, except I'm at the top of the only staircase in the house. Grandmother's bedroom door stands open. Treading lightly, I peek around the door. Mary Ann isn't there – at least nowhere I can see. The room looks just as it did before. But then my gaze lands on the closed closet door.

Some instinct pushes me towards it. I reach slowly for the door handle. Try to calm my breathing. Then, in one swift motion, I pull the door open.

There's nothing inside but old-lady dresses. No Grandmother. No Mary Ann. No monster. But I'm missing something, I'm sure. I have the strange sense that this closet goes back farther than I can see – that there's a secret part to it.

Look behind the dresses.

I shove them to one side of the rail.

And there it is. Another door. It's no more than a few boards nailed together, really, but when I push it open there's a rickety-looking staircase. It must lead to an attic. The moment I realize that, it feels obvious. Of *course* there's an attic door in the closet. I've seen it before.

I hesitate before stepping through the door, lingering dread from my dream making me wary.

'Mary Ann, are you up there?'

I wait. What would Nolan say if he saw me shivering here like some terrified child? I set my jaw, and head up the stairs. At the top, I almost trip over a stack of crates. I curse, then spot a blue object tucked away under the eaves.

'Is that my *bag*?' I pull it out, unsnap the catches and throw it open. The contents spill out onto the dusty boards, but I don't care. There are my clothes and a stack of books, as well as a few pairs of shoes.

'Who did this? Who hid my bag up here?'

There's no answer.

I taste the dust hovering in the air. Dust, covering everything, except where my footprints have disturbed it. Mine, and one other person's. Footprints smaller than my own, just like Grandmother's.

It was her. Grandmother actually hid my suitcase from me. Why? I look down at my dress. Remember how pleased she looked when I put on Lorelei's make-up. All the little slips where it seemed as though she'd forgotten that I'm her granddaughter, not her daughter. Does she even remember hiding it up here?

A faint *patter-patter* fills the silence. But it's only a tree branch blowing against the attic window, tap-tap-tapping against the glass.

It feels good to wear my own clothes again, even though it's just a shapeless black sweater and a pair of grey skinny jeans and sneakers. Not what I'd wear if I had my whole wardrobe to choose from, but at least I'm not a clone of Little Bird anymore. Or Lorelei. I don't look like I belong in Harrow Lake at all. I look like *me*.

I tried calling Carter, but he must be out of the house. Looking for me? I hope not. I don't want him to think I've disappeared like Marie. But maybe he never meant to come for me at all. Maybe he wants nothing to do with me after I freaked out in the caves.

No. Carter keeps his promises.

I've spent the last hour going through my mother's things. At first, it was just to make sure I wasn't leaving anything of mine behind, but after a while I realized I was looking for more secrets – like the one from the jitterbug shell. I've gone through drawers and looked behind photo frames and beneath loose floorboards. Searching for any other scraps of paper she might have hidden. Searching for traces of her – and what brought her back to Harrow Lake. Because in this whole mess that's one thing I can be sure of: when Lorelei left Nolan, she took me with her. If I can find her secrets, maybe they can tell me what happened next.

I find the first secret tucked into a crack beneath the windowsill in Lorelei's bedroom. I tease it out with my fingernail until the paper roll falls free. A confession about some quarrysider boy she kissed in the ruins of the church. I was there with a quarrysider boy only last night. Where I saw those twin spots of light backing into the cave. Someone watching. I suppress a shiver and try to focus.

Two secrets turn up under a board at the bottom of the closet.

I tipped over mother's planter in the yard and blamed it on Grant. He says I owe him.

From the handwriting, I'd guess Lorelei was a teen when she wrote that.

Father found out what I did. He says I'll be punished for lying.

Written around the same time. But why did she put so little detail in them? They're hardly secrets at all.

The next note is inside the frame of the photo of Lorelei with her father. As I put it back together, I feel another twinge of jealousy at seeing them so close, with the white jitterbug in her hand – that connection between them. Why don't I have that with Nolan? Why won't he let me?

But then I read the note.

He came again last night. I slept through the jitterbugs' warning.

That's all it says, but it's enough to turn my stomach over. She must mean Mister Jitters.

I continue my search of the house and find a couple more – one curled into the keyless hole in her closet door, and the other in the hollow of a lamp base in the downstairs hallway – but these are in wobbly, childlike handwriting. I'm checking under the bed one last time – slowly,

slowly – when I notice those peculiar scuff marks on the floor around the bed frame. Again, I try to imagine Lorelei bouncing on her bed and laughing, or having wild sex in this room just down the hall from her parents' bedroom. Neither seems likely.

I move to the foot of the bed, grab the frame, and drag it in line with the marks. Then I check under it again. There must be something I've missed. Maybe another hiding place, like a hole in the wall, or a floorboard that has sprung up without the weight of the bed to hold it in place. But there's nothing.

I get up, brushing dust bunnies from my knees. What am I missing?

The light slanting in through the window shows I've been searching for hours. It must be late morning by now. Where is Carter? I look at the carriage clock up on its high shelf, but it hasn't told the correct time in years, if it ever did. Why would anyone keep something so broken and useless?

That's when I notice it. The placement of the bed, and the clock, and the height of the shelf. I'm climbing in a second, ignoring the groan of springs, and balancing my weight so I can put one foot on the frame at the end of the bed and reach. I must be the same height as Lorelei because when I stretch as far as I can, my fingers just about close around the sides of the clock's casing. I slide the clock to the edge of the shelf and –

The clock hits the floor with a crack like a skull fracturing, waking the jitterbugs. Wood scatters like shrapnel, and a panel at the back of the clock bursts open, spilling out tiny folded squares of paper across the floor – dozens of them. Hundreds.

A whole heartful of secrets.

Things I learned from the broken clock

1. Mister Jitters used to come to her room at night.
2. After each visit, Lorelei carved another jitterbug. She believed their sound would warn her when he was coming. Didn't Mary Ann say that, too?
3. Lorelei desperately wanted to get away from Harrow Lake, but she was frightened Mister Jitters would find her anyway. Is that what happened? Is that why she left me in the end, and never came back?

The more I learn about Lorelei, the harder she is to understand.

CHAPTER TWENTY-FIVE

I go downstairs to call Nolan . . . Larry . . . anyone really, and find the phone line is dead. Again. Just another thing that's tightening the grip this town has on me, keeping me here. A search of my suitcase shows Larry didn't pack a phone charger, so I can't use my cell, either. Suddenly the emptiness of the house feels hungry, contagious. I need to get out before it swallows me. If the landlines aren't working, I'll just have to go and find Carter.

I hurry from the house. But as I pass the end of Main Street, I stop. Listen. That song is playing again – Lorelei's song. But that's the only sound; Main Street is deserted. I guess it's around lunchtime by now, but there's not a soul walking along the street. All the stores are closed. Nobody stands at the counters. Nothing moves behind the glass.

'Hello?' My voice intrudes on the melody. There's no answer. I'm alone.

I run. It's strange how easy it is to fly along the road. In my own clothes, my own sneakers, I can actually move. There's no lead band crushing my chest, no tree limbs wrapped around me to me hold me back.

I slow as I approach the high gates of the fairground. They're chained, and there's no sign of movement inside, only the hum of electricity coursing through the fence nearby. I turn back to the path, and, as I'm about to run again, the toe of my sneaker disturbs something lying half buried in the dirt. I reach down and pick up a small, familiar flashlight. It's hanging from a chain with a broken clasp. This is Ranger Crane's pendant. She must be nearby.

I wrap it around the bars of the gates and leave it for her to find.

Trees crowd in as I head away from the lake shore and onto the uneven path snaking around it to Carter's house. I'm running up an incline, but the void at my back drives me on. That's what it feels like, the empty town: a void. Like one of Nolan's sets the day after he wraps filming.

My vision starts to blacken at the edges, and I stop and lean against a tree for a minute. It isn't just spots dancing around my eyeballs, though. I don't need a watch to know it *can't* be late enough for the sky to be growing dark. But it is.

A vibration thrums up my legs, and it takes me a moment to realize it's the ground under me rumbling, like a creature stretching awake beneath my feet.

Mister Jitters.

Run.

I don't see Carter's house until I'm about to slam into his pickup parked out front. There are no lights on. Not here, and not in any of his neighbours' houses farther along the road. I'm about to knock on his door when it flies open.

Carter stands in the doorway, looking startled. 'Lola? What are you doing here?'

'Where is everybody? Why is it so dark?' I say. He's wearing his boots and jacket, like I've just caught him leaving the house. 'Are you going somewhere?'

'Yeah, kind of. Why are you here? I thought you'd left town already. You weren't at the house when I called by this morning.'

'I . . .'

I steel myself, preparing to tell him about waking beneath the Bone Tree, about Mister Jitters taking Mary Ann, about finding Lorelei's notes . . . but I can't. The words won't leave my mouth. They're a solid mass inside me.

Suddenly Carter's right in front of me and I'm pressing my forehead against his chest, trying not to throw up, and I think he can somehow read my thoughts. For a second, I wish it was possible, that he could just pluck all the shards from inside my head and rearrange the pieces in the right order. But he can't do that. It's something I have to do myself.

It's true dark now, even though I know that's impossible. It's like time is running away from me, leaving me behind.

'Come in a sec,' Carter says, and leads me inside. I stand in the hallway while he lights some kind of oil lamp and hooks it onto the wall.

'Where is everyone?' I ask again as he lights another in the living room. 'The whole town seems to have emptied out, except for you and me.'

'And my mom,' Carter sighs, looking out the window as though Ranger Crane might suddenly appear there. 'The whole town's under an evacuation order. A part of the hill collapsed near the quarry, and there's a high risk there'll be follow-on landslides. Major ones, like the one back in 1928. They're keeping everyone out until the risk is assessed properly.'

I look down at the bare floorboards, half expecting a gaping hole to open up right under me.

'Then why are you still here?'

'I need to go find my mom,' Carter says. 'She went into the woods earlier and she . . . I just need to find her.'

'I found her flashlight near the fairground gates,' I tell him. 'Maybe she's there?'

'I already checked the fairground,' he says, voice flat. I study his profile. Something isn't right. He's avoiding looking at me.

'Carter? Carter, what's wrong? Oh my God . . . has your mom disappeared, like Marie?'

Like Lorelei?

'No, it's not like that.' He turns slowly, giving me time to brace myself, I guess. The entire left side of his face is a swollen purple mess, his eye puffed up so badly it's almost shut.

'What happened?' I gasp, reaching out, but stopping short of touching him.

'There was this horse . . .' He tries to smile, but I guess my expression stops him. 'I just got into some trouble. It's no big deal.'

'What kind of trouble?'

Carter scratches his jaw, but drops his hand when he encounters a bruise. 'Mom and I got into it about a bunch of stuff. Her drinking, mainly.' He shakes his head. 'I should have just left it alone, but I couldn't make her listen and we needed to get out of here. When she took off, I told Cora to get a ride with Faye and her family. I was meant to find Mom and follow on in the truck.' His expression is stark when he looks at me. 'I searched for hours for her. I only came back here in case she'd come home to pass out like she usually does, but there's no sign of her. And now you show up.'

'You're telling me your mom did that to your face?' It takes me a second to make sense of this. Mothers don't do those kinds of things. I mean, they *do*. I know that. I've read about it. But it's different seeing it for myself – those marks on Carter's skin, marks put there by his mother. It doesn't fit into this strange jigsaw I've made; this picture of what a mother might be. 'She hurt you?'

'Leave it alone, Lola,' he says. He sounds so tired. 'Tell me why you're still here. I thought you couldn't wait to see the back of Harrow Lake?'

'I will not leave it alone! What the hell gives her the right to do this to you?' I shouldn't be yelling at Carter. An ugly thought unfurls itself. 'Was this because of me?'

'No,' he says, too quickly. 'Well, not exactly. When I went to your grandma's and you weren't there, Mrs McCabe called my mom and told her I'd talked you into running away. My mom had some notion that you leaving caused the land shifts, but she was just drunk and babbling . . .'

'She thought I'd left, and that pissed off Mister Jitters?' My voice comes out in a croak.

'Like I said, it was nonsense. Anyway, she kinda stormed out after . . . this.' He gestures ruefully at his face.

Carter leans back against the windowsill, the woods outside invisible beyond the glass.

'Where do you think she could be?' I say.

'I don't know. I've searched everywhere I can think of. The woods, the fairground, the ranger station, all around the lake. Man, this is a shitty time for her to wander off.'

'Maybe she didn't,' I say, and immediately wish I hadn't. Carter grows wary, like he did when I told him about Mary Ann at the church. I go on quickly. 'Maybe Mister Jitters took her.'

'Lola, no . . . Look, this isn't the first time my mom's taken off after an argument, OK? You should just forget about Harrow Lake and all its fucked-up monsters, and go home to New York.' I can't stand the way he's looking at me – like I'm being foolish. Like I'm in the way.

'But . . .'

'But what?'

I want to tell him about the eyes at the ruined church. About how I saw Mister Jitters watching us. How my mother saw him, too.

I reach into my pocket and dig out the handful of crumpled notes I'm carrying. I thrust them at Carter.

'What are these?' he asks, dubiously. 'Lola, we don't have time . . .'

'Just read them,' I say, then add, 'please.'

He takes the slips of paper over to a table by the window and begins smoothing them out, one by one, against the wood. I watch as he reads them, waiting for the moment when he understands.

I can only lie here, dreading the creak of the door opening ... never truly believed in monsters. Mother says I'm imagining it, making it up. Why can't anyone see what is happening? I just wish I could leave, get away from this place, but he won't let me go ... Nobody will believe me ...

'Well?' I say. 'This proves she saw Mister Jitters, right?'

'That's one way of looking at it.'

'*One way of looking at it?* Did you read the same notes I read?' I snatch the scraps off the table and fold them back into my pocket. 'She saw him. I've seen him, too. And now your mom is missing . . .'

Carter's words are slow and quiet when he speaks at last. 'The notes could have been written by someone who saw Mister Jitters. Or they could have been written by someone who was just very scared, and felt trapped, and couldn't see a way out of a bad situation. Someone who didn't feel safe writing about what really scared her. Someone who wanted to hide from another kind of monster . . . like an abusive parent.'

It's my turn to fall silent.

I unfold the papers again, read through them over and over, scanning for proof that it was Mister Jitters Lorelei was writing about . . . not my grandparents. Mister Jitters' name was on the note I found hidden inside the jitterbug, wasn't it? I think so . . . damn it! I wish I could read it again to make sure. But it's lost among the roots of the Bone Tree.

Then I hear my grandmother's voice again, telling me about the *special bond* Lorelei had with her father, how he adored her.

I picture the old man in the photograph on the mantelpiece, his arm wrapped tightly around Lorelei's waist. Lorelei trapped. Neither of them smiling.

Nolan has never once laid a hand on me. But maybe Lorelei's father was different. Maybe I didn't see it because I didn't think to look for it.

'Are you saying you don't believe Mister Jitters is real?' I ask Carter, my voice shaking.

He purses his lips and looks away.

No. I've seen too much for Mister Jitters to not be real. *Like I saw Mary Ann.*

'All right, what happened to Marie then?' I snap.

He still won't meet my eyes. 'She probably fell into a sinkhole, like you did . . .'

'I know that isn't what happened! I've seen him, and so did Lorelei. Why won't you admit *he's real*?'

I want to bash my head against the wall. Crack it open so all the little fragments can come pouring out like these slips of paper, and I can put them in an order that makes sense. No more secrets. No more lies.

'Carter, you're wrong. Of course Lorelei would be vague in the notes – that was just in case anyone ever found them.

She says here nobody would believe her, and they wouldn't have, would they?'

'Did your mom actually write them, though?' he says.

'What? Who else could have written them?'

He looks at me intently. 'You.'

The paper crumples in my fist. 'Why would I make up lies about my own mother, Carter?'

'I don't think the notes are about your mother,' Carter says gently. 'I think they're about Nolan. The way he suffocates you and refuses to let you have a life of your own.'

'*Me?*' It takes me a moment to get what he's saying, what he means. 'You think I wrote these things about *Nolan*?'

I raise my hand to hit him. Carter doesn't move. I think that's what stops me.

'Nolan *protects* me.' I will him to see the truth in my anger. 'He wants what's best for me.'

Safe in my little cage, like an ornament. A perfect trophy. Good job, Nolan! Such a pretty little thing, isn't she? She's so lucky to have a father like you.

Blood in the cracks . . .

Carter's frown carves ruts in his forehead.

'Jesus, Carter! Don't feel *sorry* for me. Just believe me.'

Mother says I'm imagining it . . . My grandmother didn't believe her own daughter. And Carter doesn't believe me *or* Lorelei. He's trying to twist Lorelei's words into something they're not. I won't let him. Lorelei's secrets were her truth, and she wrote about Mister Jitters. He is real. He is.

So why can't I shake that image of Lorelei sitting in her father's lap?

'Look, we can sort all this out later,' Carter says. He sounds so tired. 'But for now I need to find my mom. You should get out of here.'

I know Carter doesn't get it. Doesn't get *me*. I let a mask slide into place – not some character from a story this time. Something harder. Unbreakable.

'Don't project your own crap onto me, Carter.'

He winces like I really have slapped him. 'My dad never –'

'I'm not talking about your dad,' I cut him off. 'I'm talking about how your whole family treats you like garbage – Grant beats you; your mom does, too, and screws up any chance you have to leave this town. Even Cora talks about you like you're hopeless. What kind of life do *you* have, Carter?'

Silence falls. It's like the void I felt on Main Street has finally caught up with us.

'It's not like that,' he says quietly, close to tears. 'My mom's not well. She needs me . . .'

'She's your *mother*. She should want what's best for you.'

Carter reaches up to close his hand around the pendant hanging at his throat.

'I didn't write the notes,' I tell him. 'Mister Jitters is real, and my mother saw him. I've seen him, too. He took Mary Ann.'

I shouldn't have said that. Carter shakes off whatever pain my words caused and fixes me with a worried gaze.

'Lola, stop. There is no Mister Jitters, no Mary Ann. You need to just forget all this and *go home*.'

'Mister Jitters is real – I'll prove it!' Carter grunts as I shove past him and run out of the house. He staggers out into the front yard after me.

'Lola, stop! The hillside could collapse any second!'

I'm not leaving without answers. And I refuse to let them be buried here.

'OK, you're right!' he yells. 'Lola, *please* – I'm sorry!'

Nolan's right after all: sorry is an empty word.

CHAPTER TWENTY-SIX

The town is just as deserted as it appeared from across the lake. I take the same path as before, walking now. My clothes are damp with sweat and growing colder by the minute.

As the gates to the fairground come into view, I see a light. The pendant is hanging right where I left it – but now it glows, showing me that the gates are open.

I reach for the pendant, pulling it free. Carter said he'd searched the fairground already. Why didn't *he* see it?

Suddenly light floods the path as the fairground blazes to life beyond the fence, machines accelerating to a clatter, and the chipper 1920s jazz drags itself up to tempo over the PA system. I gape, a statue on the path. But someone must be here because the gates are open. Someone turned on those lights – someone inside the fairground.

I move as though weightless, propelled by a breeze that isn't there. Behind the music is a tap-tap-tapping that catches my footsteps. It's familiar. Hypnotic. I walk towards it.

My mother was right. Mister Jitters is real, and I need to prove it.

The entrance to the underground gondola ride is still boarded over, but the gap where Carter and I slid through last time is open. That's where the sound is coming from, that thrumming that makes my ears itch inside. There's no light in there, but a shape crosses the gap – a movement in the shadows. Jerky, unnatural. Bone-white against the darkness.

He's here.

I back up silently towards the entrance gates. I hear his chattering beneath the notes of the music, getting louder even as I put more distance between us.

Some sense alerts me to the fence at my back. I'm only one step from the crisscrossing wires that hum with current, the gates several yards away now. How did I veer so far in the wrong direction that I almost fried myself? And how is it that the gates are now closed? I didn't do that.

I hurry towards them, but when I tug at the gates they don't move. They aren't chained, I just can't get them to budge. It's like something invisible is holding them in place.

Shit.

Why did I think coming here was a good idea? What's the point in proving a monster exists if I don't make it out of here alive?

Stupid, Lola!

At the far end of the fairground, there's that stutter of movement again – the flash of a bone-white face. Then a figure emerges from behind the shed and disappears behind the ring-toss booth. He's moved away from the gondola ride. He's coming closer.

I can't get out over the gate or the electrified fence. I can't climb the sheer rock face around the entrance to the gondola ride. The only way I know to get out is through the caves, and up the steep sides of the sinkhole where I saw the church.

The lot is all lit up. If I stay here, he'll find me. By the time everyone comes back to town, I'll have disappeared like the others. Like I was never even here.

The tunnels. I need to get inside the tunnels.

I hurry over to the loose shutter of the gondola ride and slip inside, the shutter swinging closed behind me, sealing me in darkness. The noise outside is still there, only muffled through the wooden boards.

I fumble for the pendant I took from the fairground gate. Weak light illuminates the space I'm standing in.

Lorelei is gone.

The words whisper to me from the walls, written by girls who feared the monster I came looking for. I press my lips together. The sound outside hasn't changed, but I have the sense that he's nearer now. Can he hear me? I don't know, but I don't want to risk it. I need to hurry.

Whatever Mister Jitters is, and whatever he wants, he's out there right now, waiting for me.

I follow the narrow ledge lining the channel of water. It's easier in my sneakers, but the sense that someone is following me, creeping up behind me, makes the damp rocks a hundred times more slippery under my soles.

My footsteps mingle with the patter of droplets falling onto the black water. I can almost feel stiff fingers reaching out for me.

I don't remember the church being this far when I came with Carter, but everything stretches in the dark – not just shadows. I walk right into solid rock, almost dropping my flashlight. Ahead is a dead end. I need to go back, retrace my steps. Then someone calls my name through the tunnel.

I freeze. Is that Mary Ann? Was *she* the one I saw out there in the fairground? No. The figure I saw was too tall, too inhuman. But she might have followed me in here.

What does she want?

'Lola . . .' It has a sing-song quality that makes my hair stand on end. '*Lo-laaaaa . . .*'

Is she here to help me, or lure me in? Am I running towards a monster?

Twice I slip and nearly break my ankle before I stumble into a shallow part of the stream running through the caves. It fills my sneakers with icy water and sloshes up my legs. I lose my footing, landing hard on the stone path. I try not to sob. Fail. Waves of noise ebb against my skull, but the voice is now silent.

'Mary Ann?' I cry out. 'Mary Ann, where are you? What do you want?'

There's no answer. I wait, hearing only wet sounds, rhythmic and mocking. Did I just imagine it?

I don't know, I don't know, I don't know.

A sound shudders through the cavern, cracking into shards and reverberating off the walls around me. *Snap-snap-snap-snap-SNAP!*

Is that Mary Ann? Mister Jitters? Or was Carter right – is the ground shifting above my head?

The icy chill of the cave wall bleeds through the back of my sweater.

Come on, Lola. Just find the church so you can get out of this place. Not Nolan's voice now, and not Mary Ann's – my own.

I head back the way I came, keeping an eye on the ground where the light of the pendant casts a dim pool around my feet. I leave wet trails that fade into the blackness behind me.

'Damn it,' I mutter, stopping again. It's the same wall of rock facing me – the same dead end. I can't have passed it again, can I? The way into the sinkhole must be farther than I thought. It's just hard to think straight with all that noise.

The cold bites my soaked feet, draining them of feeling a little more with each step. I've only gone a little farther when I slip on a sharp stone. Pain shoots up my calf. I curse, crouching to rub the muscle. Then something brushes against my hair.

My head jerks up, but there's nobody there. I peer in all directions. Nothing.

'Mary Ann?' I whisper. 'Are you there?'

I know there won't be an answer.

I'm alone.

CHAPTER TWENTY-SEVEN

I must walk for hours, slipping and sliding from one chamber to another, with that *chatter-chatter-chatter* wrapped around me like a blanket, the noise like Lorelei's jitterbugs. Did she think that, too? Was that really why she made them? To remind her of this dark place, to warn her about monsters creeping into her room at night?

The light from the pendant is growing dimmer. I've been trying not to notice it, but it barely illuminates the path anymore. Soon I'll be swallowed by the dark. Will anyone come looking for me?

I start to sing softly, keeping myself company as my words bounce back at me:

'*He got trapped underground for a really long while,*
Then he fed on the dead and got a brand-new smile . . .'

I laugh, high and sharp. If this was an old black-and-white movie, someone would slap me now.

My ankle throbs. I have to get out of here. But the tunnels all look the same, and I've turned around and around so many times I don't know which way I came in. Was the stream running into the cave, or out of it? It doesn't matter: I can't tell which way the water's flowing anyway.

I crouch down, rubbing my ankle while I try to stem the dread. What would Nolan tell me to do? I try to listen for him. But all I hear now is the echoing chatter. Just chatter.

'Stop it,' I say. I pretend my voice is Nolan's. 'There are at least two ways out of these caves – through the church, and back out the way you came in.'

I stand; straighten my spine so the vertebrae crack. The sound joins the chatter. I walk on. It's all I can do. I keep my hand on the wall and trace the rough surface with my fingers so I won't miss an opening. I've been doing this for a few minutes when the pendant at my throat flickers, then dies.

'Don't panic,' I say to the darkness. My voice is calm. Calm. I am calm. 'Keep your hand on the wall. You'll find the way out as long as you don't panic.'

'*Panic panic panic panic panic . . .*'

The word reverberates around me. Mister Jitters is here, mocking me. He's getting closer. Too close.

'I'll never leave you like she did,' Mary Ann whispers, but then her voice changes, becomes a rattle of teeth next to my ear. '*Like they all do.*'

I sense her shifting in the dark, stretching, becoming monstrous. Becoming Mister Jitters.

I arch like a scorpion as his brittle finger traces my spine, leaving a wet trail behind. Then I run.

I make it five steps before my legs are knocked out from under me, and I fall headlong into nothingness.

I expect to hit water or wet stone, but when I land it's on a smooth surface, and it rocks under the impact. My teeth clash with the inside of my cheek, and my wrist burns where I land on it hard. Is it broken? I've never broken a bone before, and I don't know how to tell, but this hurts so, so much. My mouth fills with the taste of blood. I swallow it down, along with the whimper trying to fight its way out of me.

Good girl. You didn't make a sound.

I'm in a boat. Narrow, wooden, and long enough that I can lie flat in the base of it. I remember the one scene in *Nightjar* where Little Bird runs along the path and dives into a gondola just as it enters the caves on an underground stream. This was her gondola – a prop from the set. It saved her from the villagers hunting her with their pitchforks and their empty bellies, at least for a time. Maybe it will save me now.

I roll onto my side, bumping up against something that isn't the side of the gondola, and feel around the fabric covering it. Something rigid, cold. My hand shakes as I run my fingers over the hard bumps.

Oh God.

I bite back a sob. There's the swell of a ribcage, the ball of a shoulder joint. Then hair brushes against my knuckles.

'No, no, no, no, no . . .'

I want to scramble out of the boat and run screaming into the dark, but I force my fingers to wrap around the straw-like hair, trace a jawbone, follow the smooth line up to the temple where my fingers meet a jagged edge.

I pull my hand back with a yelp. There's a huge crack in the skull.

No. I must be imagining this. There is no body in this boat. It's just a prop from *Nightjar*.

Not a body. Definitely not *her* body.

But . . . Marie?

It could be her. I can't help hoping, though it feels wrong. But no. These bones have been lying here for *years*, not days. Long enough for her flesh to rot away, for her hair to turn brittle.

It is Lorelei lying next to me.

I sit, listening to the cave's noises for an answer that doesn't come. There's only the chatter now. Tears run down my face, but I don't wipe them away. I don't want to touch my skin after touching . . . that.

Tap-tap-tap-tap-TAP . . .

That chattering sound . . . I *remember* that sound. It unravels something in me.

'You told me we'd go on an adventure,' I whisper to the dark, but it's Lorelei I'm talking to. 'But you needed to settle some things back home in Harrow Lake first.'

More fragments of that long-ago memory unpick themselves from my mind.

'But you left me behind.'

No. The words don't feel right. Don't feel true.

She took me with her, but then Grandmother called Nolan and told him where we were and Nolan drove all

284

the way from Chicago to get us. Took us back home. And I was secretly relieved because Lorelei had seemed so unhappy in Harrow Lake. I was glad we were going home to Nolan – until the shouting started. I remember the argument, that awful record playing at full volume.

The chatter breaks down the shards, rearranging the stories I've been told, the things Nolan said over and over until I believed . . .

He lied. Lorelei didn't abandon me. We left together. If Grandmother hadn't called Nolan and told him where we were . . . The door to my room closed, protecting my little ears; the gramophone turned way up. 'T'ain't No Sin'.

But the song, as loud as it was, couldn't drown out the yelling. The banging.

'*Stop it! Nolan, don't! You're hurting me!*'

'You're hurting me,' I mutter. It was her voice – it was Lorelei screaming. An awful scream that cut off like a record with a needle scratch. And I crept from my room to see . . .

Blood in the cracks.

Running in straight lines between the floor tiles. A pale, slender hand lying limp, just visible through the gap in the door. And a shadow falling as Nolan appeared, filling the whole world. 'Get back in your room, Lola! Damn it – get out of here!'

Lorelei, lying dead.

She tried to leave him. She took me with her . . . But he found us. Then she was lying there, blood pooling around her. Blood on my father's hand as he slammed the door.

The hiss and hitch of the gramophone needle reaching the end of its journey. Nowhere else to go.

That is the sound I heard the day my mother died. The same sound I heard the night I went to knock on Nolan's puzzle door, so angry about yet another move, and his, *'Didn't I tell you?'* cracking me open, breaking through the bubble where I'd buried that secret from years before. Buried so I could keep on loving him, even after what he did. All the blood . . . the blood . . .

I see another image now: Nolan storming after me into the hallway. *'Where do you think you're going? Get back here!'*

'No. I'm leaving.'

'You think you can just walk out on me? Turn your back on me like I'm nothing? You're just like Lorelei!'

And that was it – her name on his lips. The one thing we never talked about. Buried deep, deep down. There it was.

'Why couldn't you let her go? Mom was going to take me with her, I heard her. She told you over and over again that you would crush me unless she took me away! Crush me, the way you crushed her!'

'Don't you dare speak to me that way! You'll do whatever I tell you, when I tell you. I'll NEVER let you leave me.'

Cornered at the front door of the apartment. My hand holding a kitchen knife. My head full of *NEVER*.

'Let me go!'

Oh God. It was me. It was me, it was me, it was *me*.

I couldn't stop the rage pulsing through my veins in a burning, black wave. And the moment the blade sank deep felt so *right*, so inevitable, that I did it again.

'*Stop it, Lola!*'

And again.

'Blood in the cracks,' I mumble into the darkness, and the cave swallows it. I'm so cold, so tired, and my body throbs. I close my eyes to rest. Just for a minute.

I must doze, because the cave is suddenly quiet like a tomb. The bones lie next to me, exactly as they were before. Lorelei's bones. I can't see her, but I know now that I've found her.

All this time, I've waited for her to come back for me, when deep down I always knew she couldn't. She was here, waiting to be found. And now that eavesdropped conversation between Larry and Nolan swims through my head, but in a new light – Nolan's *she was going to leave me* and Larry's *I've taken care of it.*

I know what they meant now. What Nolan did to Lorelei. How Larry covered for him by bringing my mother's body back to this place to hide her away like a shameful secret. Where, if she was ever found, it would look like her death was an accident. Or as if someone else – someone from Harrow Lake – had done this terrible thing to her.

'I can't stay with you,' I whisper.

And she wouldn't want me to stay, here in the dark. She wouldn't want me to be afraid. I know that. I remember. She was brave and wanted me to grow up to be brave, too. How did I forget her?

I reach into my jeans pocket and take out the jitterbug. I can leave that with her, at least. I open the lid and am about to lay it next to my mother when I notice the bug inside is glowing. That white-and-red pattern on the jitterbug's back glows in the dark, just like the paint inside the ghost train. The white-and-red pattern on the bug's back morphs into the face of Mister Jitters.

The pieces finally snap into place.

Daddy says I'm not to tell tales, or Mister Jitters will come get me.

Keep your secrets safe.

Carter was right. Not about me writing the notes, but about what Mister Jitters is: a darkness more real, more terrifying, than any monster.

Lorelei's father made this for her. He painted that secret message into it – the monster's face. It was a reminder. A threat.

Daddy says I'm not to tell tales . . .

He used a nightmare to keep her from revealing their awful secret.

. . . or Mister Jitters will come get me.

I didn't want to see it before, wanted so badly to have a connection to my mother – even if that connection was a monster – that I ignored the real truth in her words.

'I'm sorry,' I say to Lorelei. 'I believe you.'

Mister Jitters isn't the only monster this town has created, and Lorelei knew that.

I won't leave the white jitterbug next to my mother's body. She deserves better. I tighten my grip on it, preparing to throw it into the icy blackness. Then I hear it. That sound, *his* song, weaving black threads as it bounces from

rock to rock, thrumming over the water. I mouth the
words with trembling lips.

> 'Rat-a-tat-tat – *such a terrifying sound!*
> *With a jitter-jitter-jitter, he's stirring underground!*
> *Tick-tock, tick-tock – better watch out, he's gonna*
>   *snap-snap-snap your bones . . .'*

My heart beats like a hummingbird's wings. The cavern
is shifting, yawning awake. He's coming. The jitterbug in
my hand chatters a warning.

Then I see him. Two glinting points of light in the darkness. Coming closer. Closer. I scramble back. Away from
him. From *it*. The gondola judders as it hits a rock or a
bank. I slip, and my fingers brush against my mother's hair
one last time.

Mister Jitters is coming.

I need to run. I plunge blindly over the side of the boat.
Icy water wraps around my limbs, but I keep going, wading
away from those awful specks of light. His noise still
surrounds me. The pool grows shallower, falling away
until I'm on damp rock.

Where to? Which way?

It's impossible to see anything in this dense blackness. I
feel only cold rock at my back. But there's another sound
beneath the chatter – something else climbing out of the
water.

I scream, pull back my arm, and throw the jitterbug
shell at it as hard as I can. It hits its target with a crack.

The monster roars. I clamp my hands over my ears, but I still can't keep him out. He's not all that's inside me, though. Despite the cold, the fear, I feel something molten building in my gut, surging against him. It is a hot, venomous tide.

Because my fear isn't enough. Being trapped and alone in the dark isn't enough. Nothing that I am or that I do is enough for him, and so I let the venom out.

'LET. ME. GO!'

And my roar is louder than his. Louder than my heart trying to batter its way free of my chest. Louder than the world ending.

And now the rock beneath my feet and at my back and all around me begins to tremble. It is roaring back at the monster, too. There's a crack like thunder, and then a boulder falls from the sky. Then another. Then ten more.

The cave is collapsing around me.

I wrap my arms over my head and press myself back into the cavern wall. Whisper to the dark to *let me go, let me go, let me go, let me go, let me go!*

Shrapnel and dirt bounce off me. The rumbling goes on and on as though there will never be anything else. But then it begins to fade. Slowly, the tremors dwindle until finally I look up. Night air drifts into the cave. Dust clouds the air around me, but I can *see*. In front of me, where there had been an underground lake a moment ago, is now a mound of earth and rocks, all piled up in a slope towards the moon.

Under that pile is Mister Jitters. And, I realize with a sob, my mother.

I stumble over to the slope and begin scrabbling for a foothold, a handhold, almost digging my way up towards the sky. Soil rains around me. My wrist burns, my ankle threatens to give way with every inch I climb, but I'm almost there now. I grab onto a tree root and pull myself up, up, over the lip of the sinkhole. Up into the dawn.

I watch the light creep over the tops of the trees and I rasp in painful, beautiful breaths, lying on grass and grit and a backbone made of stories. Stars fill the sky above me, echoes from some long-dead part of the universe, stories from long ago.

The stars watch as I get to my feet and walk into the trees. Perhaps they are all monsters' eyes. Perhaps they are not there at all.

ONE YEAR LATER

NOLAN

Transcript of interview with Nolan Nox, Director of *Nightjar*, for *Scream Screen* magazine (Nightjar twentieth-anniversary special feature) – CONTD.

CJL: I heard a rumour you'll soon be returning to Harrow Lake to make a follow-up to *Nightjar* – any truth to that?

NN: Yes. The plan was for it to be released for the twentieth anniversary, but there was a scheduling issue, so obviously that hasn't happened.

CJL: Because you were attacked by a stranger in your penthouse apartment last year?

NN: I . . . what? We're not here to talk about that. Move on.

CJL: What shall we move on to? Your wife's murder? Or your daughter's mysterious disappearance after you sent her away when you were stabbed multiple times by a – quote-unquote – *stranger*?

NN: [Pause] What the hell is this? Are you trying to shock me or something? Grow up. Honestly, what were

Scream Screen thinking, sending some obnoxious child to interview me?

CJL: [Laughs] *Scream Screen* was happy to let me interview you when I promised I could deliver a no-holds-barred exclusive. Now answer the questions, Nolan.

NN: [Yelling] What goddamn exclusive? This is entirely inappropriate, Ms [paper crackle] Lahey. Wait, Cora Jean Lahey . . . why do I know that name? You're not any relation to that boy the cops looked into after Lola went missing, are you?

CJL: Carter is my brother, and – as I'm sure you're well aware – he was cleared of any involvement in Lola's disappearance. But how closely did the police look at *you*, Nolan? Or the people who work for you? Who did you have to pay off to get them to stop questioning why the women in your life have a habit of . . . *disappearing*?

NN: [Pause] What are you trying to achieve here, Ms Lahey?

CJL: [Laughs] Oh, we're back to formality, are we? OK, Mr Nox. Let's talk about the fact that your wife – who you said walked out on you thirteen years ago – was murdered.

NN: Well, no, Ms Lahey. If you'd done your homework, you would know that my wife went to visit her hometown – your hometown as well, right? – and she was never heard from again. If anything happened to her, it had nothing to do with me. Lorelei was declared deceased *in absentia*, which is just standard procedure for a case like this. For all I know, she could be living it up in Mexico right now.

CJL: Now that's funny, Mr Nox. You see, my dad died soon after Lorelei *disappeared*. Sad, yes, but he was a real asshole to my mother –

NN: Did I ask for your life story? Either make your point or get the hell out of my office.

CJL: Oh, Mr Nox, you really are dead set on ruining this, aren't you? Lola was one for telling stories – I figured you liked that. Anyway, I'll get to it. I was recently going through some of my dad's things and I found an envelope full of photo negatives. I had the photographs developed, and would you believe what was in the pictures? Go on, I'll let you guess. [Pause] No? OK then. How about I show you instead? [Sound of shuffling papers] Now I'd say that first shot quite clearly shows your assistant, Mr Lawrence Brown, next to a car previously registered in your name when you lived in Chicago. And, knowing Harrow Lake pretty well, I'd also say the car is parked up near the abandoned quarry there. Are we agreed so far? Good. And would you also agree that the body he is struggling to haul out of the trunk looks an awful lot like your *missing* wife?

NN: [Pause] What do you want?

CJL: Now, let's not rush this! We have a couple more pictures to go through first. This one, for example – I think that really captures the wound on Lorelei's head rather well. [Pause] But I think this is the really interesting one, and I've had to take a little creative licence with my interpretation, but I'm sure you'll bear with me, right? Great. You see, my mother has always told me how my dad was simply *obsessed* with Lorelei; I'm sure you can relate to that. But I'd lay money down that dear old Dad couldn't bear to think of poor Lorelei lying in the water, getting all bloated and puckered, so he dragged her body out of the quarry and laid her out in the boat as you see in the last picture. It's almost romantic, isn't it, how he folded her arms like that? Her hair swept away from her face? Or maybe Dad just wanted something more concrete to hold over you than these photos, so he made sure he could find her body again if he had to. Of course, he died before he had the chance to use that against you, didn't he?

NN: [Laughs] Oh, so I murdered your father now, too? I say 'too' as I gather I'm meant to have killed Lorelei and had my assistant dispose of her. Do I have that right? This is really quite the story, Ms Lahey. I wonder – how does it end?

CJL: Now that's the good part, Mr Nox. It ends with you paying for what you did to your wife, and my dad. And to Lola, because I'm betting you know what happened to her when she *disappeared*. And if you're wondering why on earth you would admit to any of this – because I'm sure you must be – then consider this: if you don't, I will do it for you.

NN: [Laughs] You're going public with this nonsense? I will shut you down before you've even left the building, Ms Lahey. I'll also be on the phone to your editor to make sure you never work for him, or for any other magazine or media outlet, again. How's that for an ending? Because what you have there are photos of an actress rehearsing for a part in a movie I ended up scrapping. My assistant was helping her run through a scene. Anything else?

CJL: Well, there's Lorelei's body.

NN: [Pause] What?

CJL: Oh, you didn't know about that? Funny. See, it's been a lot of work trying to rebuild Harrow Lake after last year's landslide. Long, slow work. In fact, they only got around to reinforcing the tunnel entrance at the back of the fairground a couple of weeks ago. Can you guess what they found floating in a gondola right inside the cave mouth?

NN: [Muttered curse]

CJL: I hate to be the bearer of bad news – because I'm betting this is bad news, even though there's no way it's a surprise to you – but my brother was working with the crew that found the gondola, and he tells me they discovered a woman's remains in there.

NN: That is quite a shock, Ms Lahey. Though I wonder why the authorities aren't here to break the news if the poor woman was my wife, as you seem to be suggesting?

CJL: [Laughs] Forensics take time. They'd have to be real sure before they came to talk to the legendary Nolan Nox about something like this, right?

NN: Then I don't see what you're expecting to gain from this little . . . chat.

CJL: I'm getting to that. See, I know you weren't too impressed by the photographs I just showed you, but do you know who was?

NN: Not the police, otherwise I assume they would be here to save me from this excruciating waste of my time.

CJL: No, the police weren't convinced by my photographs, you're right. But Moira McCabe was.

NN: [Pause] You showed these to Moira?

CJL: Yes. And I'll tell you, her reaction was a little different to yours. She seemed to think Lorelei had left Harrow Lake thirteen years ago – with you – after taking Lola there for a brief visit, and Lorelei then committed suicide in your apartment in Chicago the next day. Mrs McCabe was adamant that that was what you told her. And I'm wondering why, if Lorelei simply left you, as you say, would you call her mother and inform her that her daughter was dead?

NN: Well, I . . . I was upset about my wife leaving me, and . . . and no – Moira is making this up. She never liked me, never forgave me for taking her precious daughter away from her. She's lying. Besides, why would *she* keep quiet about it all these years if she knew Lorelei was dead? Can you explain that?

CJL: I can, Mr Nox. Mrs McCabe said you told her *she* was the one who drove Lorelei to kill herself. She didn't go into details, but I gather she was deeply ashamed for turning a blind eye to the abuse Lorelei suffered growing up. That was what Lorelei went back to confront her about thirteen years ago, and what you held over Mrs McCabe to keep her quiet. That's pretty callous, Mr Nox; but you'd have to be a callous sonofabitch to get your assistant to take your dead wife's body back to Harrow Lake and dump it there, wouldn't you? Was it so she'd really be stuck forever in the town she wanted to escape? Or just so you could claim she'd never left Harrow Lake if her body was ever found – and that you hadn't been the last one to see her? No one else knew you were in town, did they? I wonder what would've happened to Mrs McCabe if she hadn't taken your hush money.

NN: No . . . I . . . Shit. SHIT. [Pause] What's your angle here? Money? You want a part in my next movie? What?

CJL: You're not listening, Mr Nox. I don't want your money, or a part in your shitty movie. You have nothing I want. I'm doing this for Lola.

NN: [Laughs] You think you know my daughter? You think you're fighting her corner, little girl? You don't know anything. Lola's an ungrateful brat who ran away to Harrow Lake while I was recovering in hospital just to piss me off. I haven't seen or heard from her since. She's probably shacked up with some hillbilly by now – again, just to piss me off. That's what she's like.

CJL: Why don't you fill in some of the gaps while we wait for the cops to arrive? I'm sure they're on their way. With the forensics report, my photographs, Mrs McCabe's testimony, and this interview, I think at the very least they'll have enough to arrest you for your wife's murder, even if I haven't found out what you did to Lola yet. But, if you want to put forward your side, now's your chance.

NN: I did not do a damn thing to my daughter!

CJL: But you admit you killed Lorelei?

NN: No! Of course not! Look, take your damned photographs and your lies and get out of here. *Scream Screen* won't print a word of this without evidence, so your interview isn't worth shit.

CJL: I might agree, except I've been livestreaming it ever since we sat down.

NN: You've . . . what? [Sound of a chair scraping across the floor]

CJL: [Loudly] Mr Nox, I'm carrying a taser that'll knock you on your ass and leave a puddle on your nice carpet. Sit down unless you want me to demonstrate. [Sound of distant sirens] Ah, good. So, do you have any last words to say to your fans about all this before the cops get here?

NN: You little bitch! You don't get to threaten me! YOU DON'T GET TO DO THIS – [Thud, followed by garbled noise]

CJL: I did warn you, Nolan. Well, it looks like our listeners won't get to hear your side right now. But I expect they've heard everything they need to hear from Nolan Nox. Listeners: I'm Cora Jean Lahey, live-streaming this somewhat unorthodox interview on behalf of *Scream Screen* magazine from the office of movie director Nolan Nox. It sounds like our friendly neighbourhood cops are just about on the doorstep, so for now from me – you all have a delightful day. And Lola, if you're out there, I hope you're writing that damn book, girl.

TWO YEARS LATER . . .

Star Reads Reviews

Book of the Month: ALICE IS GONE *by L. Evangeline*

Suffocated by dark family secrets and an overbearing father, Alice embarks on a mind-bending journey to a world of monstrous creatures and terrifying magic to find her missing mother. A feminist nod to *Alice's Adventures in Wonderland*, and inspired by events in the author's own life, this exceptional debut offers an ultimately hopeful insight into a young woman's recovery from a violent trauma. With a big-screen adaptation also scheduled for release next year, *Alice is Gone* is sure to make its mark on movie-goers and readers alike.

5 STARS

ACKNOWLEDGEMENTS

Reader, if you've made it this far, you deserve to know who's to blame for *Harrow Lake*. That's me, of course – this story is my beastly child, and I take full responsibility for its bad behaviour, be that in the form of typos, factual errors, or liberties taken with the small matter of realism. But there are many more puppeteers behind the scenes, and I would like to offer them my thanks for enabling this nightmare to take physical form:

To my editors, Emma Jones at Puffin, and Kathy Dawson at Kathy Dawson Books; it was a pleasure working with you both to unleash this monster on the world. Huge thanks also to the teams at Penguin Random House UK and US for their part in shaping this book inside and out, and getting it into the hands of readers: Stephanie Barrett, Jane Tait, Sarah Hall, Michael Bedo, Simon Armstrong, Geraldine McBride, Becki Wells, Amy Wilkerson, Karin Burnik, Anne Bowman, Jacqui McDonough and Alex Murray at Puffin in the UK, and Rosie Ahmed, Regina Castillo, Mina Chung and Elaine C. Damasco at Kathy Dawson Books in the US.

Thanks as always to my agent, Molly Ker Hawn, for being a kind, brilliant, unstoppable force, and to my early readers: Jani Grey, Kate Brauning, Jeanmarie Anaya, and Dawn Kurtagich. Thanks to my cousin Candice for 'Did I ask for your life story?' and other beautifully delivered burns. And love and thanks to my husband, friends, and family for indulging my dark brain and supporting my huge dreams.

Finally, thanks to Literature Wales, who saw promise in an early draft of this book and awarded me a Literature Wales Writer's Bursary supported by the National Lottery through the Arts Council of Wales. Without the bursary, I'd probably have one less kidney right now. So thank you, from the bottom of my kidneys.

ABOUT THE AUTHOR

Kat Ellis studied English with Creative Writing at Manchester Metropolitan University before going on to work in local government communications. When not writing, she can usually be found exploring ancient ruins and cemeteries around North Wales, or watching scary films with her husband. *Harrow Lake* is her fourth novel.